The News Where You Are

CATHERINE O'FLYNN

PENGUIN BOOKS

PENGUIN BOOKS

Published by the Penguin Group
Penguin Books Ltd, 80 Strand, London WC2R ORL, England
Penguin Group (USA) Inc., 375 Hudson Street, New York, New York 10014, USA
Penguin Group (Canada), 90 Eglinton Avenue East, Suite 700, Toronto, Ontario, Canada M4P 2Y3
(a division of Pearson Penguin Canada Inc.)
Penguin Ireland, 25 St Stephen's Green, Dublin 2, Ireland (a division of Penguin Books Ltd)
Penguin Group (Australia), 250 Camberwell Road, Camberwell, Victoria 3124, Australia
(a division of Pearson Australia Group Pty Ltd)
Penguin Books India Pvt Ltd, 11 Community Centre, Panchsheel Park, New Delhi – 110 017, India
Penguin Group (NZ), 67 Apollo Drive, Rosedale, North Shore 0632, New Zealand
(a division of Pearson New Zealand Ltd)
Penguin Books (South Africa) (Pty) Ltd, 24 Sturdee Avenue, Rosebank, Johannesburg 2196, South Africa

Penguin Books Ltd, Registered Offices: 80 Strand, London WC2R ORL, England

www.penguin.com

First published in Viking 2010
Published in Penguin Books 2010

3

Copyright © Catherine O'Flynn, 2010

The moral right of the author has been asserted

Grateful acknowledgement is made for permission to quote from the following:
'She Wears Red Feathers', written by Bob Merrill, © 1952 Chappell & Co. by kind permission of
Warne Chappell Music Ltd; 'Nature Boy', written by Eden Ahbez, © Crestview-Music Corp (NS).
All rights administered by Chappell-Morris Ltd. All rights reserved: 'The Old Fools', from *Collected Poems* by
Philip Larkin, reprinted by kind permission of Faber and Faber Ltd

Typeset by Ellipsis Books Limited, Glasgow
Printed in Great Britain by Clays Ltd, St Ives plc

A CIP catalogue record for this book is available from the British Library

ISBN: 978-0-141-04636-5

www.greenpenguin.co.uk

LOTTERY FUNDED

PENGUIN BOOKS

The News Where You Are

'...eet and shot th...ugh with ...shes of comedy'
Literary Review

'A slice of modern life that fans of Jonathan Coe will adore' *Elle*

'A tender, funny tale' *Grazia*

'An insightful exploration of the foibles of contemporary society delivered
with a fantastically dry wit' *Easy Living*

'Wry and poignant' *Good Housekeeping*

'Darkly funny' *Sunday Independent*

'Its gentle wit and melancholy are beguiling' *Daily Express*

Catherine O'Flynn was born and raised in Birmingham, the youngest of six children. Her parents ran a sweet-shop. She worked briefly in journalism, then at a series of shopping centres. She has also been a web editor, a postwoman and a mystery shopper.

Her first novel, *What Was Lost*, won the Costa First Novel Award and the Jelf First Novel Award, was shortlisted for the *Guardian* First Book Award, the South Bank Literature Award and the Commonwealth Writers' First Novel Prize, and was longlisted for the Orange Prize and the Man Booker Prize.

Catherine O'Flynn won the Galaxy British Book Newcomer of the Year Award in 2008.

For Edie and Peter

Prologue
April 2009

He gave up any pretence of jogging now and walked slowly along the lane, following in the wake of an empty crisp packet blown along the tarmac. Without its example he wasn't sure he'd have the will to move forward.

His steps were heavy and the elasticated cuffs of his tracksuit made his wrists itch. He looked at the loose flesh on the back of his hand pinched by the bright red polyester and found the contrast grotesque.

Mikey had let him down again. Finally he understood that Mikey would never do it.

The sky had darkened as he walked along and now the first fat drops of rain splattered on the road around him. Phil nodded his head. Rain was all that had been missing.

He heard a car approaching. Its passing force would whip the crisp packet away and he didn't know what he'd follow then. The driver was making the most of the straight country lane and picking up speed. Phil moved slightly closer to the hedgerow on his left. He knew he cut a pitiful figure – an old rain-soaked man dressed head to toe in Nike. Jimmy bloody Savile.

The car was getting closer now and as it did it veered slightly towards Phil's side of the lane. Phil smiled blandly in its direction – force of habit. As it drew down upon him, he realized that the driver wasn't going to swerve away. In the last few seconds, the sky's reflection on the windscreen vanished, and Phil saw the familiar face behind the wheel, white with fear and running with tears.

Six months later

Frank's daughter sat in the front passenger seat humming the same tune over and over. The notes spiralled upwards and then abruptly plummeted, before starting the ascent again. Frank drove towards the city.

'What's the tune, Mo?' asked Frank.

'It's a song by The Beatles. It's a man asking questions about when he gets old.'

'What? "When I'm Sixty-Four"?'

'Yeah. That's it . . . Dad, do you want to know something?'

'Erm, yes, please.'

'When I'm sixty-four, I'll be eight times older than I am now. Eight times eight is sixty-four.'

'That's true.'

She looked out of the window. 'Eight hundred per cent!' She shook her head in amazement and began to hum again.

Frank frowned. 'But "When I'm Sixty-Four" doesn't sound anything like that.'

Mo beamed. 'I know! I invented a new tune. It's better.'

'Oh, okay.' Frank paused. 'It's very different to the original. Are the words the same?'

'I don't know, I'm just humming.'

'I know, but in your head are the words the same?'

'No. They're better too. He wants to know will there be robots, and will his cat be able to talk and will his car fly.'

'It's quite a strange tune.'

'It's how he thinks music will sound when he's old.'

'Oh, I see, future music. That explains it.'

Mo hummed another few bars and then, to Frank's relief, stopped.

'Dad?'

'Yes.'

'Do you think Gran ever listens to music?'

'Not future music. I don't think so.'

'No. I mean any music.'

'Yes, I'm sure she does sometimes. She has a radio in her room.'

'I know, but it's all covered in dust. She should listen to music. I think it would make her less sad. She could listen to stuff she remembered when she was young.'

Frank said nothing.

'Maybe I could take her some old music and she could listen to it on my headphones.'

Frank glanced at Mo. 'Sometimes old music makes people sad. It reminds them of the past and things that have gone.'

'Oh,' said Mo.

Frank reached across and squeezed her hand. Mo spent a lot of time trying to think of ways to make his mother less unhappy. It was a project for her.

'Are we going a different way to the supermarket?'

'I want to show you something first.'

'Okay.'

Frank put the radio on and they listened to a comedy programme. Mo laughed when Frank laughed.

He parked on a meter in a back street and then walked with Mo down to the busy ring road. A pedestrian bridge spanned the six lanes of traffic and Mo and Frank climbed the zig-zagging concrete steps to the top. Halfway across they stopped. Frank bent down towards Mo so she could hear him above the roar of the traffic. Her hair blew into his face.

'Remember I told you about my dad.'

'That he had a dog!' said Mo excitedly.

'Yeah, that's right. He had a dog when he was a boy. But do you remember what I said my dad's job was?'

'Yes. He was an architect. He made buildings.'

'Can you see that block over there? The tall one with the dark glass.'

'Yeah. I can see it.'

'That's called Worcester House. My dad designed that building.'

'Did he live in it?'

'No, he didn't live in it. We lived in a house. He made this for people to work in.'

'How many floors has it got?'

'Twenty.'

'Are there escalators?'

'No, there are two lifts.'

'Can we go up in them?'

'No, I'm sorry. We can't go in the building now.'

'Can we go and look at it?'

'That's where we're going.'

Mo ran across the rest of the bridge and then waited for Frank to catch up. The building was a little further away than it seemed from the bridge, tucked amidst a cluster of other blocks, converted townhouses and car parks. Worcester House was a classic mid-period Douglas H. Allcroft and Partners creation. Built in 1971 it was an uncompromising, thuggish-looking block, clad in precast concrete panels and devoid of all exterior decoration. Despite its height it appeared squat and defensive, occupying a large plot on the corner of Carlton Street and Newman Row, glowering down on the few Georgian blocks still remaining in the centre.

As they drew closer to it at street level, Mo noticed the white boards all around the outside of the building:

'Why are the boards there, Dad?'

'They're there to protect people when they demolish the building.'

Mo stopped walking. 'They're demolishing it?'

Frank nodded. 'That's why I brought you today; it'll be gone soon.'

'But why are they knocking it down? Is it broken?'

'No, it's not broken; it's fine. It's just . . . they don't need it any more.'

'But, Dad, loads of people could work here. Or they could use it to put homeless people in – that'd be better than sleeping on the streets. They could sleep under desks and go up and down in the lifts.'

'They want to build new homes in the city now – apartments for the people who work here – and this building isn't right for homes. Dad didn't build it for that, and so they say it has to be taken down and started again.'

Mo thought for a while. 'Does that happen to all buildings? Do they all get knocked down?'

'Some stay for a long time. Like Aston Hall. But lots don't. It's a bit like clothes. You know, you wouldn't wear the clothes Mom and I used to wear – they'd seem really uncool to you – and sometimes that happens with buildings. People just don't like them any more; they aren't fashionable.'

Frank realized that unfashionable wasn't quite adequate. People did not feel about his father's buildings the way they felt about marble-washed denim or ski-pants. They might smile ruefully and shake their heads about their own lapses in taste, but not those imposed on their city. Aside from the family home he built in Edgbaston, only two of the eight buildings his father had created in the city remained. In a few weeks there would be only one.

Mo was squinting at the building, counting the windows. When she'd finished, she turned back to Frank. 'But, Dad, sometimes things come back into fashion. Like Mom always says the clothes in the shops now are the same as twenty years ago. Maybe if they waited this building would be in fashion again.'

Frank nodded. 'Maybe. People don't always agree, though. A few of us thought it should be saved, but others didn't and . . . well, they won in the end.'

'I don't think this building is uncool.'

Frank got out his camera. 'Anyway, I want to take a photo of you and the building behind you. So however many different buildings come and go you'll always know this building was here, and that you and I stood on this spot and talked about it one morning.'

Mo wouldn't smile for the photo. She said it was for when she was grown-up and serious. Afterwards she said: 'Dad, are you sad that it's going to be demolished?'

Frank looked up at the top floor of the building and remembered looking out from there as a boy. 'Yes, I am.'

Mo held his hand. She looked at the other buildings in the street. Worcester House was the only one surrounded by boards. 'Me too.'

Two days later Frank listened to the countdown on his earpiece, took a swig of water and stowed the bottle under the desk. In the last few seconds his expression became attentive with the hint of a frown. He spoke on cue.

'Now on to a remarkable story of survival. Sixty-five-year-old Alan Purkis had something of a shock when he discovered a thirty-foot-deep hole had opened up in his back garden. The retired electrician from Droitwich was only saved from a plunge into the abyss by the timely arrival of a cuckoo.' Head inclined to one side, his quizzical expression segued into a reassuring smile: 'Scott Padstow gets the full story for us.'

The package ran. Frank had a headache and thought he should have eaten something before they went live. He thought of the Mars bar that had sat on his desk all afternoon and was filled with sharp longing and regret. He turned and looked at Julia's exposed arm and could imagine with terrible clarity ripping into it with his teeth. When he looked up, she was staring at him. He gave a little shake of his head as if coming out of some private reverie. He looked, he hoped, as if his thoughts had been on something distant and intangible or, failing that, on anything other than eating her flesh. He gave a slight sickly smile. Julia was still in a foul mood.

'Great story. News that almost happens. A man doesn't fall down a hole.'

The producer's voice sounded in their earpieces. 'Come on, Joolz, can we get over this? The man almost falling isn't the story – it's the hole. Why is it there? Is it going to widen and open up in other gardens, maybe swallow entire houses? I think that is of some interest to people in our region.'

'Right – but that's not really what the link focused on, is it? It bills it as a "remarkable story of survival", and what about the cuckoo? Where's the news value in that?'

Another voice cut in: 'Back with you, Julia, in five, four, three, two . . .'

Julia introduced an item about a pub in Wolverhampton whose steak and kidney pies were doing well in a national competition.

Frank thought that a pie might be an option. Beef and Guinness. He knew he didn't have one at home, so that'd mean a trip to Tesco, and that was too depressing a prospect. He wished, not for the first time, that he had a local pub that served decent food. He thought of the Rose and Crown whose menu consisted of three types of frozen pizza – brittle seven-inch singles of misery that resisted any attempts at cutting. They came topped with a mysterious molten substance that clung to the roof of the mouth and burned straight through. Frank didn't expect much from food, but he thought it shouldn't injure you.

The story about pies was coming to a close. Frank read the next link just ahead of his cue and braced himself. He tried too late and too half-heartedly to apply a mischievous smile and instead achieved only a half-cocked imbecile grin.

'Reaching the national finals of that competition is *pie* no means a small achievement!' He turned and beamed at Julia who looked back at him with bare-faced contempt. His grin faded. 'But seriously, well done to the Bull's Head there and good luck on the night.'

After the bulletin he apologized to Julia. 'You know I don't want to do the jokes.'

'Well, I wish you fucking wouldn't, then. There is no humour there, Frank; they are not recognizable as jokes. The only way I can tell that's what they're supposed to be is because otherwise what you've just said makes absolutely no sense. What the hell am I supposed to do? If I laugh, I look as if I'm mentally ill. If I don't laugh, I look as if I hate you.'

'Maybe just smile, pityingly. The viewers would understand that.'

'It's not easy to smile, Frank; believe me, it's not easy.'

'Try and imagine it's an illness. That's what I do.'

Julia shook her head as she got her coat. 'See you tomorrow, Frank.'

The door closed behind her and Frank was left wondering what to do for the evening. His hunger had mysteriously evaporated and he didn't feel like going straight home. That morning Andrea had taken Mo to visit her aunt in Bradford and they wouldn't be back till the next day. He found the house just about bearable when his family were there; with them away he avoided it as much as he could.

Sometimes he'd grab a drink with the crew, but tonight the thought of being that particular version of himself, of talking and listening and laughing in the right places, seemed too much effort.

He got in his car and headed for the Queensway. The car seemed to guide itself – gliding up over flyovers and swooping down into underpasses. The lights of the tunnels passed through his windscreen and across his face. Familiar glimpses of the city slid by and as they did stray names and faces associated with them from old news stories combined with memories from his own past. He was at his most susceptible to nostalgia and melancholy when he was tired.

The car pulled in at a garage and for a moment Frank had no idea why he was there, until he saw the buckets of flowers and realized that tonight he would pay his respects. He was too weary to resist.

The young man at the till recognized him and Frank switched his face on.

'I seen you on the telly, man.'

'Right, yes, that's me.'

'What's that other one? The babe. Julie, is it? She fit, mate. Flowers for her, are they?'

'These? No, actually they're for someone else.'

'Ahhh – you bein' a bad boy? Sniffin' up some other telly lady?'

'Yes, that's right. These are for Esther Rantzen.'

'You tell that Julie, if she's getting lonely, to come down

here and ask for J and I'll show her a sexy time. Tell her I know what she likes.'

'Well, I'll certainly pass that on J. She's a busy woman, but you never know.'

As he walked away, Frank heard the assistant say to his colleague: 'She could do a lot better than him, man.' Frank smiled, knowing how much that would amuse Andrea when he told her.

He drove out of the city on the Expressway and was surprised to find he remembered the way, despite the passing of time. The street was lined with parked cars on both sides, but he managed to find a space within sight of the house. It had changed since the first time he'd seen it. Then paint had peeled from the woodwork and the privet hedge in the front garden had expanded in all directions, covering the bay window and half the pavement. He didn't know how many people had come and gone in the intervening years. The windows were UPVC now, the front garden gone altogether and replaced by some slabs providing not quite enough space for a 4x4, which was wedged in at an angle, jutting out onto the pavement.

Frank was sure that whoever lived there now would know nothing about William Grendon. No one had noticed him when he lived and no one had noticed him when he died. The single thing that had brought his existence to the notice of the wider world was the smell of his decomposing body. He was discovered sitting upright in a high-backed chair with a twenty-six-day-old newspaper on his lap. Frank remembered there was no photo of William to show on the bulletin, so instead he had delivered the story in front of an image of the outside of the house.

He pulled the flowers from the cellophane and then carried them loose in his hand to the front of the house. He looked at the houses on either side, the blue light of a television flickered through the gaps in the curtain of one. He dropped the flowers on the slabs.

Frank stood and thought of William Grendon. Something invisible had disappeared, but it left a mark. There was always a mark.

3

On Saturday he drove out to Evergreen. His mother sat in her room, a book on her lap, the same one she'd been reading for a year. She looked at Frank with a pained expression. 'Is it still sweltering out there?'

'No, Mom, it's October; it's cold.'

'I can't bear it. It suffocates me. I can't breathe. How do people live in those places like Spain? Why do people go to those places? Sweating on the beaches, roasting like chickens in an oven. I'd die. I'd die.'

'Do you want me to open the window?'

'We need some rain. God, anything to freshen the air. What I'd give for a downpour now.'

'Mom, it *is* raining. Look out of the window.'

Maureen moved her head slowly and looked out. 'Oh,' she said. 'Thank God.' Then after a pause: 'It makes my joints ache so.'

'What does?'

'The rain.'

Frank pulled up a chair beside her. 'So what have you been up to this week?'

'Sitting here, dying slowly. Too slowly.' Frank exhaled and his mother looked at him. 'Oh, I know it must be very boring for you to have to come and visit me, endlessly clinging on. I've told you before, forget about me, leave me here, live your life. I'm dead already.'

Frank ignored this and looked over towards the window. 'They could do with someone clearing up the leaves out in the grounds. It all looks a bit grotty out there at the moment. Do the gardener and his mate not come out so much now?'

She shrugged. 'Maybe they leave them there deliberately. Maybe they think that dead leaves are exactly what we should be contemplating as we sit in here waiting to fall off the branch.'

'Mom . . .'

'You see how you fare. You'll be old one day. You see how you cope when all your friends are dead, and your senses are gone.'

'Your senses aren't gone, Mom. You're in excellent health . . .'

'Ha. That's a joke.'

'. . . You're in much better shape – physically and mentally – than most of the other people here, but you lock yourself away in your room. You're seventy-two, Mom – that's nothing. They sit and talk in the lounge, they listen to music, they walk in the garden.'

'"Why aren't they screaming?" Frank, "Why aren't they screaming?" Do you know who wrote that?'

'Larkin. You quote it every time.'

'Well, I'm an old fool too,' she snapped, 'and I forget.'

They fell silent for a while.

'Have you read this one?' said Maureen, indicating the book on her lap.

'No, no, I haven't.'

'Oh, it's terribly involved and clever. I can't wait to get to the end. It's about a man who discovers that he had an older brother that his parents never told him about and he tries to find this brother and it turns out that he's a . . . a . . . oh, blast . . . What do you call it?'

'A palaeontologist.'

'Exactly! I thought you said you hadn't read it.'

Frank smiled at her. 'I haven't. It was just a lucky guess.'

'Remarkable, of all the things he could have been.'

They fell silent again.

'Andrea sends her love. She's had to go on a course today.'

'Oh, Andrea, she was always one for the books, wasn't she. Is she still a great reader? I remember some marvellous conversations we've had about books. She'd love this one.'

'Well, you can tell her about it on Wednesday when she comes,' said Frank, knowing that Andrea had not only read the book, but had given her copy to his mother and listened to the same description of the first chapter each time she visited. The flowered bookmark she had given along with the book remained stranded at the same page in the book week on week.

Maureen looked towards the window. 'The rain should cool things down. It's good for the gardens.'

'It's October, Mom.'

'I know. I'm not a fool,' Maureen snapped. 'It's still needed, isn't it? We can't go all through the winter without rain, can we? We'd shrivel and die. Become withered husks.'

Frank didn't respond. His mother looked at him. 'I saw you on the television the other day. Something very sad.

A terribly sad story about a child waiting for an operation.'

He thought for a moment: 'Oh, Leanne Newman. Yes.'

'Will she get the operation in time?'

'I don't know, Mom.'

'I can't watch your programme – it's too sad. Always sick children, or horrible people hurting each other and dogs eating babies and young people losing their homes. It's a very upsetting programme. And that woman!'

'Which woman?'

'That wretched woman who sits next to you.'

'Julia?'

'I don't know how you bear to work with her. She smirks. She listens to those awful stories and then she smirks. She enjoys it. Pure evil.'

'Mom, she doesn't smirk. That's just her face. She's very professional.'

'Oh, she's a devil. I liked that other one.'

'Which one?'

'Oh, you know. The coloured lady. She was nice and cheerful. The programme never used to be sad when she was there. But that's just West Indians, isn't it? They're just lovely cheerful people. Beautiful singers as well.'

Frank drew in a deep breath and steadily exhaled.

'Your father had a lovely voice too.'

'I don't think I ever heard him sing.'

'He used to sing to me before we married. A lovely baritone. He'd sing "On the Street Where You Live". Poor Douglas. A beautiful voice. He used to sing for you too when you were very tiny. On long car journeys. Don't you remember? You'd cry out, "Monkey, Daddy, monkey," and he'd sing "Little Red Monkey". You loved it. You'd laugh and clap your hands like the monkey in the song. You made us so happy. We were all so happy then.'

She was crying now. Frank held her hand. They looked out of the window together at the rain rolling down the glass.

Corny jokes had been one of the trademarks of Frank's predecessor, Phil Smethway. Each programme would contain at least one baffling pun or tortuous play on words. Smethway got away with it somehow – he'd look rueful and his co-presenters would groan and it was a nice bit of shtick. Phil had had some kind of televisual gold dust – viewers loved him; there had been something in his DNA that seemed to make him affable to everyone. He'd long ago moved on from regional to national television and from news to entertainment. He had been hosting a primetime blockbuster show every Saturday night when he was killed in a hit and run accident six months previously. Frank missed him. He had lost a friend and a mentor.

Frank often thought back to the days they worked together, with Frank as reporter and Phil as presenter. Every day around the same time Phil received a phone call from someone called Cyril. Phil never mentioned the calls, and always conducted them in a low voice. Frank asked him about it once.

'Who's Cyril?'

Phil tapped the side of his nose.

'It's very mysterious. Are you having an affair?'

'With a bloke?'

'You wouldn't be the first married man to do that.'

'With a bloke called Cyril?'

Frank shrugged and Phil said nothing more about it.

Phil had made his move from *Heart of England Reports* in 1993 and the phone calls stopped. One morning a few months after he'd taken over from Phil as main anchor, Frank received a call at his desk from Lorraine at reception.

'Hello, Frank, sorry to disturb you.'

'Lorraine? Can you speak up a bit?'

'Not really, love. Can you hear me?'

'Just about. Are you okay?'

'I'm fine. Listen. We've had a few phone calls for you over the last few weeks.'

'Oh right. Sorry, I didn't get the message.'

'No, no – there wasn't a message. It's the same man that kept calling, but he never wanted to leave his name and number – always just said he'd call back – which was quite annoying, to be honest. But you know it was probably just a little power thing with him, maybe wanted to feel like he was in control.'

'Maybe he just liked speaking to you, Lorraine. You know you have a very attractive telephone manner – particularly this new husky whisper – most affecting.'

'Yeah – funny – well laugh away, because he's here now, waiting to see you.'

Frank stopped eating the Frazzles he'd been enjoying.

'I can tell him you're busy if you like.'

'But he'll be back, won't he?'

'Oh yes, he'll be back.'

'I suppose I should get it over with, then.'

'Might be for the best.'

'Where would you place him on the scale?'

There was a pause. 'It's hard to say.'

'Is he wearing a baseball cap?'

'No – no hat at all.'

'Okay – that's not too bad. How many carrier bags?'

'Er . . . none. He has a briefcase.'

'Oh – a briefcase – that could be worse. What do you reckon's in the briefcase?'

'I don't know.' She hesitated. 'Do you remember the one with all the coat hangers?'

Frank sighed. 'I remember. Okay. I'm coming out.'

Lorraine was right. On first impressions the man was hard to place on any scale of eccentricity. He was maybe in his mid-sixties, wearing a leather blouson jacket and Reactolite glasses that had yet to react to the light. Frank walked over to him and held out his hand.

'Hello there, I believe you're here to see me.'

'Oh, hello, Frank. Good of you to see me. I was a business associate of your predecessor Phil Smethway. Cyril's the name. Cyril Wilks.'

Frank hid his surprise. 'Hello, Cyril. Pleased to meet you. How can I help you?'

'Well, as you know, Frank, Phil's moved on to bigger and better things now. I always thought he would. No offence to you, but regional telly was too small for him.'

Frank agreed. 'No, I understand. Phil has star quality – always had.'

'He certainly does. Phil Smethway's A-list now and of course he has a whole team of people surrounding him.

I've had to face up to facts: he doesn't really need me any more. I won't lie, it hurts a little, but I understand.'

Cyril looked as if it hurt more than a little. He looked like a dog left locked in a car. 'Phil and I go back a long way – back to the Jurassic era – or pirate radio as it was known in those days. Phil had his morning show and I was a glorified tea boy, but that's how it started.' Cyril stopped. 'I'm sorry, Frank, I'm wittering. I'll cut to the chase. The point is, I'm sure Phil told you all about the kind of service I provide and, well, not to beat about the bush, I was rather hoping you might pick up where he appears to have left off.'

Frank wasn't sure how to handle this. He didn't want to hurt Cyril's feelings. 'I'm afraid Phil was always very private about his business affairs.'

Cyril sighed. 'I should have guessed it. Course he wouldn't say anything. That's the curse of our profession, always the dirty secret hidden in the corner. No one wants to confess to hiring us.'

Frank tried to suppress the alarming notion that Cyril was some kind of senior rent boy. 'I'm afraid I still don't understand. What was it that Phil hired you for?'

Cyril seemed to experience a small flush of pride as he answered: 'Gags.'

Frank took a moment to let this sink in. 'Gags? As in jokes? The kind of jokes he used to tell on air? He paid for those?'

'Well, Frank, if you want quality, you have to pay.'

Frank's mind was reeling. It was overstating it to even call them jokes. Half-puns and leaden one-liners. To have planned them in advance. To have paid for them.

Cyril appeared oblivious to Frank's incredulity. 'It was a very reasonable rate; he'd pay a pound for each joke, three if he used it. I'm willing to maintain those prices for you.'

Frank had to think fast. 'Look, Cyril. Thanks for the offer, but it's not really my thing. I can't tell jokes; I'm terrible at it. They just die on me – turn to dust on my tongue.'

'Nonsense,' said Cyril, 'no such thing as a bad comedian, just bad material!'

Frank resisted pointing out the obvious.

Cyril continued. 'Name a great comedian. Go on, name one. I've written for them all. Name one British comedian of the last forty years and he'll have hired me as a gagsmith.'

Frank thought for a moment. 'Okay, Ronnie Barker.'

'No, not Barker. Someone else. Go on. Name one.'

'Tommy Cooper?'

'Keep going.'

'Eric Morecambe . . .?'

'No. Try again. Name one.'

'I've named three!'

'Yes, but you managed to pick the three I never wrote for. Uncanny.'

'Cyril, look, it doesn't matter, the point is . . .'

'Bryce Spackford – do you know him?'

'Erm . . . no, sorry.'

'What about Big Johnny Jason, "the lad with all the lines"?'

'No.'

'Paddy "Sure, I'm only having you on!" O'Malley?'

'I don't think so, sorry.'

'Do you watch any comedy, Frank? These are big names. Look at this.' Cyril started rooting in his briefcase, pulling out a blurred photograph of what appeared to be a TV screen. 'Do you see that there?'

'I can't see anything; it's just a blur.'

'With respect, Frank, it's not easy; the titles were flying past pretty fast. Here.' He held the photo a foot in front of Frank's face. 'Now let your eyes unfocus, like a 3D picture. Do you see it yet?'

'I don't really know what I'm looking for.'

Cyril grinned and shook the photo for emphasis. 'Those, Frank, are the credits for *You Gotta Laugh* 1988 Grampian TV. And that, my friend,' said Cyril, pointing to a particular patch of pixels, 'is my name.'

Frank looked at Cyril and then spoke slowly. 'Cyril. It's good of you to come in, but the truth of it is that I'm not going to buy any jokes from you. I don't need a gag writer. I don't want a gag writer. I'm not Phil Smethway. I'm a local news presenter, not Paddy O' . . .' His mind had gone blank.

'Malley! Paddy "Sure I'm only having you –"'

Frank cut him off. 'I'm not him. So I'm afraid I'll have to say no.'

Cyril stared at a point above Frank's head, his lips pressed together tight and then his eyes started to leak. Frank looked over at Lorraine in panic, but she shook her head and ducked behind her monitor.

Frank found a handkerchief in his pocket and handed it to Cyril. He got him to sit down and tried to calm him. 'Come on, Cyril. Come on now. It's not that bad.'

Cyril continued to cry and it was some time before he could control his voice enough to speak.

'I'm so sorry, Frank. I'll go. What a ridiculous spectacle. I'm just . . . sorry.'

Frank put his hand on Cyril's arm. 'It's okay. You don't have to go. Get your breath back. It's all right.'

Cyril tried to breathe deeply. 'I'm so embarrassed. I don't know what's come over me.' His voice went high again. 'I don't go around crying like this, you know. Please don't let Phil know. I couldn't bear for him to think of me like this.'

'Just take it easy for a few minutes. It'll pass.'

Cyril sat with his head down taking deep breaths. Frank went and got him a plastic cup of water. When he returned, Cyril seemed to have collected himself.

'Are you feeling all right now?'

'Yes, thanks. Again, I'm so sorry. I was just taken unawares.'

'I wasn't expecting you to take it so badly. I mean it's only a few quid a week. It can't be that big a blow.'

Cyril shook his head. 'It's not the money – I can get by on my pension. Phil and I went back a long way – he was all I had left. Since he's moved on I've tried some of the old clients, but they've all got new writers or packed it in. Paddy O'Malley's training to be a geography teacher. Can you believe that? Phil kept me going. I could meet with the other writers once a year and hold my head up knowing my material was still out there.' He paused for a moment to take a long drink of water. Afterwards he looked into the empty plastic cup. 'Writing jokes is what I do. What have I got aside from that?'

Frank grimaced. 'I'm really sorry, Cyril, but I just don't think I could say those things.'

Cyril sniffed and looked Frank in the eye. He sensed that Frank was softening. 'Frank, look, if you're not comfortable doing jokes, I'll give you really subtle lines – those that aren't looking won't even notice them, but those that miss Phil's gags will appreciate the odd little play on words, just a hint. Not every day, just once a week, on a little story, tucked away somewhere, just enough so that I can still say I write.'

Frank said nothing.

'Please, Frank. I won't make you look a fool.'

That had been fifteen years ago. Since then co-presenters had come and gone, the studio set had been transformed by various makeovers and just six months ago Phil Smethway had died, but the jokes remained. If anything, they were even more noticeable than when Phil used to drop them in as they were now only occasional and Frank appeared so ill at ease with them.

Shortly after he started inserting the occasional joke, Frank's producer discovered through a friend of his son's that Frank was developing a cult status amongst students in the city – the bad jokes were actually pulling in more viewers. Eventually a website was dedicated to him – www.unfunniestmanongodsearth.com – with clips of Frank delivering his more excruciating one-liners. One forum thread focused on his 'anti-timing' and some contributors thought that Frank must in fact be a comic genius to be able to misplace the beat so unfailingly in every gag. Frank went from a dull but credible newsreader to a bit of a joke in a matter of months and the increased viewers meant his bosses had no intention of letting him make the step back. He started being asked to do more public appearances, and he found it hard to say no. He'd managed to develop a persona that fitted him as poorly as the cheap suits he'd worn as a reporter, but neither the suits nor the persona ever really bothered Frank. He held on to the belief that people saw beyond the surface.

5

Frank had started working on *Heart of England Reports* in 1989. Since then he'd learned to smile patiently at the remarks about cats stuck up trees, presenters in bad toupees and roller skating ducks. He knew there was an assumption that anyone who spent their working life in regional news was either unambitious or had suffered thwarted ambition, but he knew also that neither was true of him. Local news was where he had always wanted to be.

His mother always maintained that it was something in his father's dedication to the large-scale and concrete that had pushed Frank in the direction of the small-scale and human. It was true that as a boy, surrounded by plans and drawings, what had fascinated him wasn't the shape of the windows or the relationship of the interior to the exterior spaces, but the people who might live and work in those buildings, of the potential stories they might contain.

Frank thought he'd made a good local news reporter. He had met many of the great and good of the city as a child through his father's work and because of that link many of them had trusted him alone amongst local journalists. His promotion when Phil moved on made him the youngest presenter in the programme's history. He knew he should be proud of the achievement, but part of him always missed reporting.

After twenty years in regional TV, though, he was no longer the bright-eyed enthusiast he once was. He appreciated that the small-scale and the local often equated with the banal and the inconsequential. He started to question the choice of what was featured in the news and what was omitted. It seemed to him that it was often the stories that didn't make the broadcasts that said the most about the region and its people. In this too he sensed the shadow of his father. As his buildings were bulldozed one by one, Frank began to suspect that often what vanished revealed more than what remained.

In May 1991, around the same time as the first of the demolitions, Frank reported on the death of Dorothy Ayling. He was used to the ways in which news stories could creep up on him. The murdered women, abandoned babies and teenagers caught in the crossfire would not affect him whilst at work. In the preparation and delivery of his report, caught up in the adrenalin pulse of the newsroom, his mind was all on the job. It was later in the evening, having a drink with colleagues, or at home with Andrea, his mind spooling of its own volition through the events of the day, that something would snag. He would feel himself suddenly anxious, a small panic that something was terribly wrong, and then he'd remember the story, hearing the words of his report for the first time and finding himself affected by the details. He was used to this, and dealt with it as his audience did, by trying to think of something else. But Dorothy Ayling was different.

She was found nineteen days after her death. As often happened, the neighbours reported a bad smell. When the police broke in, they found her lying in bed. In the years to come he would find it strange how often the isolated were discovered in positions of repose – sitting in an armchair, lying in bed or on a couch. Their deaths had not surprised them in the middle of making a cup of tea or watering a plant. They seemed instead to be ready, waiting perhaps to see if anyone would notice their absence from the world.

He presented the report live from the studio itself. Just a few words into the report he felt an unbearable lump in his throat and for a horrifying moment thought he was going to cry. He managed to disguise his emotion with a coughing fit, and was able to compose himself enough to continue. Afterwards, though, his mind would not move on. As he read the item, he was overcome with a powerful sense that he was uttering the last record of her existence, that no one would speak of Dorothy Ayling again. A death so isolated and solitary that it seemed less like death to him and more like extinction. As the autocue scrolled and her name disappeared, so, Frank felt, did she.

He didn't understand the anxiety he felt, but it lingered and grew. After Dorothy he started to keep a record of any similar deaths he came across, writing their names, dates and whatever other details he could find in a notebook. Sometimes there might be two in six months and then nothing for another year. Most never made it onto the bulletin, only the few that happened to be discovered on sufficiently slow news days. For the majority, their solitary deaths created no more ripple than their solitary lives. Frank thought they should be remembered, though. Something in him would not accept that people could vanish without leaving some trace. He made a note of all of them, even attending their funerals when he could, or taking flowers to their doors.

Dorothy Ayling's funeral took place four months after her death, after all attempts to trace a next of kin had failed. The service was short and simple. The vicar recited the twenty-third psalm. Frank would come to know those words by heart. He would learn the different versions, the cups that overflowed and the cups that runnethed over, he would notice the different lines emphasized by the different ministers. He had always thought the words were intended to reassure the flock left behind, but over time he came to believe that their purpose was to comfort the Shepherd himself. A reassurance to him that this sheep had not felt abandoned, had not been lost and scared, that he had not failed in his duty to care and guide. When Frank heard the psalm as he would many times in the years to come, he wondered if the Good Shepherd was consoled. Could he believe that the person lying now in the plain coffin with no one but a stranger to mourn them had truly felt 'Thou art with me'?

There was one other mourner at Dorothy Ayling's funeral. A plump woman with blonde hair and an open face. Frank spoke to her afterwards and learned that her name was Jo Manning, a technical support officer at the coroner's office. She always tried to get to the funerals of such cases when her workload allowed. For her, attendance was a simple mark of respect. Frank found his attendance less easy to explain but Jo seemed to understand. In time they grew used to seeing each other on separate benches in cold rooms. Jo would tell him of small triumphs in the cases of those where a next of kin was located – sisters who had lost touch, brothers who had moved abroad, as well as the sadness of those where no one was found.

Andrea asked him once about the list of names and dates he had in his notebook and he told her.

'Is it very weird?'

She hesitated before answering. 'A little.'

'I'm not sure why I do it.'

She smiled. 'Because you have a melancholy disposition.'

'You make me sound like my mother.'

She looked at him. 'Perhaps this has more to do with your father.'

Frank put the notebook away and gave a little laugh. 'I'm hoping I'll grow out of it.'

Andrea touched his face. 'You'd say, wouldn't you, if you ever found the job was getting to you? If it was making you too sad or depressed.'

He told her he was fine.

6

It was a forty-five-minute drive from Frank and Andrea's home to Evergreen Senior Living. Today an hour had passed already and they remained trapped in the Crufts gridlock around the NEC. Andrea and a Great Dane in the next car stared at each other morosely. The same advert for a carpet showroom had been playing on the radio for what seemed a very long time. Mo sat in the back engrossed in her comic and Frank hummed a tune as the engine idled.

In the advert a sales assistant showed a husband and wife around a showroom. The husband was a reluctant customer. The sales assistant extolled the virtues of different floor coverings to which the husband invariably replied in a dour, no-nonsense Northern accent: 'Oh aye? And how much is that going to set me back?'

Hearing the amazing low price would cause him to faint and his oblivious wife to say: 'Come on, Jim, this is no time for a lie down.'

The scenario was repeated over and over again. The final revelation of nought per cent finance was too much for Jim who fainted for the last time and was unable to be revived. It was left unclear whether he was in fact dead, but his wife seemed unconcerned as she told the sales assistant: 'I think we'd better take the lot.'

The voice-over gave the location of all the stores and then a helium-voiced speeded-up garbling of credit terms and conditions.

Andrea tore her eyes away from the Great Dane and looked at Frank. 'Do we have to listen to local radio?'

'I just wanted to catch the news. I want to see if they've picked up on the school closure protest.'

'I can't take much more.'

'They'll play some music soon – it's not all adverts. It's golden-oldie hour.'

She sighed. 'Great – fingers crossed for some Phil Collins.' A song started and Andrea instantly recognized the pizzicato strings. 'Oh God, it can't be . . .'

Frank beamed and turned the radio up. 'Amazing! T'Pau! Hey, Mo, this is our song!'

Mo shuffled forward in her seat. 'What?'

'Your mother and I – this is our special song.'

Andrea turned round. 'It isn't, Mo. Ignore him.'

Frank looked at Mo in the mirror and nodded conspiratorially.

'Why is it your song, Mom?'

'It isn't our song. Your father's just saying that to annoy me.'

Mo listened to the song for a few moments.

'How can you have China in your hands?'

'Who knows, Mo.'

Mo listened for a few more moments and then wrinkled her nose. 'I don't like it, Mom. It doesn't make sense.'

Frank shook his head. 'You two have got no soul.'

*

It was 1988 when Frank met Andrea, but behind the smoked-glass doors of Birmingham FM every day was 1983. The playlist favoured the current top forty, but would squeeze in a power ballad from Tina Turner or Bonnie Tyler every chance it got. The women who worked at the station favoured big hair, and a kind of leather-and-lace rock-chick-gone-to-seed look. The men had blotchy blond highlights, wore large red-framed glasses, sky-blue jeans and colourful knitwear. Andrea soon noticed the uneasy contrast between the dour off-air personalities of many of the DJs and the larger than life clothes they chose to wear.

Frank was a recent graduate in his first job as a reporter; Andrea was still a student doing a work placement at the station. They instantly picked each other out as misfits. Andrea's clothes and hair had something of the 1950s about them and she seemed to Frank intimidatingly cool and collected. He was incredulous to later discover that Andrea thought exactly the same of him, though less incredulous to subsequently find that this had been based on a mistaken impression.

When he'd got the job at the station, Frank had assumed that he should wear a suit and tie every day. His budget being tight, he bought his two suits at the local branch of Oxfam. As far as he was concerned, a suit was a suit and aside from checking that they didn't have holes and weren't outright flares he didn't notice the width of the trousers or the shape of the lapel. The team at Birmingham FM, merely five years out of date, smirked behind Frank's back at his ten-years-out-of-date clothes. For Andrea, however, never suspecting that Frank could be as clueless about clothes as he turned out to be, he was cutting edge in his adoption of new-wave retro style.

Like all work placements, Andrea was taken advantage of. Many producers and presenters believed the best experience they could offer her was either to be left ignored and forgotten in the corner of a room 'observing' or fetching drinks and lunch for the team. Aware that they should be providing something more enriching for her, but unwilling to take the time to do so, most staff felt irked by her presence and passed her on to another party as soon as possible. She eventually turned up at Frank's desk. On their first morning together he got her a tea and asked her how the placement had been going. Andrea was surprised by the question; in three weeks there no one else had asked her.

'It's been really useful.'

Frank hadn't expected her to be so positive. He'd observed her regular errands to the shops for coffees and chocolate bars. 'In what way?'

'Well, before I came here I couldn't decide what I wanted to do after university and now I know.'

Frank couldn't see her as a presenter. 'Are you thinking of producer?'

Andrea shook her head vigorously. 'No. A translator. Spanish. My degree is a big mistake. I never want to work here. Or anywhere like here. I'm not interested in working in the media. I'm going to quit and re-enrol on a Spanish degree. I should have done that in the first place.'

Frank nodded. 'Right. Good. Well, that's a positive outcome, then.'

★

Andrea worked with Frank for the remaining week of her placement. Despite her decision about her new career direction she appreciated Frank's genuine efforts to tell her about his job and the way he worked, and she found going out with him to cover stories to be a welcome relief from the studio where the voice of Carol Decker seemed to boom from every speaker. Although younger than most of the rest of the staff, Frank seemed more solid and mature in ways that Andrea couldn't quite put her finger on. He took his job seriously not just for the sake of ambition and advancement, but because he cared about the work he did and wanted to be good at it.

Frank discovered quickly that Andrea was not as intimidating as she had at first seemed. She had an acute ear for the vocal tics and traits of those around her and was a brilliant mimic of certain presenters. She had a keen sense of the absurd but also appreciated the ways in which the apparently trivial and laughable were often nothing of the kind. By their third day of working together Frank realized that he kept finding new things to like about Andrea. He tried to stop, but still they mounted up, unignorable. He liked her Leeds accent, he liked the way she unwrapped Kit Kats, he liked the perfect clarity of her face. Although it made him slightly nervous he even liked the way that she assumed he knew about the kinds of obscure bands she liked. He had no idea where she'd got the impression that he had a clue about such things, but he couldn't help but be flattered.

*

Mo shuffled forward on the rear seat again. 'Mom?'

'Yes.'

'What do you think is yours and Dad's special song?'

Andrea thought for a moment. 'I don't know. I'm not sure that we have one.'

Mo was insistent. 'I think you should have one. I think it's important. Try and think of one.'

Andrea thought again and then smiled. 'Okay. I think maybe something by the Pixies.'

Mo looked happy. 'Can we listen to them when we get home?'

'Yeah – you'll recognize them – I've played them before.'

'Why is that your song?'

'Oh, your father was a big fan when we met. A big expert on the Pixies.'

Frank shook his head slowly and glanced at Andrea. 'You're a regular funny guy, aren't you?'

Andrea smiled sweetly and hummed 'Gigantic'.

Frank thought back to the final lunch hour of their week working together. Andrea had been sitting reading a music paper, something Frank always found unnerving. She looked up at him and asked, 'Have you heard *Surfer Rosa* yet?'

Frank considered various high-risk strategies in answering this, but decided in the end for the simplicity and honesty of a simple head shake.

Andrea continued. 'It's an amazing review, but you know, I don't want to be disappointed.'

He picked up on the doubt in her voice and thought he

could safely venture something here without revealing his ignorance.

'Yeah, I mean can she really live up to that kind of hype?'

Andrea looked at him for a moment and then burst out laughing. He liked her laugh – it was a deep, open giggle that always made him laugh too, though in this case the effect was slightly more disconcerting.

When she'd stopped, she said: 'You're a regular funny guy.'

He shrugged, having no idea what was funny, but unwilling to rebuff the compliment. He didn't like pretending to be something he wasn't, but he thought he could save letting her know for another time. He was almost sure there would be other times.

Mo had finished her comic now and was waving halfheartedly out of the window at a large poodle who was in turn ignoring her.

She moved forward in her seat to speak. 'Dad, there won't be anyone in the building, will there?'

'What building?'

'The one we looked at. When they demolish it. There won't be any people still inside?'

Andrea gave Frank a warning look before saying. 'You asked me that the other day. Do you remember what I said?'

'You said there won't be. You said they emptied it months ago, but I just thought what if a homeless person went in there to shelter from the rain? Or what if some little boys went in to explore? Or what if one of the people who worked there realized that they'd left their umbrella and they went back to get it?'

Frank answered. 'But no one could get in. You saw it – there are big high boards all around, and the men will go and check last thing before they demolish it. Buildings get demolished all the time and never, ever in all the time I've been doing the news has anyone ever been trapped in the building.'

'What if a pigeon flew in the window, or a dog jumped in?'

'There are no stray dogs in town, and a pigeon could just fly straight out again.' Frank thought for a moment. 'Do you want to come and watch it being demolished? You'll see then and you can stop worrying.'

Straight away he realized he'd said the wrong thing. Mo's face was horror-stricken. 'People watch it being demolished? But what if it falls on them?'

'It won't fall on anyone. The people have to stand a long way away, and the men are clever; they know exactly which way the building will fall.'

Mo was shaking her head. 'Don't go, Dad. Mom, tell Dad not to go. It's dangerous. I don't want to go. I don't want to see it.'

Frank looked at Mo's eyes in the mirror. 'That's okay. We won't go.' He suddenly felt as if he might cry. He reached back and squeezed her leg. 'I don't really want to see it either.'

7

Mustansar the transport correspondent was walking past Frank's desk when he reached out and grabbed the sandwich packaging littering his work surface. 'Frank, quick, without thinking, what are you eating?'

Frank looked at Mustansar. 'A sandwich.'

'Yes, yes, but what's the filling?'

Frank thought for a moment. 'I can't remember.'

'Excellent. That's what I wanted. So, just on taste – what are you eating?'

Frank took another mouthful and chewed slowly.

'What can you taste? What's the filling?'

Frank thought hard. 'Wet and cold?'

'Ha!' shouted Mustansar louder than was necessary. 'That is not what it says on the box! This is what I'm talking about. That woman. What's she doing to our food? Has she got a syringe down there that sucks out flavour? Can anyone distinguish cheese and coleslaw from tuna mayonnaise? Or does it all come from the same vat of cold porridge that she ladles into damp bread every morning? And do you know the best of it, my friend? We pay her! We actually give her money! We are fools!'

Julia was seated at the next desk and looked up. 'To be fair, I don't think she actually makes the sandwiches

– they're just bought in along with the rest of that snack-bar crap. At least in the old days of the staff canteen you could get some fresh vegetables.'

Mustansar wrinkled his nose, but Julia didn't seem to notice. Frank took another bite of his sandwich. 'I don't mind them; they fill a gap.'

Julia shook her head. 'You're wasting your time, Mustansar. Frank's exactly the reason why there has never been a revolution in this country. A deluded peasant, happy with his gruel. If you want a nice sandwich, go down to Entice, they do beautiful stuff – freshly baked bread, locally sourced vegetables, all organic ingredients.'

Mustansar pretended to consider it for a moment before saying: 'No, fuck that. I'm off to McDonald's. Does anyone want any real food?'

Julia sighed and returned to her screen. Frank asked Mustansar for an apple pie and went back to scanning the stories ahead of the morning's production meeting.

It looked as if the lead was going to be a hospital story. West Birmingham was apologizing to a patient for the distress caused to him when he overheard staff laughing about his weight and referring to him in offensive terms. Frank had watched the package already. It included an interview with the man, who said that whilst he acknowledged he was overweight he didn't expect to overhear members of staff laughing about it like children. His central message was that members of the caring profession should be more caring and professional. Frank found it hard to argue with that, but worried that by appearing on the evening news the man was exposing himself to more unkind comments. Viewers could be quite cruel; Frank knew all about it.

Next was the expected sentencing later that day of a man found guilty of throwing a pan of hot oil over his wife's head. Footage from the trial showed a small man in a tracksuit covering his face with his jacket. A picture of his wife before the assault showed a woman with tired eyes and the ghost of a smile.

Next an uneasy gear change into a light-hearted story about obesity in pets and a canine gym that had opened up. It was a quiet day. Or, as Julia put it, 'A load of old bollocks.' The difference between a busy news day and a quiet one had a big impact on people's lives. Today was lucky for the doggy gym, which on another day would have gone unreported; unlucky for the wife abuser.

Through the years Frank had started to detect patterns and recurrences in the news. The same things happened over and over with little regard for originality. Sometimes he'd feel sure that he'd presented certain items before; sometimes he thought he remembered entire programmes. The faces changed but the stories were the same. Another sick child hoping to get an operation abroad, another old couple swindled out of their life savings, another bare paddock of neglected horses. Sometimes he almost anticipated them. Like counting cards and knowing when to expect the next king. The different incidences became compacted in his mind to form generic news staples and the faces merged to form the composite face of a local news victim. He had not, though, become desensitized. Whilst he recognized the patterns, he still appreciated, albeit hours after the show, the pain, or the loss, or, very occasionally, the joy in each story. He remained, he hoped, despite it all, human.

He was interrupted by a call on his mobile. He took it out of the office. It was Cyril.

'Aye, aye, Cap'n.'

'Hi, Cyril.'

'Anything in the net today?'

Frank wasn't sure when the fishing metaphors had started, but he didn't think they made these exchanges any easier to bear. 'Not really, Cyril, sorry.'

'Oh, come on, Frank. It's been a week. Toss me a sprat.'

Frank closed his eyes and tapped the bridge of his nose with his finger. It had been a week. It didn't seem that long to him. A new joke was due. For a little while a few months back Cyril's calls had become less frequent and Frank had briefly held the hope they were dying off, but now they were back to at least once or twice a week. He gave up the obvious victim.

'Well, there's something about a gym for dogs . . .' He couldn't go on; Cyril was giggling at the other end of the phone.

'A gym for dogs? You're having me on! You couldn't make it up!'

Frank sighed. 'No, I don't suppose you could.'

'Oh, Frank – people, eh? Barking mad.' Another gale of laughter. 'This is a goldmine. Let me go away and have a think. I'm getting possibilities already. I'll get back to you in an hour – on the dog and bone!' He was laughing helplessly.

Frank rested his head against the wall. 'Cyril, remember, just something subtle,' but Cyril had already hung up.

*

Frank picked up the local paper in the hope of finding a new lead to suggest at the production meeting. He had leafed through over half of the pages before something caught his eye. The body of a seventy-nine-year-old man had been discovered sitting on a bench on Smallwood Middleway. The police estimated that the man had been there for two days before anyone noticed he was dead. The man was named as Michael Church and the police were appealing for information. Frank reached for his notebook to take down the details. The newspaper carried a photo of the man. It was a poor-quality passport-style image, taken presumably from his bus pass. It showed an old man in a V-neck jumper and shirt leaning slightly to one side, neatly parted hair, red cheeks and piercing blue eyes. Frank lifted the paper closer and stared at the image. He recognized the man. He quickly read through the article again. The name meant nothing to him, but he knew he had seen those eyes before. They were unusually large, giving an almost comic look of mock-innocence to the face. He tried to think where he had seen Michael Church before.

Julia noticed him peering at the paper. 'Found anything of news value at all?'

'Sorry?'

'The paper, Frank. Impossible though it seems, is there anything in there of more pressing import than cross-trainers for dogs?'

Frank looked again at Michael Church's face. Completely unknown, dead for two days already. 'I suspect nothing that Martin would consider newsworthy.'

Julia went back to typing and Frank continued to look at the old man's eyes. He felt his blood moving more quickly through his body. Perhaps this time he could do more than simply lay flowers.

8

'"Call the banker! Call the banker!"' cried Henry, his eyes shining. 'Is that it? Did I get it right?'

Frank shook his head. 'Sorry, no, that's someone else.'

Henry punched his open palm. 'Ooh – you're good. You're too good for me. Give me another go. Here we are now, how about: "It's good but it's not right!"'

Frank shrugged his shoulder. 'No, sorry. Wrong again.'

Henry looked shocked. 'Balls! I was sure I had you then. Oh, wait there, wait there: "Hello, good evening and welcome." Eh? Eh?'

Frank wondered how long this might go on for. Every time he visited his mother, he spent some time in the residents' lounge. The manageress thought he lifted their spirits. Andrea thought it was more likely that he drove everyone to their rooms for a nap. Henry recognized Frank from TV but could never place him, or possibly pretended not to. There was a diabolical glint in Henry's eyes and an edge to his grin that led Frank to believe that Henry knew very well who Frank was and was mercilessly mocking him.

'Oh God. Oh no. You're not that insufferable little prick, are you?'

Frank looked apologetic. 'Possibly.'

'Oh Christ. "Remember, don't have nightmares." What an utter shit! Is that you?'

Henry was interrupted by Walter's approach.

'Oh, for God's sake, Henry, leave the man alone and give it a rest, will you.' Henry immediately sidled off. Walter shook a box of dominos at Frank. 'Fancy a quick one?'

'Why not?' Frank pulled up a chair to their usual table by the window. Walter distributed the tiles and hummed 'I Just Called to Say I Love You' with gusto. Sometimes Frank wondered if this was how it might have been had his father lived to old age. A quiet game of dominos, small talk about the weather, an easy companionship, but the image never quite rang true.

His father had died at fifty-one in a room full of people. Standing in front of a screen, illuminated by the glow of a projector, he was pointing with a fine baton at his design for the headquarters of a legal firm when his arm suddenly jerked towards the upper part of the plan. The assembled partners focused their attention at the baton's end and squinted to see what was now being called to their attention. They jumped in shock as the gentle whirring of the projector's fan was abruptly drowned out by Douglas's roar of pain, and he collapsed sideways, crashing through the screen, the pale blue lines of his design momentarily framing his stricken face before he hit the ground. He was dead before the ambulance arrived.

Frank was eleven when his father died, but in truth Douglas had been absent throughout much of his life, his passion for his work taking up most of his time and energy.

Frank and his mother stayed on in the house that Douglas had built for them, a modern two-storey flat-roofed home set on a gentle slope in Edgbaston.

Even before his father's death, Frank had noticed the way Maureen often seemed elsewhere in her thoughts. He had become aware as a young boy of days when his mother would watch the television without seeing anything, would ask him where he was going without listening to the answer or open cupboards and stare into them for minutes at a time. Some days she would be fine, but on others he would return from school to see her at her bedroom window, looking out at the sky, an expression of terrible loss on her face. As he grew older, he began to suspect that his mother was doing all this for his benefit – that he alone was her intended audience. Sometimes friends or work colleagues would visit and she seemed a different person with them, laughing and chatting. Whilst he believed she often was unhappy, and could even see that she perhaps had grounds to be so, he also felt that she wanted him to see her that way. It was a feeling he could never quite shake.

Walter was winning as always. Frank wasn't sure what Walter got from playing against someone so weak at the game, maybe just the novelty at his age of anything being effortless.

'I saw your mother in here the other day.'

'Oh, good. She does leave her room occasionally, then?'

'Oh yes. She's not in here all the time, but she comes down every now and again, and it's always a pleasure when she does. She has such a sense of humour.'

Frank had heard this many times. 'Apparently yes.'

'Yes, oh, she makes me smile. Very quick witted. Very dry.' Walter laughed to himself. 'You should hear what she says about the management here. "The Cabal" she calls them. I know she has her blue days. We all do. But on her good days she's like a crisp, clean gin and tonic.'

Blue days. Frank had always thought of them as purple. He smiled at the thought of the gin and tonic; it was a good description – sparkling and fresh. He saw that side of her very rarely now, but he knew what Walter meant.

After Douglas's death Maureen continued to work part-time at the local doctor's surgery and had many friends and colleagues around her, but despite this she often spoke as if her life was almost over – referring to herself as old as far back as Frank could remember. At times her melancholy bordered on self-parody, descending into Eeyore-like gloom. Andrea asked Frank not long after they married if he thought his mother was depressed and Frank had said: 'She's not depressed; she's just miserable.'

But after retirement, whatever constituted Maureen's condition – grief, depression, loneliness or just a pre-disposition to melancholy – was exacerbated by an increase in her alcohol consumption. Late in the evening, after she'd had a bottle of wine, Frank would receive phone calls from Maureen telling him that she didn't think she'd live much longer, or that she wanted to be cremated not buried, and he would find himself ensnared in her circular monologues.

Gradually the house became too much for her. She no longer had the energy or the will to keep the large windows and the parquet floors clean. More of Frank and Andrea's visits were taken up with cleaning and shopping for food. Maureen started to lose weight and never seemed to know when or what she'd last eaten. One day Frank received a call from the newsagent near his mother's house, telling him that Maureen had tried to pay for her paper with a bus ticket.

The doctor didn't rule out Alzheimer's but diagnosed Maureen primarily as depressed. Frank asked her to come and live with his family, but Maureen refused point blank. She said she would rather he smothered her with a pillow than become a burden on him. And so after much investigation and thought, aged just sixty-seven, Maureen moved into Evergreen Senior Living.

Evergreen had started off in the States before importing their variety of deluxe privately run care homes into the UK. Maureen's home, by virtue of being in the Midlands, had been branded Evergreen Forest of Arden. It was a vast purpose-built facility, with over one hundred permanent residents and more making brief stays for respite care. The home was divided into two zones. Maureen, Walter and Henry were in 'Helping Hands', whilst those with more advanced dementia or greater dependency were housed in a separate, secure area called 'Golden Days', inevitably referred to by residents as 'Gaga Days'.

For some historical reason never explained to Frank the home had always attracted a significant proportion of residents retired from the entertainment business. Frank had first heard of Evergreen through Phil Smethway, who had himself heard of it through someone else, word of mouth being the way that most people came across the home. Retired magicians, dancing girls, musicians and technicians now found themselves all at the same endless after-show party, drinking tea and trying to identify the latest presenter of *Countdown*.

Once a month a cabaret night was staged by the residents. Maureen had attended one once and told Frank it had all the charm and entertainment value of being buried alive. Frank noticed the poster for the next one on the wall:

The Great Misterioso
(aka Ernie Webster)

will be presenting a dazzling array
of his greatest tricks in

✶　✶　✶

THE MAGIC NEVER DIES

✶　✶　✶

Saturday 24th 4 p.m., Shakespeare Lounge

'"The magic never dies". Are you going to that, Walter?'

'No, it's been cancelled.'

'Why?'

'He died.'

'Oh dear,' said Frank.

Walter broke into a wide grin. 'So that proved that bugger wrong, didn't it?'

9

It was almost midnight. Frank undid his bow tie, took off his dinner jacket and flopped onto the sofa. His head was filled with the static of the evening's exchanges – scraps of banal conversation, half-hearted banter, empty words that continued to jangle. His face ached from smiling for the camera. G. E. Jones Industrial Solutions had got their money's worth. The drinks reception was interminable, followed by a dinner of overcooked beef, and he'd thought he'd be able to escape after his speech, but then came the photos. He had posed for at least forty, and at least half of those, it seemed, with men called Derek.

Frank was always amazed by the non sequiturs and bizarre remarks that tipsy managers and board members blurted out whilst posing next to him and waiting for the flash. The close physical presence of someone hitherto seen only through a television screen seemed to have a strange impact on conversational skills. One insisted on saying 'Penis' rather than the more traditional 'Cheese' as the photo was taken; another asked Frank: 'Do you piss in a bottle under the desk?' whilst another muttered inexplicably: 'The wife won't like this.' Frank knew he wouldn't sleep until the buzzing in his head subsided. He didn't want to wake Andrea with his tossing and turning and so sat in the cool, dark living room waiting for a calm to descend.

He looked at his cufflinks and cursed Phil Smethway whose gift they were. He felt bad for cursing the dead, but couldn't help blaming Phil for every PA he did. It was easier to blame Phil than himself. He knew that he could say no, as Julia did. But Phil had said yes to everything and Frank had simply carried on unthinkingly. Phil always said it was part of their job; he emphasized the many charities he supported through appearances. But most of the charity dinners were naked exercises in corporate PR and Phil's true motive, Frank suspected, was that he simply enjoyed the glitz and glamour even as low level as it often was. It was after all at a launch for a new car showroom where Phil had met his last wife, Michelle, almost forty years his junior.

When Julia had joined the team, she'd made it clear that she wouldn't be doing any PAs – she considered them a compromise of her neutrality and integrity. At first Frank had dismissed this as more of Julia's pompous earnestness, but as time had gone on he'd felt more and more uncomfortable cutting ribbons and making speeches. It was a ridiculous way to spend an evening. It was also more time away from Andrea and Mo. He now tried to only accept those invitations that had become annual commitments.

He removed the cufflinks and played with them in his palm. They had a nice weight and surface finish. They were solid silver, made by Hermes, and he was sure they had been horribly expensive. They had been Phil's farewell gift. It was typical of Phil to not only buy everyone else presents at his own departure, but for those presents to far outstrip in both thought and value the tacky landfill purchased with the proceeds of the office whip-round for him. Inside the box Phil had put a small note saying: 'Have some class for once in your life.' And even though Frank knew Phil had bought them to mock his singular lack of panache, he thought they were beautiful.

Phil Smethway's career had been marked by a combination of good luck, personal charm and an amazing ability to adapt. He had started out in insurance before taking detours through estate agency, concert promotion and pirate radio. He'd suffered setbacks in his career like everyone, but his ability to shed his old skin and move on meant that they were never more than fleeting. His move to national TV came at the age of sixty-three, a time when most men would be considering retirement, but for Phil it was just the start of his greatest work. Phil was born only five years after Frank's father and yet Frank would never have placed them in the same generation. Phil always seemed entirely of the moment.

When Frank joined *Heart of England Reports* as a reporter in 1989, Phil had been on the show for fifteen years, the last nine of those as the main anchor. Frank had grown up watching Phil, and the easy charm he had on screen made Frank suspicious of how he might be in person. Frank had come to recognize a certain strain of presenter in local radio. Some of those who possessed a greater fluency, who were able to communicate a smile through the microphone and achieve a close rapport with listeners, developed a strangely exaggerated view of the rarity and specialness of their gifts. They had seen too often how others groped and stumbled at something they found effortless and this knowledge worked on them. They began to see their personalities as the commodities they were and to ration and exchange them only for hard currency. Off air they aspired to be as charmless as plastic forks. This combined with a suspicion of newcomers and a generalized paranoia that one day someone would come along with all the natural, easy, unmeasured grace they had once possessed. Perhaps luckily for him, Frank had presented no such threat and so suffered nothing more from them than mild contempt.

Frank learned quickly that Phil was not of this school. His on-screen warmth was a contained and diluted version of his off-screen self. Away from the camera Phil had a wicked sense of humour, dry and relentless, a constant jabbing. He found something to needle everyone around him and kept at it, and yet no one got angry or found it tiresome, but reacted instead like puppies having their stomachs tickled. Phil was a lover of the finer things in life and he never ceased to get comic mileage out of Frank's lack of discrimination. Frank would enter the office and Phil would look genuinely concerned and ask if he was happy with the tie he was wearing. On the occasions when they grabbed a bite together he was both amazed and appalled at Frank's utter indifference to food.

His greatest skill, though, was in capsizing co-presenters and correspondents, something he would do only very occasionally and which he swore was unintentional. In the last few seconds of a video package, as the action was about to return to the studio, he would say some small thing, his face a deadpan mask. They called them 'grenades' as there was always a small delay before detonation. The co-presenter would launch into the next item, successfully holding it together for five or maybe ten seconds before issuing an abrupt bark of laughter, and Phil would frown and apologize to the viewer and take over the link. The baffling thing was that the lines were never that funny, at times even made no sense at all, but some combination of delivery and context was devastating. Often their humour lay simply in the glimpse they offered of Phil's internal mental landscape, which seemed always at a far remove from whatever report was running. He'd done it to Frank just once, back when Frank was the sports correspondent. They sat and waited in the studio whilst a report ran about a fatal stabbing outside a fish-and-chip shop. Their crime reporter was at the scene speaking to overexcited eye-witnesses and speculating as to the motive for the attack.

As the reporter was about to hand back to the studio, Phil turned to Frank and said as if in response to something he'd said, 'The problem is that saveloys turn your piss red.'

Frank could only remember one occasion on which some-one had taken offence at something Phil had said. A floor manager once told him to fuck off for a fairly innocuous crack. Frank was amazed at Phil's reaction.

'Oh God, Frank, he thinks I'm a complete dick.'

'Don't be daft. He's just having a bad day.'

'No, you didn't see the way he looked at me. Like he really hated me. He said it with real venom.'

'I was there! There was no venom – he just snapped. It was nothing.'

'I don't like the thought of him hating me.'

Frank was laughing. 'He doesn't hate you, and even if he did – so what? What do you care about his opinion? Everyone thinks I'm a dick and it doesn't bother me.'

Phil gave a small smile. 'Yes, but it's factually accurate in your case.'

Frank nodded in acknowledgement of the open goal. After the conversation, though, he felt he'd glimpsed another side of Phil. Not the effortless charm on the surface, but a hint of the frantic paddling underneath. It would never have occurred to him that someone so assured and confident felt such a need to be liked.

He put the cufflinks on the coffee table and finished his drink. The whiskey had worked to smooth out the edges of the evening. He looked in on Mo, pushing some strands of hair from her face, before gratefully climbing into bed and drifting off to sleep.

10

Maureen had never been like other mothers. As a general rule, the kinds of things that made other mothers happy tended to have the opposite effect on Maureen. Frank had known this since he was a little boy. He remembered visiting the homes of classmates and being shocked and puzzled to see their finger-daubed paintings stuck on walls and fridges. Whenever he took a picture home from school to his mother, she'd ask: 'What am I supposed to do with this? Why do they make you bring these things home?'

It never occurred to Frank to be upset by this, in fact he agreed. His paintings were rubbish; he could see that. They were rushed things, done under duress, and never looked remotely as he had intended.

Maureen couldn't stand boasting. She tried to compensate for her husband's professional confidence by deprecating herself to a brutal degree. Similarly Frank's modest achievements, such as they were, were not the source of joy they might be to other mothers, but a cause of real anguish to Maureen. She was mortified to discover that Frank had done better than many of his classmates in his O levels.

'Don't tell anyone what grades you got! Oh, how can I face the other mothers?'

Frank could see definite advantages in this. His mother never fussed in the way that other mothers did. She never embarrassed him in public by singing his praises and ruffling his hair. She rarely turned up to watch the dreadful school plays he was forced to participate in. She didn't stand on the touchline and shout silly things that the other boys could tease him about. She hated any acknowledgement of Mother's Day, which she considered artificial and American. She had no interest in boxes of chocolate or bath salts or cookery books.

She was not an easy mother to make happy, but Frank used to think he might prefer that to a mother who was indiscriminately delighted by everything. The few things that did please her seemed to count for more. She loved books and if Frank managed to buy her one she liked her happiness and gratitude were sincere. She enjoyed watching old films on television. She passed this love on to Frank, along with a wide knowledge of British B-list actors of the fifties. In latter years Frank would buy her videos and then DVDs of films she'd seen at the cinema as a girl and she would gasp in delight and amazement as she unwrapped them and saw the title, always saying: 'Now that was a film.'

But as she grew older the short list of things that made her happy diminished. Since her move to Evergreen Frank had been at a loss to find anything to lift her gloom. She said she no longer had the concentration to read books or watch films. As had always been the case, she made no effort to appear happy for the sake of Frank or anyone else. She was quick to pour scorn on any ideas aimed at improving her lot, and either didn't notice, or pretended not to notice, how upsetting this could be for others. Frank would often leave Evergreen furious with her refusal to acknowledge how hard both Andrea and Mo had tried to make her happy, and her lack of grace in even pretending the occasional success.

Frank frequently found himself now wondering why she couldn't be more like other mothers. The other women in the home were delighted to see their families and took evident pleasure in their grandchildren. Frank developed an almost bloody-minded insistence on making his mother do things that other mothers and grandmothers would enjoy. Chief among these was his determination that she should take occasional trips out from Evergreen.

Once a month he took her out for a drive, and every time she put up the usual objections: 'Where is there to go?' 'What is there to see?' 'I don't want to go out in that heat/rain/fog etc.' None of which moved Frank. He and Andrea would come close to physically dragging her from her wingback armchair and Maureen would give every impression of being kidnapped. 'Where are you taking me?' Calling out to other residents: 'I don't know when I'll be back.' The other residents smiling and calling: 'Have a lovely time, Maureen.' And Frank wondering why he couldn't have a parent that said and felt things as straightforward as that.

On their trips out Frank and Mo would sit together in the back, Andrea would drive and Maureen would be wedged into the front seat, tucked in with a blanket that she insisted on and was pure theatrical prop.

They tried quaint market towns, grand stately homes and charming woodland walks, all of which Maureen endured like so many visits to the dentist. She would generally soften at the inevitable stop-off at a tea shop, which gave her the rare opportunity to take tea as weak as she liked it and to make catty comments about the other customers. What anyone else might consider heart-warming, the sight of an elderly couple enjoying each other's company and a slice of fruit cake, would incite scorn from Maureen.

'Look at them. Bored out of their minds. Nothing to say and nothing to do, just trying to get through another bloody day.' Or the inevitable. 'Why aren't they screaming?'

Although she rarely enjoyed the destination, Frank noticed that Maureen seemed quite placated by the drive. In particular she appeared to enjoy driving along residential streets and looking at the suburban houses.

Today as they drove through Yardley she said: 'That's a nice little house, isn't it, Andrea? A nice pitched roof and a little garden path.'

The house was an unremarkable semi. Andrea glanced at it. 'It's nice enough, but you lived in a spectacular house. You featured in style magazines.'

Maureen nodded. 'It was beautiful I suppose, but I always felt that Douglas thought we ruined it by living in it. We just seemed to upset the clean lines and sharp edges.'

Mo shuffled forward in her seat. 'Granny.'

'Yes, dear.'

'You know Douglas.'

'Yes, dear.'

'Grandad.'

Frank sensed his mother's patience growing thin. 'Yes, dear. I know who we're talking about.'

'I never met him.'

'I'm aware of that.'

'But I've seen photos.'

'Yes, I'm sure you have.'

'He smoked a pipe, didn't he?'

'He did.'

'Why did he do that?'

'I don't know. I suppose he must have liked it.'

'Was he like Sherlock Holmes?'

'Not really, no.'

Mo slumped back in her seat, disappointed. Maureen turned her head slightly to see Mo and smiled at her.

'You know you look very much like your grandfather?'

Mo looked at Frank. 'Is that true?'

Frank shrugged. 'You do a bit. You just need the pipe. Would you like that? Sitting at home puffing away whilst eating your spaghetti hoops on toast?'

Mo pulled an exaggerated face of disgust. She spoke in a whisper so Maureen wouldn't hear. 'How can I look like him? He was a man, and I'm a girl.'

Frank whispered back. 'Well, you don't look like a man, you know. You don't look exactly like him – you just have similar eyes and mouth. You have some of his expressions.'

Mo pulled some strange faces, as if trying to find the expressions she shared with her grandfather. Frank looked at her and tried to imagine his father as a child, but couldn't. When he thought of his father, he found it hard to think of anything but his work, impossible to separate the man from the buildings. Douglas had been one of Birmingham's key post-war architects, one of the ground-zero visionaries along with Madin and Roberts, welcomed with open arms by the city engineer Sir Herbert Manzoni.

Frank had once come across a quote from Manzoni: 'I have never been very certain as to the value of tangible links with the past. As to Birmingham's buildings, there is little of real worth in our architecture.'

It seemed to Frank that Manzoni had a particular lack of certainty about the value of the city's Victorian heritage. Landmark buildings, elegant department stores and elaborately embellished public buildings were torn down and replaced with the kind of stark buildings favoured by Douglas and his contemporaries. Birmingham was where the future would be built.

It hadn't worked out that way, though. The demolition frenzy of post-war development was now seen as a disaster, the concrete collar of the ring road and other schemes revealed as flawed or obsolete even before they were completed. But the craving to wipe clean and start again wouldn't die; it was too deeply ingrained in the city's character. The target had merely shifted. Now it was the turn of the post-war buildings, the clean lines and concrete which had replaced the Victorian ornamentation. The future that Frank's father had spent his life building was being shown as little sentimentality as the Victorian past he had tried to replace.

Andrea looked at Mo in the rear-view mirror.

'Maybe you'll grow up to be an architect like your grandfather.'

Mo shook her head. 'I don't want to be an architect.'

'Why not?'

'Because after you die they demolish your buildings.'

'That doesn't happen to every architect,' said Frank.

'No, dear,' added Maureen, 'some are still alive when the demolition starts.'

11

He was having to pull over every few minutes to check the A–Z, then with the next few twists and turns committed to memory, he'd set off again, driving slowly through the heavy rain. Despite the downpour the windscreen wipers protested at every sweep, squawking as they dragged themselves with ill grace over the glass, a sound that had a special ability to jab at Frank's nerves. He realized he was blinking in time to the wipers. He decided to pull over and walk.

The Hilltop estate was a compact sixties development on the very edge of the city. It was set, as its name rather overplayed, on an unremarkable bump in the landscape offering views back towards the city in one direction, and out to ploughed fields in the other. Due to some combination of the whims of its developers and the con-tours of the land the Hilltop estate had something of an experimental feel. As Frank had looked at the page of the A–Z, he saw the steady Euclidean geometry of the road network descend into a spaghetti of ellipses and ox-bows at Hilltop. It was no clearer off the page. Crescents bloomed from crescents in a tangled Mandelbrot soup.

With the street map in one hand and an umbrella in the other Frank set off to find 12 Lysander Avenue. At first it seemed as if the neat houses and maisonettes were not playing their part in Hilltop's mission to disorientate. They were not the melting Gaudi confections that Frank thought would better complement the street design. It was only a matter of minutes, however, before their role became clear. Whilst every house had a number, they weren't as far as Frank could tell in any discernible order. He found number 2 Lysander Avenue, which was followed by number 4 and number 6 creating a momentary illusion of a world in balance, before number 54 loomed up. After further increasingly damp investigation Frank discovered that number 54 belonged to Titania Close, which appeared not simply to intersect Lysander but to dismember it entirely, scattering the remains all over the estate. Frank eventually found number 12 embedded in the heart of Oberon Drive. A woman in a grey trouser suit, with long red hair, answered the door.

'Mr Allcroft?'

'Frank, please.'

'Hello, Frank. I'm Rebecca – you spoke on the phone to my colleague Simi.'

'Hi, Rebecca, I'm sorry I'm late. I couldn't find the place.'

Rebecca frowned. 'Did you not have the address?'

'Yes, it's just this place, you know; it's a labyrinth . . .' Frank laughed.

Rebecca looked at him blankly. 'Well, it's no problem anyway. I'm here all morning sorting through things. We really appreciate your offer to help – it could lead us to a relative.'

'I'm glad to help. Hopefully this will jog my memory. I

see a lot of faces in my work, but I usually remember them eventually.'

Rebecca nodded. 'Okay, I've collected some stuff on the table in the living room there – have a look through. I need to get on and clear the rooms upstairs, if that's all right.'

She turned and walked up the stairs, trailing the scent of some hair product Frank recognized from home. He left his dripping umbrella at the door and walked through to the living room. It was not as he had imagined. He realized that he had been expecting a scene of squalor. He had envisaged piles of mildewed newspapers, empty soup tins on the windowsills and mouse droppings in the kitchen. Instead the living room was sparsely furnished and spotless. A single high-backed orange armchair in front of a wall-mounted gas fire, a teak-effect dining table with two chairs, a matching side cabinet with what looked like a seventies-era music centre on top. He looked at the dustless smoked plastic lid of the record player. He thought of Michael Church diligently cleaning a house that would only be visited by strangers after his death. He thought that squalor would have been less sad.

On the table was a pile of paperwork. The woman from the council had said they'd found nothing there to indicate a next of kin. Frank sat carefully on the edge of a chair at the table and wondered what he was doing in this dead man's house. The chances were that Michael Church had once featured in some news report and Frank would be able to add nothing new to his story. Perhaps Frank had interviewed him back when he was a reporter and all they would learn is that this man once had a lorry crash into his dining room, or had protested about a school closure, or been taken to court for cruelty to dogs.

He pulled the pile towards him and started sorting through the papers and envelopes. He touched the documents gently as if handling ancient relics. It was the usual tangle of paperwork built up over a lifetime. Policy booklets, TV-licence reminders, a letter of thanks for a recent donation. He had a fleeting memory of sitting at another table, many years ago, the afternoon sunlight pooling on the floor as he helped his mother sort through the policies and payment books left behind after his father's death. He looked for Michael Church's past addresses; he thought that place would be the key to his memory. Instead, in an A5 Manila envelope he found some photographs. A black and white one of a young woman sitting under a tree, the wind blowing her hair. The woman was laughing at whoever was taking the photo. Another one showed a couple of young men in army uniforms, neither appeared to be Michael. Another was in colour, a toddler, probably a boy, though it was hard to tell, holding a bucket and spade and looking delighted with himself. Another black and white one showed two young boys. The boy on the left was clearly Michael Church. He was wearing a tank top over a short-sleeved shirt and smiling shyly at the camera. The boy on the right was taller with an arm round Michael's shoulder. His smile was wide and he seemed to have all the confidence that Michael lacked, his eyes looking straight through the lens. Frank had seen that look a hundred times. The boy was Phil Smethway.

Frank leaned back in the chair and closed his eyes. Now he remembered. It hadn't been anything to do with a news story. It hadn't even been that long ago, maybe eighteen months. Phil had been up in Birmingham on one of his visits and they'd arranged to meet for lunch. They were walking past St Philip's Cathedral, heading down to the Jewellery Quarter when Phil called out to a man walking towards them. The man looked lost for a moment and then slowly broke into a smile as he recognized Phil. As he came towards them, Frank noticed his eyes – bright, big and blue and somehow too young for the rest of his face. Phil and the man shook hands vigorously, both laughing, and Phil introduced Michael to Frank as his 'most longest, lostest, dearest pal'. Frank remembered how strong Michael's grip was when he shook his hand. Michael said something about seeing Phil on telly and Phil was demanding to know why he'd never got in touch. Frank felt a bit of a spare part and so told Phil he'd go on ahead to the restaurant to get a table. He'd asked Michael if he'd join them, but he said he couldn't. He left the two of them trying to work out how long it had been since they'd last met.

Frank looked again at the photo. He wondered if they'd stayed in contact after the chance encounter in the church-yard. He thought of the contrast in the way they had looked that day: Phil with his perma-tan, Rolex and white polo neck; Michael pale and slight in a cagoule. Michael didn't look like the kind of person Phil had in his life; he didn't look like he played golf or drove a Mercedes. Frank looked at the room around him and wondered if Phil ever discovered that Michael was living such a solitary existence. Michael must have heard of Phil's death and yet Frank was sure he wasn't at the funeral. He felt an itch to know more about Michael. To see if there was anyone alive who knew him and might give some clue as to who he was and how he ended up slipping out of life unnoticed. Frank could tell himself he was doing it as a favour to Phil.

12

Michael
October 2009

It's a strange place for a bench. He's walked past it hundreds of times and never seen anyone else on it. He wonders if it's been waiting for him.

The seat is lower than he's used to. He bends his knees as far as he can and then allows himself to fall the rest of the way, hitting the bench hard, rocking back with the momentum. Black specks swim in the air around him. He closes his eyes and waits for the buzzing in his head to stop. When he opens his eyes, he assesses the view. Three lanes of cars hurtling towards town, and another three fleeing in the opposite direction. Not something many people are keen to gaze upon.

The carriageway marks the eastern edge of the housing estate. The houses and most of the streets he knew were cleared decades ago, even the old name of the neighbourhood has been lost, but still he likes to look for traces of the places he used to know, places he and Elsie used to meet. He finds them now and then: the birch tree on the corner of Ellesworth Street, the small section of iron railings in the park, the blackened bridge over the canal. He sees himself as an unlikely archaeologist, searching for worthless treasure.

He's started revisiting the area since Elsie's death. Most

weekends he catches the 86 into town and then walks the rest of the way. He can't get used to the empty spaces. His memories are of houses built on top of one another, families crowded upon families, but now he finds a landscape dominated by gaps. The flats and maisonettes stare at each other over vast concrete quadrangles and landscaped hillocks. The wind blasts across the open spaces, bending the sapling trees and choking the weeds with litter. He doesn't know what the spaces are for; no one seems to use them. He doesn't understand where the children are.

Down the road a little from the bench remains a chunk of the past still intact. Edward Street School, it seems, is no longer a school. The sign outside speaks of opportunities and resources for the unemployed, but the building itself is the same Victorian redbrick lump it always was.

He looks over at its familiar silhouette and he remembers the sounds most of all. He closes his eyes and he can still hear the familiar footsteps behind him. There are three of them. His heartbeat speeds up in time with their approach and as he turns he gets the full weight of a satchel of books square in the side of the head. He smells leather and ink as he fights to keep his balance. He's dazed but lashes out, flailing wildly, using every part of himself to inflict as much damage as he can in the few seconds he has before they bring him down. He rams his knuckles into somebody's face and catches someone else in the balls with his boot. For a moment he feels invincible and lets out a victorious roar, but then he tastes the blood in his mouth and the horizon begins to shift.

Once they have him on the ground they begin in earnest.

He catches glimpses of their grim faces as they lay the boot in and he almost respects their dedication to something they seem to get so little pleasure from. They breathe noisily through their open mouths, putting all they've got into the job at hand.

They see him lying there curled up on the wet surface of the playground taking a beating, but it's an illusion. Michael is far away. His name is Rusty and he rides through Monument Valley on his Appaloosa horse. He saves the life of his trusty dog Pancho after he's bitten by a snake and they team up with a Cherokee scout to capture a dangerous outlaw by the name of El Capitan. They free the beautiful girl that El Capitan has locked away and she rides with Michael on the back of his horse, her arms clasped tightly round his waist. Her name is Maria. Her heart beats hard against his back and it feels good. The setting sun casts strange shadows on the valley floor and Pancho barks and wags his tail.

The kicks have stopped. He stays on the ground, clinging to the image of Pancho's shiny eyes, but it fades fast and instead he sees the chalk smear of a hopscotch grid trickling towards him. He sits up slowly and checks himself. His back hurts and his head throbs, but Rusty would take far worse and never complain. He touches the back of his head and the pain shoots out. He closes his eyes for a moment and when he opens them there's a pair of legs in front of him. Phil pulls him up. He holds Michael's chin in his hand and turns his face from side to side.

'Nice work, mate. You're getting better. They didn't get a decent kick into the face today.'

Michael rolls up his jumper and shirt and asks Phil to check his back. Phil breathes in sharply.

'Bloody hell, Mikey. The bruises have already come up and one's a big bugger.'

'I don't think they broke anything.'

'They had a good go, though, didn't they?'

'Did you see it all?'

Phil's quiet for a moment. 'Well, most of it.'

Michael looks at him. 'It's all right. It's not your fight.'

'Three against one, that ain't a fight. They're just cowards.' He stops for a moment. 'I'm a coward too, just watching it happen.'

Michael shakes his head. 'You're not a coward. You stick your neck out – you talk to me.'

'The rest of them are idiots.'

Michael smiles at that. 'It doesn't matter. They don't bother me.'

'You know you're mad, don't you? You could outrun them.'

'I was always told that was the worst thing to do with bullies.'

'Well, I'm saying that's bollocks. "Stand your ground," they say. "Fight back!" Well, you do that and look where it gets you. "Run away," I say – that's what they want. They don't even enjoy it any more, mate. They'd take any excuse to stop.'

'I don't think my dad would have liked me to run away.'

Phil is exasperated. 'What you talking about? Your dad ran away. Left your mom before you were even born.'

'She said he missed Germany. He went back to be a shepherd.'

They look at each other. 'A shepherd?' says Phil. He shakes his head. 'Baaa.' He and Michael start laughing.

They walk out of the school gates and start heading home. Phil wonders if they're going to be evacuated again and asks Michael if he remembers all the odd bods in Belbroughton when they were there in 1939. As if Michael could forget. Then Phil starts on about the bulgy-eyed vicar in Evesham when they were sent there. He does the vicar as a crazed, toothy Alastair Sim and he knows it always makes Michael cry with laughter. He begs Phil to stop as it hurts too much.

Phil spots the girls first. 'Come on, Mikey, let's go and impress them with your bruises.'

They're sitting under the tree in the park. Michael looks across and sees her chatting to her friend. She's smiling and moving her hands and her hair bounces as she laughs and he feels as if he's been kicked in the stomach again. He stops walking and Phil looks at him.

'Come on. What you doing? All right, we won't show them the bruises. We'll just tell them how you took three of them on and you were the only one left standing.'

Michael thinks he needs to sit down. It's hard to breathe.

Phil's smiling. 'Come on. You know she likes you. God knows why when I'm around, but she does.'

Michael manages to shake his head. 'She never looks at me.'

'Exactly.'

Michael doesn't move. 'I don't think I can.'

Phil pulls on his sleeve. 'Just walk with me. I'll do all the talking. You can be the strong silent type. The other one's sweet on me anyway; she has better taste.'

Michael looks in Phil's eyes. 'You'll do all the talking?'

'Do you think I'd let you blow it?' He straightens his collar. 'I told you to protect your face, didn't I? Those eyes of yours – the girls go for those. They make you look innocent – you can get away with anything.'

Michael buries his hands in his pockets and walks up with Phil.

A lorry pulls up and the school disappears behind it. The traffic is heavier now and the queue for the roundabout reaches right down to the bench where Michael sits. He can't remember a single word of what Phil said to Elsie and her friend. But he remembers Elsie's eyes settling on his for the first time and he remembers the shock of the knowledge that passed between them.

13

The motorway was quiet, but he stayed in the slow lane tucked behind a beaten-up van travelling at fifty. Frank secretly held a strong suspicion that he should not be in charge of a vehicle after dark. On city streets all was fine, but on country lanes or unlit stretches of motorway he was alarmed at the sullen lack of communication between his eyes and his brain. Something had gone wrong between them in the last year or two and now the brain would periodically choose to ignore or wilfully misinterpret visual input. The familiar patterns of tail lights, road signs, catseyes and oncoming headlights had broken down into a free-form floating abstract projection through which Frank hurtled wide-eyed on leather upholstery. At times he mistook the retreating tail lights of the car ahead for headlights coming towards him, at others he would mistake reflections on his side window for vehicles swerving into his lane. His progress along a deserted stretch of motorway was often punctuated by sudden braking at phantom hazards on the road ahead. He waited for the day the police pulled him over, breathalysed him, and imagined their disbelief slowly turning to unease when they discovered no trace of alcohol in his blood.

He indicated and took his exit from the motorway,

making his way along the A-roads and country lanes to-wards home. His journey tonight was even longer than usual after having to attend a work 'away day' in Surrey. His daily commute however was fraught enough and just another reason for him to dislike where he lived. He was always happy to get back to Andrea and Mo, but dearly wished that this nightly reunion could take place some-where other than their home. He had never felt so little affinity with anywhere he'd lived before, not even the bleak shared houses of his student days with their swirling carpets and pungent sofas. He and Andrea had moved out of the city when Mo was born with some vague idea of the country being a better place in which to raise a family. They bought a five-bedroomed detached new build on a large plot of land thirty miles out of Birmingham. It certainly wasn't the city, but neither could it be called the country. It was handy for the motorway and that had seemed like a good idea.

That first damp, grey day that they'd moved in Frank had felt a terrible emptiness to the place, but put it out of his mind. In the first few months Andrea settled in easily and Frank had high hopes. He'd always lived in cities, but he held in his head an ideal of country living. He looked forward to doing all the things he thought people who lived in the country must do.

He bought a book of local walks and set out many times in the early days in full Gore-tex regalia, but found the landscape charmless. Try as he might he could find nothing inspiring in trudging over ploughed fields or along narrow lanes with cars screaming past at murderous speeds. He would walk through a field, cross a stile in the hedgerow to emerge into another identical field. Apart from the screaming crows, he saw no other living creature. Sometimes he imagined that he was the last person living after the bomb had dropped, and such thoughts inevitably failed to lift his mood. After persevering through each weekend in October and November, he gave up. There was, he concluded, nothing to see out there.

His other efforts centred around the local facilities, such as they were. The nearest village was three miles away. He was intent on shopping locally and imagined how much better food would taste when sourced from nearby farms. The hub of the local village consisted of a post box, a phone box, a franchise convenience store, a Chinese takeaway and a small pub. The shop sold nothing grown locally. Frank learned that the surrounding farms were producing food on an industrial scale to service the large supermarkets. The local shop had little to distinguish it from the convenience store he used to live by in the city except, Frank noticed, for an alcohol selection twice the size and the presence of serious porn titles alongside the usual lads' mags. He bought a tin of baked beans and a Yorkie bar on his one visit. After that he drove the ten miles to the nearest twenty-four-hour Sainsbury's.

Andrea and he had realized too late that this was not a good environment for Mo. Although she was happy enough at school, none of her friends lived nearby and when Frank thought of the future he could think of nowhere worse for her to spend her teenage years. He'd often see two or three forlorn characters in hooded tops sitting on the back of the bench in the village, lighting matches and throwing them in the gutter as they passed a bottle of Thunderbird between them.

He pulled on to the drive now past the faded 'For Sale' sign. After two years he'd given up hope that anyone would come and take the place off their hands. Andrea was in the kitchen and greeted him with a raised ladle.

'How was the away day?'

He kissed her. 'Utterly inspiring.'

'I bet. Were there jumbo flip charts?'

'Oh yes.'

'A PowerPoint presentation?'

'Several.'

'Did you learn anything new?'

'Only that I'm getting too old for all this.'

'You knew that already.'

Frank took off his jacket. 'Have you spoken to Mo? Is she having fun?'

'Yes, she's happy. She was very excited about something Laura's mum had given them for tea. Potato with a face apparently. She was delighted by it. I think that might be the highlight of the whole sleepover for her.'

Frank sat down heavily and stared at the reflection of the room in the black window. After a few minutes he became aware that Andrea had been talking.

'Sorry. What were you saying?'

Andrea looked at him. 'Are you okay?'

'Yeah. I'm fine. It was just a bit weird today.'

'What? Gritting your teeth through all the corporate piffle?'

'No. Not that. It was on the way back. I ended up driving down the road where Phil died.'

Andrea sat down next to him. 'Oh.'

'The conference venue was a big house in the middle of nowhere and I got lost on the way back. Well, very lost, in fact, driving along endless country lanes – no signs anywhere – and at some point in the midst of all this I saw bunches of flowers and photos stuck to a tree. I thought nothing of it at first, but then I caught a glimpse of Phil's face on some of the photos. I wouldn't have thought there'd still be any trace, but there were loads – some of them looked quite new.'

'I wonder if it's local people who leave them there or if people travel there especially.'

'I don't know.'

'I don't understand it – this need to leave flowers for people they've never met.' She stopped. 'I don't mean you. I mean that's weird too, but in a different way. At least you're remembering the forgotten; Phil was hardly that.'

'Perhaps it's a way of people feeling close to him. They had no tangible connection with him when he was on television, but maybe by putting flowers at the spot he died they feel some link to him.'

She shrugged. 'It seems odd to me.'

Frank looked at Andrea and smiled. 'Oh, people are odd. All of them.'

Andrea grinned. 'Not like us.'

Frank shook his head vigorously. 'No, not like us. Everyone else. Not us.' He poured a glass of wine. 'I couldn't understand how it happened, though.'

'What?'

'The accident. The hit and run. I always assumed it was on some winding lane, but it's not. It's long and straight. If Phil was killed at the spot I saw today, I don't know how the driver didn't see him.'

'Maybe they did see him, but they just lost control of the vehicle. Or maybe they fell asleep at the wheel.'

'But then they'd have crashed as well. It just seems mad that they could drive down a perfectly straight road, kill a pedestrian who would be completely visible and then drive on.'

Andrea went back to her cooking. 'Poor Phil. Of course he would be jogging. Couldn't just age gracefully. Seventy-eight years old and still trying to look forty-five. Why couldn't he just let himself go to seed? I can't wait to start sprouting biscuit crumbs and money-off vouchers cut from *My Weekly*.'

Frank smiled and turned on the worktop TV. He stared at the screen, but found that all he saw were fluttering images of Phil's face glimpsed on a tree on a long straight road.

14

He sat in his parked car and looked across at the banner declaring the grand opening. It described it as an exciting new leisure development. What that amounted to was a casino with a gym on top. Black and silver balloons bobbed frantically in the sharp wind. A few women with straightened blonde hair and suntans were dressed as bunny girls to lend glamour to the occasion. They clustered shivering in the shelter of the entrance. Stretched behind them he saw the pink ribbon that he would soon cut. The letter 'o' in the neon sign above the casino door was a roulette wheel. Above the glare of the sign, discreetly carved into the stone portico, were the words: Royal Children's Hospital.

The Regal Casino was the latest and perhaps most audacious in a series of reimaginings of city landmarks. Birmingham was trying to change its reputation for the way it treated its architectural heritage: the famous lack of sentimentality that bordered on self-harm. The city now adopted a more sensitive approach to its Victorian heritage. Those notable examples that had managed to survive the post-war purges were protected and cherished.

One of the consequences of the current doctrine was a drive to find new uses for Victorian buildings. Many had stood empty for years, their original remit expired, obsolete or transferred to newer facilities. Now private development companies with names like Urban Heritage, Regeneris and New Concept were finding new ways to use old spaces.

Frank looked at the small crowd now assembling over the road. He always donated his PA fees to charity and that made him feel guilty for rejecting lucrative offers. He'd agreed to open the casino as a favour to an old colleague of his father's whose son now owned Regeneris, but he couldn't suppress his distaste for the development. He'd felt ambivalent in the past about some of the strange reinventions of old buildings. The eye hospital that became a luxury hotel, the imposing hilltop edifice of the Victorian mental hospital turned into apartments. He could never pass the grand driveway to the gated condominiums without remembering walking past as a boy and seeing the patients standing behind the chain-link fence shouting strange words and asking for fags. He wondered who would choose to live in a place of former suffering. What level of hubris was required to feel so utterly undaunted by the past?

Of them all, though, he found something particularly hard to take about the metamorphosis of a children's hospital into a casino. It seemed to aspire to a new level of inappropriateness. The hospital had moved to larger premises five years earlier, but Frank always thought of it in its former home. He'd been there as a child to have his appendix out, and again as a panic-stricken father when Mo had fallen downstairs as a toddler. He'd also covered many stories there. In particular he remembered Lucy Smallwood, a ten-year-old with leukaemia who had spent her time in hospital engaged in one sponsored event after another, raising funds for other sick children. There was regular coverage of her attempts on the programme and in the local press and Frank would always remember the silence in the newsroom on the day she died.

He gazed at the images of dice and chips hanging in the windows and wondered who could feel lucky in such a place. Looking at his watch he saw there were still another ten minutes to go. He spent much of his life killing small blocks of time. It was a consequence of his punctuality. He wasn't sure that punctuality was the right way to describe it: he was always early, which was, he supposed, as unpunctual as always being late, but he inconvenienced only himself and not others.

He'd been brought up to arrive fifteen minutes ahead of any appointment, but people didn't want personalities to arrive early; they expected to be kept waiting. Now, after twenty years, he was able to recognize the unease that the public experienced when they saw celebrities – even of his minor variety – out of certain clearly defined realms. They understood that celebrities existed primarily in the spotlight – shuffling papers officiously as the intro music faded out, emerging from behind curtains, smiling on a sofa behind a pile of unread magazines. They understood also that celebrities had a 'real life'. But this was a certain type of real life glimpsed only in photos in magazines with short one-word titles. Celebrities with no make-up on, with strange scars visible and shameful rolls of fat falling over expensive bikini bottoms. It was understood that celebrities existed in these separate and clearly defined realms, but the PA – the charity dinner, the restaurant opening – blurred these lines. The exotic and the mundane came together for a short while and it was essential that the celebrity balanced perfectly on the fine line between the two.

Frank used to arrive whilst the photographers were still setting up, quite happy to wait a few moments and exchange pleasantries with the staff of the shop or restaurant he was opening. He'd be there in his role as celebrity, but not quite 'on' yet. Eventually it was a restaurant manager who spelled it out to him. Frank had arrived ten minutes early and the manager whisked him off to the staff changing area to wait. 'They don't want to see you like that,' he'd said, and for a moment Frank thought he'd spilled something down his suit, but then he realized what he meant. He had to emerge, fully formed and glistening, at the appointed hour, not hover awkwardly for ten minutes beforehand.

And so Frank had become practised at a form of invisibility. He had no control over his early arrival – it wasn't something, at his time of life, that he had any power to change – but he did seem able to manage his visibility, to choose to be seen or unseen. He'd kill time in nearby shops, or read a newspaper in his car, and no one would notice him until he switched on his beam and stepped up to the ribbon. He remembered when he was a boy that he had written a list of superpowers on a piece of paper ranked in order of how much he craved them. He could only think of a few now, the obvious things: the ability to fly and to travel through time. He recalled clearly, though, that top of the list had been the gift of invisibility. Sometimes at night he'd pretend that he was wearing magic invisible pyjamas. He'd lie alone in his bed and be sure that no one could see him. He'd will his mother or father to come in the room and panic at his apparent absence, just so he could have proof of his invisibility. He'd lie and wait and the longer he waited the more he wondered if he really was invisible. He would start to worry about how he could know he was visible, that he even existed, if there was no one to see him. He'd fall asleep in a state of confusion unsure about himself, his imagination and his pyjamas.

He got out of the car now and walked purposefully towards the man he had identified as the owner. He was a fleshy figure, pigeon-chested with no neck, attempting some kind of *Miami Vice* look that Frank didn't think suited him or the bitter weather. Frank reached out to shake his hand and as the man turned and recognized him Frank noticed the brief look that crossed his face. A momentary flash of amusement as if Frank had just been the subject of some humorous conversation. It was a look he was used to. After a few introductions, Frank stood up at the ribbon and gave the speech he'd been asked to give – combining an upbeat economic forecast for the area with corny jokes. He gave his best cheese-eating grin as he cut the ribbon and the cameras flashed.

Afterwards he drank tasteless cava and chatted to an investor in the development called Eddy and the generically glamorous woman at his side who was not introduced by name.

'There seem to be casinos cropping up all over the city now,' Frank ventured.

'Yeah, well, there's only so many tits a city can take,' said Eddy. 'Did you know Birmingham has more gentlemen's clubs per capita than anywhere else in Europe?'

'Really?' said Frank.

'Thing is that women's bodies are being devalued.' Frank was momentarily wrong-footed, before Eddy made his meaning clear. 'Some of the skanks these clubs employ, they cheapen the experience, put the punters off. I run five lap-dancing establishments, but they're classy. The girls keep themselves nice and spruce-looking. But it's all too available now. A man should feel special that he has the currency to pay a beautiful woman to dance for him, but there's nothing special about it now. It's lost the glamour and the magic. The punters feel sordid.'

Frank had always assumed that was the point.

'But casinos, Frank, that's a different game. They have that glamour and magic and they have it in spades. People think of casinos and they think of James Bond, they think of George Clooney and Sharon Stone. They think of all these things and, while they think, they are pouring money on those tables faster than we can bank it. Course, I could've done without the recession, but you never know; desperate times sometimes call for desperate measures – like putting it all on red.'

Eddy continued to speak, but Frank drifted off. He looked around distractedly at the faces around him. He wondered how many of them had been in the hospital as children, or had maybe brought their own children there, running every red light in the empty night-time streets. His attention was caught by a figure with a shopping trolley making his way along the pavement towards them. The man was tall, perhaps in his fifties, wearing an anorak covered in badges and a Boyzone baseball cap. He stopped to look at the spectacle before him. After a moment he dragged his trolley up to one of the bunny girls and Frank heard him ask: 'Is the kiddies coming back, love?'

'Sorry?'

'The kiddies. The hospital. Is them opening it again?'

'The hospital?' She was speaking loudly as if the man was deaf. 'Is that what you're asking? The hospital's moved now . . . This isn't the hospital any more,' she added slowly.

The man looked at her as if she was simple. 'I know that, love. I remember it closing. I thought they wuz reopening it like. What's happening, then? What's all this in aid of?'

'It's a new casino opening today.'

The man frowned at her. 'A casino? Here? You joking, bab?' And then he started to laugh. He laughed so much that one by one the conversations began to trail off until eventually everyone had stopped speaking and all eyes were turned on the laughing man with the trolley in their midst.

15

Andrea, Frank and Mo had driven out to the canal for a walk one afternoon the previous summer. They followed the canal out through the suburbs where Mo enjoyed giving a running commentary on every back garden they passed. She loved the ones with stone ornaments in the shapes of hedgehogs and badgers and waistcoat-wearing frogs carrying wheelbarrows. She also loved the gardens that had small wooden jetties at the end and row boats tied up. The idea of just getting up in the morning and going out in a dinghy seemed entirely magical to her. She disapproved fiercely, however, of those gardens with trampolines, believing their proximity to the canal was a terrible accident waiting to happen.

Frank had said: 'What? Boing, boing, splosh?' and Mo had nodded solemnly.

At some point the houses petered out and the canal continued its course through countryside, alongside empty fields and tangled hedgerows. They had walked for some miles through the filtered green light of overhanging leaves when the landscape on the opposite towpath abruptly changed. Modern apartment buildings in the style of old warehouses and wharves rose up from the towpath. An opening in the block revealed a colonnaded plaza built around a grand stepped waterfall, which led down to the canal. Enormity appeared to be the key design feature.

The three of them stood and stared for some time before crossing the bridge to explore. Mo ran up and down the steps at the side of the waterfall while Frank and Andrea looked around the shopfronts of the plaza. All were empty except for the office and estate agents of the development company itself, and a shop selling leather furniture. They laughed at a lime-green sofa that cost £6,000. They wandered on through the estate, which stretched far back from the canal. Signposts told them they were in a village and directed them to the centre. They passed through an empty zone called Waterside, through another called Gardenside and reached the apparent centre, which branded itself as Marketside. Here they found more empty shopfronts, two designer clothes shops, a Sainsbury's Local and a bar yet to be opened. They saw no one apart from the shop workers that stared as they passed. Andrea said it was as if a neutron bomb had fallen. Mo liked it. She liked the neatness of the houses and shops and she liked the clock tower in the middle. She said she felt like a Playmobil figure and started speaking in a strange, presumably Playmobil, accent. Frank walked into a shop like someone fallen from the sky to ask where they were. The answer was Byron's Common.

Now Frank was back again. The bar was open for business, serving food all day, and he sat waiting to meet Phil's widow Michelle. Byron's Common was a little busier now, though still had the feel of a stage set. Most of the shop units were still empty, but Frank could see a chemist and a Chinese takeaway had opened on the parade. There was a slow trickle of people passing by and a few other tables were occupied in the bar. For no reason that Frank could discern, the upholstery in the bar was covered with what appeared to be cow hide, and bleached cattle skulls hung on the bare brick walls. Their hollow sockets gazed out at the Sainsbury's Local across the street. Frank wondered if it was a reference to the Old West, with Byron's Common cast as a frontier town. Had he missed out on the gold rush? He couldn't help but notice that the women in the bar all looked similar. Blonde hair, deep tans, jumbo handbags, tight dark jeans and heels. A few of them recognized him. They caught his eye, looked away then looked back. He pretended to read the menu.

It was twenty minutes past their arranged meeting time when he saw Michelle pull up in her convertible Audi and park illegally on the pavement outside. She created an enormous disturbance in the atmosphere as she entered the bar jangling with keys and earrings and beads. She bustled up to the table. 'I'm sorry, Frank love, bloody workmen. Take my advice: you want a new kitchen? Fit it your bloody self. Couldn't do a worse job! Oh God, I need a drink.'

Frank smiled and stood up to kiss her. 'Don't worry. I've been enjoying the ambience.'

'Oh, I bet.' Michelle sat with her back to the other tables and ordered a spritzer. She asked lots of questions about Frank and Andrea and Mo before Frank was able to speak.

'What about you? How have you been?'

'Fine, yeah fine.'

Frank frowned at her.

'You don't have to say that.'

Michelle smiled. 'Okay.' She thought for a moment. 'Well, since the funeral, in chronological order, I've been bad, really bad, terrible, better and now okay, I think, or close to it.'

'We tried calling, but it was always the answerphone. You should have called us when you were having a rough time.'

'No offence, Frank, but what could you do? What could anyone do? I had to get through it. I went away. After the circus of the funeral I had to get out of the country. The scale of the reaction just freaked me out. I know it wasn't that extreme – Phil wasn't Princess Di – but even at his level of fame it felt so inappropriate, so invasive.'

'Were people bothering you?'

'I'm probably overreacting, but I never really got it. I never got who those people were who used to write to Phil when he was alive – his agent got letters every week from fans. Who writes to TV celebrities? Maybe if you're a kid and you have a crush – but to Phil? I can't see him being a teen pin-up. So it was just more of that, much more. Death seems to bring them all out of the woodwork. I had letters from people saying they'd cried more than when their own fathers had died. Can you believe that? Maybe I should have been touched, but I just thought they were tapped.'

Frank thought of the kinds of letters and emails he received each day, the endless ways in which people construed and interpreted you once your face was on television. The baffling array of purposes they thought you served. He had letters asking him for directions and for recommendations of dry cleaners, letters telling him about Jesus, letters telling him he was a wanker, letters telling him he brightened up their mother's day, letters asking for photographs and letters containing photos of their own. He knew the number he received each week would be nothing to the volume that Phil had got. Phil hadn't looked and certainly hadn't acted like a man in his early sixties when he made his transition to national TV. In just fifteen years he'd become an institution. The nation's favourite older man, twinkly yet suave.

Michelle shrugged. 'I suppose people can't deal with the shock of death. Even at seventy-eight. It's something that we never really absorb. He was on telly every Saturday night; he couldn't just suddenly die.' She fell quiet for a moment. 'I felt the same way.' Tears started to leak.

Frank gave her a tissue.

'I still can't believe it. It's so stupid. Of course I knew the age difference when I met Phil. Nearly forty years – you can't overlook that – but I always just thought of that in terms of him being elderly before me. I never thought of him dead. I thought I'd have to look after him in his old age and that was fine. I know it's corny, but I believed in the wedding vows. It never occurred to me that he'd go so suddenly, before I even had a chance to take care of him properly, when he needed it.'

Frank shook his head. 'You were together twenty years. You took care of him.'

Michelle smiled, but she looked unconvinced. 'So, anyway, I went abroad – Spain, Portugal, Italy. I don't know what the hell I was doing. Running away, I suppose. Lying on beaches, eating too much, drinking too much, feeling lonely and a mess. I came home, spent time with friends, got my head straight, sold the house and then this whole TV thing came along.'

The TV thing was a new career for Michelle as the host of a makeover programme called *Tough Love*. During her marriage to Phil she had become a regular guest on chat shows and celebrity quiz shows. She was pretty, laughed in the right places and was married to a famous man; no other reason was needed. Since Phil's death, though, her career had taken off with *Tough Love*. Andrea loathed it; Mo loved it.

'Now *I* get the bloody letters. Only mine are more extreme. I'm their inspiration or they want to kill me. Women are so vicious. Anyway, I've got a place here that's handy for the studio, a place down in London and a villa in Almeria. I'm busy working and sorting the houses and busy is good.'

Frank smiled. 'How do you like life in Byron's Common?'

'It's weird, isn't it? Toytown. My sister visited and said she thought a big white ball would chase us if we tried to leave. I like it, though. It's wipe-clean.'

'Yeah, I know what you mean. Mo liked it for the same reasons.'

'You know, on the programme, it's all before and after. And the before is always rubbish and ugly and sad. I like it here because there's no before, only after.'

Frank thought that with him it was always before. It was after he had a problem with. He remembered Michael Church. 'While you're here, I wanted to ask you something. Will you look at a photo for me and tell me if you recognize

95

a face?' He pulled the photo out and placed it on the table in front of Michelle.

She looked puzzled for a moment and then smiled. 'Oh my God, it's Phil. Wasn't he handsome when he was young? I mean he was handsome when he was old, but just look at him. Those eyes. I've never seen one of him this young before. His old photos got lost along the way somewhere. What a charmer. Who's the other boy?'

'That's what I was hoping you might tell me. His name is Michael Church. Do you recognize him at all? Can you remember Phil ever mentioning him?'

Michelle peered at the photo for some time. 'No, sorry. I don't recognize him.' She was silent for a moment. 'Maybe the name . . . I don't know. "Michael" is ringing a vague bell, but I can't think from where. It's not an uncommon name, though, so it's probably the wrong one.'

Frank shrugged. 'Don't worry about it. I was just trying to figure out who he was. It's not important.'

Michelle looked at her watch and swore. 'Shit, I've got to go. My whole day is half an hour out of whack. There was something else I wanted to talk to you about, but it will have to wait. I'll call you, okay?'

He stood up to kiss her goodbye. As she left, all the women in the bar turned and watched her go, their faces as unreadable as the skulls on the walls.

16

Phil
December 2008

There isn't any discernible transition between sleep and consciousness, no gradual surfacing, no sudden disturbance. He just finds himself fully awake, lying in bed, and when he looks at the clock it's always around three. It's jet lag without the long-haul flights. His body clock has shifted to a rhythm that beats out of time with his life and his routines. He's had a year of it now. He knows that nothing he tries will send him back to sleep until the half hour around six, when his thoughts will lose their edges and he'll drift into dreams for two hours before he hears Michelle moving around and making their morning cup of coffee.

Michelle has a remarkable aptitude for sleep. Like a doll her eyes seem to close automatically as she lies down, and then stay shut for the nine hours or so until she sits up again in the morning. She is able to sleep at will, and Phil has often envied her ability to simply switch herself off for the duration of long, dull journeys or tedious plays. He knows she won't wake, but still he moves the duvet gently and shuts the door quietly behind him.

He's never sure which is worse, lying in bed awake, or wandering around the house in the middle of the night. He seems to feel more isolated when he gets up. When he lies awake in bed, he knows that he is at least in the customary place and position for three in the morning. Once he's up he feels as if he is setting himself against nature. Something about turning lights on in cold, empty rooms and seeing the blackness outside the window makes him feel nauseous.

After getting a glass of water he goes to his office. He pulls down the blind before turning on the desk lamp. For a while he moves about listlessly, adjusting the angles of photos, moving piles of paper from one place to another. All the while, though, he feels the pull of the locked door. He doesn't put up much of a fight before getting the key from his drawer and opening the cabinet. He knows Michelle disapproves of him watching this stuff. She allows that once might be okay, but anything beyond that is damaging, is essentially unhealthy. He twists his head to better read the labels. His eyes drift past the DVDs back further in time to the shelves of video tapes. He plucks one at random, puts it in the machine and flops back onto the leather sofa with the remote control. He holds a cushion on his lap.

The tape hasn't been rewound from a previous viewing and it starts with a crackling of distortion and white lines before the image settles down. It's the old *Heart of England Reports* studio. Phil looks at the suit he wears on screen and the shape of his haircut and is able to date the broadcast to somewhere around 1985 or '86. He and Suzy are out from behind their desk and standing in the small circular studio area reserved for all manner of nonsense. Phil is halfway through a sentence as the picture clears.

'. . . of course invited John, Peggoty and Roland down to the studio.'

Suzy looks off camera and starts laughing delightedly. 'And here they all are now!'

From the back of the studio a man slowly walks in a crouched position waving a celery stick at ground level. Behind him emerges a complicated arrangement of wheels and fur. The camera closes in to reveal a guinea pig harnessed to a miniature cart upon which sits an immense white rabbit. The guinea pig pulls the rabbit along following the celery.

Phil laughs. 'My goodness, I hope you can see this clearly at home. Here he comes now, our very own Ben-Hur of the hutch.' The camera closes in on the dissipated face of the rabbit.

Suzy turns to John. 'John, thank you so much for coming down to the studio today and bringing Peggoty and Roland along with you. What an extraordinary sight they make. Now Peggoty's the guinea pig, is that right?'

'That's right.'

'And is she or he quite . . .'

'Her's an her.'

'Right, good, is she quite comfortable there? Roland looks like he's eaten more than a few carrots and Peggoty's really very small.'

'Her loves it!'

'Perhaps we should let poor Peggoty have her celery reward now.' John seems reluctant, but eventually drops the stalk on the studio floor, where the guinea pig seizes upon it. 'Gosh, she's enjoying that, isn't she?' says Suzy.

'John, I have to ask,' says Phil, 'how on earth did all this start?'

John starts to give his answer, but Phil, sitting in the

dark, isn't listening. He looks instead at his own youthful face on screen. He watches how his eyes are focused on John until Suzy says something causing Phil to turn, smile and then look to camera before making his own comment. He freezes the image and then rewinds it a few seconds to play the reaction shot and his turn again and then again. The look at Suzy, the smile and then the full turn of that smile to camera. Every time he watches it his heart seems to take a gasp. The simple combination of ease, grace and timing in those few seconds captures something he feels he has lost forever. He watches it over and over again as if repeated viewing will bring it back to him, but he knows it is not something he can relearn. The clip shows him in his fifties with all the confidence and sureness of successful middle-age. He freezes the screen and looks at the face he had over twenty years ago. Surgery has provided him with a poor, tautened imitation of that face, lacking the fullness and fleshiness it once had. He reaches up slowly and runs his fingers over his stretched skin, feeling only the skull beneath it.

He drops his hand onto the cushion on his lap and stares at the back of it. His mother always said to look at the hands to know the real person. She would notice the bitten fingernails of glamorous starlets, the small feminine hands of certain leading men; she saw hands, not eyes, as the windows of the soul. She was right, of course. His hearing aid is invisible, his need to piss every half hour easily covered up, but his hands dangle there at the end of his arms for all to see. The skin on the back of them is loose, covered in coarse grey hairs and dotted with liver spots. He wonders why cosmetic surgery is never offered for hands. He stares at them until they seem entirely alien to him. Two lumps of bone and gristle lying on a purple velvet cushion. He imagines them touching Michelle's smooth skin. He sees them cupping her breasts, stroking her stomach and he closes his eyes to try and block out the image.

When he opens them, the freeze frame has released and the tape is playing again. There is mild chaos on screen as Roland has leaned too far to the side and pulled the cart over with his substantial weight. He lies inertly on the studio floor, allowing John to scoop him up, while Peggoty drags the capsized cart around behind her looking for more celery. The camera closes in on Phil's face to block out the scene behind him. He's unflustered, with a wry smile, as he hands over to the weather report.

Phil turns off the TV. He sits for a few moments and stares at the dark screen, but the silhouette of his head is still reflected by the light of the lamp behind him. He reaches back for the switch and turns it off. His reflection disappears. He stays there awake and upright in the dark, blessedly invisible to the world and to himself.

17

Frank found it harder each time he went to locate his father's headstone. He visited the cemetery so rarely that the rows of graves expanded in vast leaps between each visit. They proliferated faster and further than Frank ever managed to predict, always leaving him struggling to navigate his way around the featureless landscape. Once his father had been a pioneer, breaking new ground for the dead on the far west of the cemetery, but now he had been overtaken by legions of newer recruits advancing steadily down the gentle slope.

After fifteen minutes of wandering, he found his father's stone looking nothing like he had remembered it, in a place he wasn't expecting. It was a dark, flecked, rose colour, not the black he had thought. In front of the imposing stone was a plot-sized rectangle of stone chippings, surrounded by a low chain. Frank had no idea what that was supposed to be; he lacked any understanding of cemetery aesthetics. He thought of it as a kind of front garden to the headstone's house and it seemed ridiculous to him. Were the loved ones supposed to put deckchairs on the shingle and admire the stone? Perhaps lay a towel down on it and recline there just a few feet above the deceased?

He'd always felt resentment at the idea that this was the place he was supposed to reflect on his father, that this anonymous plot was where he should care. He felt no connection there. In his experience the only thoughts that cemeteries inspired were of the physical remains beneath the ground, not the lives that once animated them. The sole reason he came, albeit occasionally, was that to not come, to allow the grave to fall into total neglect, would suggest an utter lack of respect or care for his father. It would make a false statement. As it was, the plot looked pretty bad compared to its near neighbours. The bottom of the stone was caked in dried grass cuttings and blackened stalks poked from the holes of the mildewed flower container.

Today would have been his father's eighty-fourth birthday, though the date was as meaningless as the location. He didn't think of his father any more or less on certain days. It was just habit that he came on this day, a habit started by his mother and continued now by him. What he remembered about the visits with his mother was the silence. They would stand by the grave saying nothing. Frank would wonder what he was supposed to feel. He would look at his mother's face and find no clues there.

He looked at the headstone now, picked from a brochure of similar stones, made in a factory in Wales, and reflected that as his father's buildings were torn down, there was every chance this mass-produced slab would be the only monument left bearing his name.

He knew he should clean the stone. Should walk over to the stand pipe, splash water over his shoes as he tried to capture the sputtering flow in a plastic bottle and then labour with whatever tissues and old business cards he could find in his pockets to remove the worst of the accreted dirt, but he felt himself paralysed. He was trying to will himself to move when his phone rang, making him jump. The cheery tone, always grating, seemed particularly out of place in the setting. He fumbled in his pocket to silence it quickly:

'Hello.'

'Hi, Frank, it's Jo from the coroner's office. Is this a bad time?'

'No, it's fine. Actually I'm at a cemetery.'

'That's appropriate . . . Oh no. Are you at a funeral? I'll call back.'

'No, no – no funeral. There's no one else here.'

'Then why are you whispering?'

Frank hadn't realized he was. He tried to speak in a normal voice. 'Sorry. I don't know.'

Jo laughed. 'You're not going to wake them up, you know.'

Frank looked around at the massed ranks of headstones and tried to ignore the sense of disapproval he felt radiating from them. 'What's up?'

'That guy you were asking about. Michael Church.'

'Oh yeah?'

'Well, I just thought I'd let you know that the post-mortem's been done. Nothing really to report – heart failure.'

'Oh – okay, thanks for letting me know.'

'We'll hold off on the burial, though, until the search for next of kin is completed.'

'Have the police got anywhere, do you know?' He heard Jo blow smoke.

'Ah, Frank – you know what it's like. They have pretty limited resources – I mean they'll give him a reference number, they'll look for paperwork, but you know there's not going to be some dogged investigator pounding the streets and knocking on doors. He lived in local-authority housing and there's no estate, so there'll be no probate researchers getting involved. If you're interested, you should look into it. I mean you already know he was once a friend of your mate, which is more than anyone else knows. Maybe you could find something out.'

'Yeah, I wondered that. I didn't know if it was stupid, though – I mean, if the police find nothing, why would I?'

'Like I say – just because you have the time and the interest. I'm not trying to pressure you, but I just mean if you think you might find something out do it and don't worry you're going to get in the way of the police. I really don't think there's any danger of that.'

'Okay, Jo, maybe I will.'

'All right, well let me know if you find anything. It usually takes the police a couple of months before they give up and tell us to release the body. It'd be good to get someone at the funeral.'

Frank walked over to the nearest path and sat on a bench. He thought of Michael Church growing more and more isolated, occupying a progressively smaller space in the universe until finally he vanished altogether. It reminded him of the TV set they'd had at home when he was growing up. When you turned it off, the image would rapidly shrink down to a small white dot and then, after an unguessable interval of time, disappear. He knew, though, that the programmes were carrying on somewhere; he could just no longer see them. Sometimes he'd press his ear against the screen to see if he could hear the tiny voices of the television people hidden by the dark glass. For a moment he found himself doing the same now as he looked out upon the massed ranks of headstones, but all he could hear was the distant rumble of traffic.

He stretched and walked over to the stand pipe. He was eager to get out of the cemetery, to see Andrea and Mo, to go and push their way around a crowded shopping centre, to stake their place in the world, eat pizza, buy something they didn't need and be among the living.

18

Francis
1975

Douglas works long hours at the office. In the evening Francis sits waiting for his father's return, listening for the key in the door. When Douglas enters, Francis always pretends to be busy with his homework, sitting with his school books open and arrayed on the floor around him in the hope that something there might catch his father's eye and engage his attention. Sometimes it works. Douglas will pick up Francis's maths book and talk animatedly about some concept that Francis doesn't understand but pretends he does and nods his head appreciatively. Francis sees it as a weakness in himself that he prefers English to maths.

He's never visited his father's office and has no clear idea of exactly what goes on there. Douglas always reeks of cigarettes when he returns from work and Francis pictures him spending his days in a room full of serious-looking men, smoking and wearing hats, whilst his father tells them very important things about streets and houses. He imagines his father visible only in silhouette, his voice issuing clearly through the blue smog.

Over dinner Douglas asks Francis how his day at school has been, and Francis can never think of anything to say beyond, 'Fine.' His father never asks him about things on which he has interesting observations to make – like cars or vampires. Francis listens to the conversation between his parents. His mother uses more words, but she too often seems at a loss to respond to Douglas's polite enquiries about her day, and he in turn seems not to listen to her answers. Francis hides his peas under his mashed potato and wonders when he might be allowed to turn the television on.

After dinner his father retires to his study to continue his work. Francis can't imagine how there is so much work to do, or why his father never seems to finish. Sometimes he worries that maybe his father is a bit of a slow coach – like Simon Harris at school. He imagines his father frowning and chewing his lip over piles of exercise books in his smoke-filled office and feels a pang of sympathy for him.

He isn't allowed in his father's study on his own. The only time he gets to see the room is when his mother sends him in with a cup of tea. On such occasions he's under strict instructions to create no disturbance. He is to knock, enter when summoned, place the cup and saucer on the desk and then leave. Sometimes his father is too engrossed to notice Francis. At others, he might engage him in conversation. Francis likes it when his father tells him something about whatever project he happens to be working on, but he lives in fear of being asked questions about it. His father sometimes holds up two sketches and asks him which aspect he prefers. Francis studies the images closely, hoping that an opinion will form in his head, and that it might be the right one. He can rarely tell the difference – they are just pictures of buildings.

He has been told that his father will be very busy for some time. He is working on designs for a new town. Before that he was very busy because he was working on Rhombus House and before that Worcester House and before that somewhere else that Francis can't remember now. Sometimes at dinner his father speaks about the new town. He talks about gyratory road systems and enclosed shopping precincts; he talks about pedestrian bridges and shared recreation space. He has taken Francis to see the stretch of Worcestershire countryside where the new town will be built, but Francis finds it hard to imagine. There are no roads or streets, no green studded plastic Lego base board – just grass and mud. The idea that a town can appear fully formed in the middle of fields and trees is strange to him. He thinks of the dead leaves and the bones of animals lying buried in the soil underneath the pavements and playgrounds and it makes him shiver. There are no houses for miles around and he wonders who will live there. He imagines his father designing the inhabitants. Making them the right size and shape. He wonders what his father's ideal citizen would look like and he wonders if he could ever be one.

19

He stuck the two photos of Michael Church to the wall of his office at home. He'd seen this done in TV cop shows and it seemed a good start. One was a copy of the black and white photo he'd found in Michael's house of him and Phil as boys. The other was the newspaper shot of Michael as an old man in a photo booth. He looked at the two faces of Michael Church and wondered at the distance travelled between them.

He tried to guess how old Michael and Phil had been when the first photo was taken. It was hard to gauge. The photo was taken in the era when boys passed from child-hood to middle-age sometime around their tenth birthday. Frank tried to disregard the Ministry of Defence side partings and old men's clothes and focus only on their faces. He thought they might be fourteen, though they seemed simultaneously both younger and older than that.

He was struck by how little there was to distinguish the boys at the moment the photo was taken. Perhaps Phil's smile was more confident whilst Michael seemed shy, but essentially they were equals. He thought about their deaths and how the great contrast between them made each seem more extreme: the front-page headlines that followed Phil's set against the utter indifference that greeted Michael's. As Frank looked at the photo, he imagined Phil's image expanding to fill the entire frame while Michael shrank down to a pixel.

Andrea came to bring him a cup of coffee. She frowned at the photos. 'Is that the guy?'

'Yes. And look – that's Phil in that one.'

Andrea squinted and laughed. 'My God, he looked cocky even then.' She carried on looking at the photos. 'So what is this?'

'What?'

'The photos, the interest. I mean you've remembered where you know him from now.'

'They've got to find a next of kin.'

'Yes, I know they have – the coroner's office or the police or whoever . . .'

'Well, I thought I might help. You know, they can't always devote much time or resources to this kind of thing, and I did meet him one time, so it feels a little bit more personal and I thought maybe as a favour to Phil I . . .' He noticed Andrea's face and trailed off. He looked down. 'No.' He gave a little laugh: 'It's got nothing to do with me really. I just think someone should remember him.'

Andrea nodded. 'Maybe he wouldn't want to be remembered. Not just him, maybe the others too. Maybe their dearest wish was to pass unremarked and unacknowledged. Many of them chose to live alone; maybe they wanted to die alone too.'

'I know. It just bothers me.'

Andrea smiled. 'Is this how it's going to be now? Not just taking flowers or attending strangers' funerals, but actually investigating their lives? It's a crap hobby, Frank. Couldn't you just take up golf?'

'I thought this might get it out of my system. Maybe if I did something tangible to help for once then I could let it go.'

'You think you're Columbo, don't you? This is playing detectives.'

'Like the lieutenant, I have a bumbling almost irritating exterior that masks a brilliant mind.'

'Almost irritating?' Her smile faded and she looked away. 'Don't turn weird, Frank. Don't get all obsessed.' She was silent for a few moments. 'Your past weighs us down a lot. Weekends spent with your mother, letters sent to defend your father's buildings. It feels like enough history and melancholy without actively seeking out more. Maybe we should spend the time we have with each other and Mo.'

He reached out for her hand and pulled her to him. He held her and said quietly: 'I only ever want to be with you and Mo.'

After she'd gone he drank the coffee and thought about what she'd said. He looked at the face in the photo. Had Michael really hoped for the gentle fall of other deaths and other stories to cover his quickly and soundlessly, to be lost forever in that endless layering of beginnings and ends? Every day at work Frank added more news, more facts, more faces to the vast multi-layered mosaic of the city and amidst all this Michael was an empty space. It was always the gaps that drew Frank's attention. They seemed to matter more than the other pieces.

Michael
October 2009

Rush hour's ended and the traffic has loosened once more to a steady flow. The sun has dropped and Michael sits right in its line, the whole bench bathed in warm, golden light. He experiences it as a gentle hand pushing him back down against the bench, not letting him leave.

The sun in his eyes always reminds him of their first few days in Port George, stationed in the transit camp. Phil thought life would be less regimented once they were posted overseas, but he was disappointed. Michael coped better with guard duty and the mindless marching. He found the strict routine allowed him to absent himself, to be somewhere else with his thoughts. Sometimes on shit days of endless drill he'd remember the characters he used to daydream about as a kid – soldiers and cowboys and tough guys called Buddy, and he could still imagine he was one of them.

Off duty, though, Phil found things to enjoy about Port George. The other lads didn't like the atmosphere when they went into town. Most of them had barely left their hometowns before and found the constant attentions of Arabs trying to sell them lighters and dirty postcards disconcerting. But Phil could more than match the bullshit and bluster of the street traders and on the first night he was the man every other soldier asked to negotiate their purchase of a new lighter or a watch. He liked haggling with the vendors. The next time he was in town he'd remember their names and strike up conversations with them, asking about the best bars and places to visit.

Michael feels the golden light pressing against his eyelids and is once more with Phil exploring the back streets of the town on their own. They find an open-air café free of other soldiers and Phil is delighted at the discovery. At Phil's insistence they share a hookah and Michael finds the orange-scented smoke working its way into the creases and folds of his brain. He closes his eyes and sees Elsie on top of Adam's Hill, the wind blowing her skirt against her legs. He's not sure how much time passes before he opens his eyes and looks at his watch.

'The lorry's picking us up in fifteen minutes.'

Phil shrugs. 'We can get a taxi.'

'Have we got enough money?'

Phil laughs. 'Do I look like some sap who's going to get us ripped off? I'll negotiate a price. Just sit back and relax. We're going to travel back in style, not like cattle in a truck.'

Later they find a taxi willing to take them back out to camp. Phil manages to barter a good price and they get in. Michael feels woozy from the smoke and the heat, and the inside of the taxi spins just a little. He sits with his head back on the seat behind him and looks up out of the window at the stars flying past overhead. He wonders what Elsie is doing right now; he wonders if she can see the same stars. He can't remember ever seeing stars like them in Birmingham. He doesn't know what time it is there. Maybe it's not night. Maybe she's on her lunch, sitting under their tree in the park, polishing an apple on her sleeve.

Suddenly Phil is whispering urgently in his ear. 'We're going the wrong way.'

Michael carries on looking out at the stars. 'Why are you whispering?'

He whispers louder. 'We're going the wrong way. Away from the camp.'

Michael raises his head and gives a brief look out the front of the cab: 'Nah. He knows where he's going.'

'He knows where he's going all right, but it ain't to the camp.'

'How can you tell?'

Phil hisses: 'Because it's the wrong fucking way!'

Michael sits up properly and looks at him. He notices Phil's face is pale and moist. 'What's the matter with you?'

'We're going to die.'

'What?'

'We're going to die, Mikey. Jesus Christ, he's going to kill us.'

Michael starts to laugh. 'Why are you saying that?'

'Cos that's what's going to happen. Have you not heard the stories? British soldiers get picked up in taxis, taken out to the desert, robbed and killed.'

Michael stops laughing. The taxi stops spinning. 'What stories? What are you talking about?'

'The stories – everyone's heard them.'

He stares at Phil. 'Why didn't you tell me about the stories when you said we'd get a taxi?'

Phil looks down at his lap. 'I forgot.'

Michael leans forward and says to the driver: 'Mister, I think you're taking us the wrong way. Can you turn round, please.'

He's ignored.

Phil is muttering: 'Jesus Christ, Mikey, bandits.'

Michael tries again. 'Oi, mister. Where you going? Turn round.'

He sees the driver's dead eyes in the mirror as they start to slow down. 'Don't worry, please. We are here now.'

Phil and Michael look out of the window at the blackness beyond and both see that 'here' is not where they want to be.

The car pulls in at the side of the road where two men stand waiting. One of them opens the car door and signals for them to get out. The three men stand around Phil and Michael. One of them holds a large knife. He speaks in English. 'Take off clothes, please.'

Neither Phil nor Michael moves.

'Take off clothes, please, or I cut throat.'

Michael looks into the darkness, trying to see where the two men could have come from. He sees no houses or cars nearby. He wonders how far they've travelled to the rendezvous. Have they walked all the way from town? He starts wondering about the man's English. Does he only know vocabulary related to robbery? Michael wonders if the robber looks forward to these little opportunities to practise his stock phrases.

He's shouting at them now. 'You! Take off clothes! I ask nicely last time.'

Michael smiles. The Hollywood school of English. He'll

be coming out with some Jimmy Cagney line next. He turns to share his amusement with Phil only to see Phil standing naked apart from his baggy cotton shorts, shaking despite the heat. Michael has no idea what Phil is playing at. He has a strange feeling, as if he's watching the scene from a distance. The man keeps shouting at him, his face now inches away from his own. Why does he keep telling him to take his clothes off? Michael can think of no earthly reason why he would do such a thing.

Phil turns his head a fraction. 'For Christ's sake, Mikey, do what he says. Do you want to get us killed?'

Michael looks at Phil. It seems a strange thing to say. Michael is filled with a desire to be back in his tent eating the bar of chocolate he knows he has in his tin. He realizes he's starving. He thinks about the shepherd's pie his mother used to make. Then he thinks about her apple crumble and custard. What would he give for that right now? Or even just a single decent cup of tea and a nice coconut ring. He's irritated to find his thoughts interrupted by the man with the knife screaming at him: 'Take off!' The man reaches across and plucks at Michael's jacket and without making any conscious decision Michael finds his fist shooting out, hitting the man full force in the face.

The impact is a shock to both of them. Michael is suddenly alert. He lunges forward and manages to grab the knife before the other two men have dropped their fags. He feels their hands on his arms, but is able to kick and hack his way out. He waves the knife and they back away. He looks around and sees that Phil has already started running towards the road. Michael starts to run after him. He checks over his shoulder, but the men have no interest in the chase. Instead they hunch down, picking over Phil's uniform.

Michael and Phil run along the dark road, managing after half a mile to flag down a passing truck. They climb into the back and collapse exhausted on the flatbed, trying to catch their breath. It's a while before Phil is able to speak.

'Bloody hell, Mikey. You could have done your John Wayne bit before I dropped my pants.'

'I didn't get the chance. You don't need much persuasion, do you?'

'They had a knife, for Christ's sake, that's enough persuasion for me.' He's quiet for a moment and then adds: 'Thanks, Mikey.'

'What for?'

'You saved my life.'

Michael smiles. 'They weren't going to kill us, you daft sod. Their hearts weren't in it.'

Phil shakes his head. 'You saved my life.'

Michael looks at Phil and starts laughing.

'What's so funny?'

Phil's face and body are smeared with whatever animal's shit is all over the back of the truck and clumps of feathers are sticking to him.

'We showed the others, didn't we? Let them travel like cattle – we'll get back in style.'

21

He ordered a beer and took it to a table by the window overlooking the queues of cars nudging their way round the roundabout. As always, he was early to meet Andrea and as always she would be late. The hotel bar played its early evening selection. Frank was familiar with the track-listing now. He knew that 'Mas Que Nada' would be followed by the Lighthouse Family. The smooth early evening playlist. Andrea hated that kind of music; she said it made a vein throb in her face. Frank quite liked it. He tapped his foot.

The bar was charmless and yet he and Andrea always met there when in town. It was on the fourth floor of the hotel and Frank enjoyed the view. He liked that part of the city centre – an area where small scraps of the past were still visible at the margins of the newer developments, like unfashionable trainers peeping out from under a new suit. All the office blocks around had been converted into apartment complexes, their windows made larger, their surfaces lighter. Frank looked out at a building now calling itself Westside One. He remembered it as the office of an insurance company. He wondered what the people who had worked there, who had once sat at desks dreaming of escape, now thought of the dream of champagne flutes, leather sofas and wooden laminate flooring that was being sold back to them. He wondered if any of them had bought an apartment there and looked down now on the view they once hated with new eyes. He suspected not; no one seemed to be buying any more. An enormous banner hung on the outside of the building announcing that the 'last few' still remained two years after the first residents moved in. The banner boasted the development's selling points, one of which was that it overlooked another more prestigious development.

In the centre of the roundabout was one of the city's few remaining sunken mini-parks. A faded sixties mosaic of an imagined Victorian past, horse-drawn carriages and children chasing hoops with sticks, formed the backdrop to a now stagnant water feature. Empty cans lay motionless on the black surface of the water in the concrete pond. Benches waited for anyone who might enjoy a moment's rest in the eye of the traffic's storm. The city's many subways were once a source of pride, decorated with public art and seating areas. Frank had seen archive footage from the sixties of the opening of a subway under one of the busiest roads in the centre. A race to cross the road was staged between two councillors. One went by surface, the other by subway – and won. The results were clear: subways were quick, safe and modern.

Frank could see now that three of the subway tunnels that led into the underpass were sealed off. New pedestrian crossings had been installed on the busy roads. The ethos of separating people from cars that Frank's father had thought the solution was now seen as the problem. People wanted the right to roam the surface of the city and not be shuttled below or above the roads out of the sight and minds of motorists. Frank remembered covering a murder in one of the tunnels some years ago. The victim had tried to resist his mugger and ended up dead. He wondered how long it might be before all the entrances were sealed off and the sunken garden covered over. He imagined it remaining intact under a new layer of development, as empty and forlorn as it stood now, waiting for future archaeologists to unearth and invent complex mythologies about.

He didn't hear Andrea approach and jumped slightly as she touched his shoulder.

'Sorry I'm late.'

He stood to kiss her. 'You're not really sorry. You think making me wait keeps me keen.'

'Does it? Were you sitting there thinking longingly of me?'

'I was thinking about pedestrian underpasses.'

'Naturally.'

He smiled. 'Do you want a drink first or shall we go to the restaurant?'

'Let's get a drink and I can ring and check on Mo before we go.'

When Frank returned from the bar, Andrea was staring at the muted TV screen on the back wall. He followed the direction of her gaze and saw Phil's face. He felt himself begin to smile before the memory of Phil's death returned and he experienced a small jolt of shock once more.

Andrea spoke without turning her head from the screen. 'They're showing *An Evening With . . .* again. He looked great, didn't he?'

'He'd have loved to hear you say that.'

Andrea smiled and looked at Frank. 'God, he was funny, wasn't he? I bumped into him once in Rackhams and blimey you couldn't miss him. He had that ridiculous suntan, and was wearing this enormous white padded jacket and gold-framed sunglasses. You'd think it was Tony Curtis, not the local newsreader. Everyone was staring.'

'I know. He loved it. He was totally shameless about it. He knew it was shallow, but he didn't care.'

'Did I ever tell you about my auntie and Phil?'

'No.'

'You know Margaret? She loved him, thought he was the cat's pyjamas. She only had to hear the name "Phil Smethway" and her face would light up. She used to watch *Heart of England Reports* every night just for him and was absolutely devastated when he left.'

'But I took over after Phil.'

'Yeah. I know. Anyway, obviously she stopped watching after Phil left.'

'Obviously.'

'She assumed he'd retired, gone off to live in Monaco or somewhere glamorous. Then shortly afterwards she and Uncle Matt were on holiday in Brighton and they saw him presenting *South-East Reports*.'

'I'd forgotten that. He only did it for a few months.'

'Uncle Matt said she was furious. She felt so betrayed – it was as if she'd discovered an affair. When he moved to national telly after that, she'd never watch him. If ever he cropped up on an advert or a trailer, she'd do this thing, wiping her lips with her fingers as if to wipe off a kiss.'

'Well, you see, there's a lesson for her. Don't be dazzled

by these entertaining types – with their charm and their wit – stick with people like me, stolid and dull, we won't let you down. Haven't I always told you that?'

Andrea smiled. 'God, I couldn't have lived with Phil. I mean he was lovely and fun to be around, but he was always checking out his own reflection, always fussing with his hair or his shoes. I couldn't be with a vain man.'

'He was sending himself up a lot of the time.'

'I know he played up to the role – but it was based on truth. He and Michelle were like the perfect accessories for each other. I was never sure if there was much to their relationship beyond the surface.'

'I think there was. Just because they were glamorous, it doesn't mean they didn't love each other. I remember the way Phil used to talk about Michelle. I'm sure he loved her.'

Andrea shrugged 'Well, you knew him better than me, so maybe he did. Maybe all that gloss just distracted me from the substance underneath.'

As they headed towards the restaurant, Frank thought back to one of the last conversations he'd had with Phil. After they stopped working together they kept in regular, if occasional, contact. They met maybe once or twice a year. Sometimes at each other's houses with Andrea and Michelle there too, at others just the two of them for lunch or a drink when they happened to be in each other's part of the country. Frank would tell Phil about developments on the programme: who had left, who had joined, the latest budget cut, the sinking morale. Phil would tell Frank funny stories of A-list celebrities, monstrous egos and associated bullshit. Inevitably, though, what they talked about most were the old days. The fortune-telling parrot that bit Frank, the skateboarding dog that caught Phil in the balls, the alcoholic sports correspondent, the philandering weatherman, the stories that broke nationally, the unsolved mysteries, their favourite interviews.

A few weeks before his death, Phil phoned Frank. Phil normally called during the day, but this call came late one evening as Frank was about to go to bed.

'Howdy, pardner.'

'Hello, mate.' Frank glanced at his watch. 'Shouldn't you be in your lead casket by now? Cucumber slices placed carefully over your eyes.'

'Sadly, Frank, the days of cucumber slices are long gone; they just don't cut it any more. I sometimes look in the mirror and have to accept that I'm not the man I once was. I console myself, though, with the thought that I look a hell of a lot better than you will when you reach my age.'

Frank noticed Phil was slurring his words. 'I suspect you look better than I do now.'

'Well, you will insist on wearing those cheap suits. I've always told you how ageing poor tailoring is.'

'And I've lost sleep over it. What are you ringing for anyway?'

There was silence for a moment, then Phil said: 'You know I love Michelle, don't you.'

Frank frowned into the receiver. 'Of course I do. Have you been drinking?'

'I have, actually. I've just finished off a bottle of Glen-farclas, but that's beside the point. I love her very much.'

'I know. It's good that you love her. She's your wife.'

'I mean . . . you know she's a lot younger than me; she could have married a young man, but she chose me. I never want her to regret that.'

'Why would she regret it? She loves you. Why don't you go to bed?'

'I'm going, I'm going. I just wanted to call you. I wanted to tell you, because you're a mate, one of the best. You know that, don't you? I mean all joking aside. We take the piss, don't we? We have a laugh at each other. We always have, but you know, don't you? Don't you?'

Frank was smiling at his end of the phone. He'd never heard Phil so drunk. He was relishing the prospect of reminding him about the call when he was sober. 'I know what?'

'Oh, you're trying to make me say it. You're a tease. You know what I'm talking about. Shush . . .' Phil whispered the next bit: 'I love you.' His voice went back to normal volume: 'There, I've said it! Not in a funny way. You know that. Man to man. Mates. I know you think I'm a flash bastard. But I love you, Frank. Oops. Said it again. I love Michelle too. I never want her to regret it. She won't regret it.'

'No one's going to regret anything, Phil. Except you in the morning. Go to bed now. Go and have a sleep, okay?'

'Okay, Frank. I've embarrassed you. I know, I know. That's okay. We're mates, Frank. You know the funny thing? I'm going to tell you a secret. All my life I've been scared, but tonight, when I've got something to be scared about, I'm not scared at all. I'm not scared, Frank.'

'All right, Phil, well done, not scared, very good, now

go to bed. Don't worry about anything. Go and have a lie down.'

'Night, Frank.'

'Night, Phil.'

A quiet Phil phoned a few days later to apologize.

Frank laughed. 'Don't worry about it. I'm a loveable man, why wouldn't you ring me up late at night and tell me how you feel? I'm amazed you've suppressed it so long.'

'I'm sorry, Frank.' Phil seemed entirely lacking in bounce.

Frank found it impossible to take the piss when Phil wouldn't bite back. 'It's okay. It was funny.'

'It was pathetic.'

'Well, maybe, but that's okay. Are you okay? You seem down.'

'Yeah, yes, I'm fine. Probably still hungover. What an idiot.'

'Well, you're making me feel bad now. Almost as if you didn't mean what you said.'

'To be honest, Frank, I don't even remember most of what I said.'

'Oh, it was nothing. You love me, you love Michelle, that's all.'

'I'm ridiculous.'

'Bloody hell, Phil, don't worry about it. I enjoyed it; I thought I'd be able to mock you for years, but you're taking it so badly you're ruining all the fun.'

Phil said nothing – his breathing was heavy.

'Phil? Are you sure you're okay?'

'Yeah. Honestly, I'm fine. Sorry, just tired.'

'There was one thing you said on the phone that was a bit odd.'

'What? What did I say?'

'Something about not being scared even though you had every reason to be. What have you got to be scared of? Are they discontinuing Grecian 2000?'

'God knows. I was talking rubbish. Bloody Glenfarclas. Never again.'

Within a month Phil was dead. His apology call was left hanging in Frank's memory as their last conversation. It was a strange note on which to end. Frank felt guilty for his facetiousness. He squeezed Andrea's hand. 'I thought a lot of Phil, you know.'

Andrea looked at him, surprised. 'I know. Of course you did.'

Frank opened the door to the restaurant and wished he'd said the same to Phil.

22

Frank worked through his in-box. In a bid to appear relevant in the digital age, the email addresses of the show's presenters appeared on-screen underneath their names, as well as on the website. Aside from spam, he typically received between ten and twenty mails a day from the public and the policy was to reply to all but the outright abusive or threatening. Today he had three requests for personal appearances, four suggestions of stories to feature, one asking about the shirt he'd worn on the programme of 2 October, one obscene request pertaining to his female co-presenters, one veiled threat, one unveiled threat and a racist joke. He was left now with the 'unfriendlies', which needed more time and care. An unfriendly wasn't straightforwardly abusive and thus warranted a reply, but a generically bland response would lead more often than not to a rapid escalation of hostility. Julia received roughly the same amount of mail as Frank, but the content tended, even Frank would concede, more towards the bizarre. Reporters and correspondents got their share of mail too and at any one point someone on the show would always have a stalker, but it was naturally enough the presenters who attracted the most attention.

In total there were seven presenters covering the various

bulletins and programmes across the team's output. Frank and Julia were the regular presenters of the evening show as well as presenting some of the other brief post-network news bulletins throughout the week. Frank liked working with Julia, even though she gave no sign of this being mutual. They were an odd couple, but with an on-screen dynamic that seemed to work. She was younger, earnest, frosty, but concerned. He was older, sincere, awkward and corny. As a pair they seemed to convey the right blend of warmth and authority and both had enough self-awareness to know that they were better together than apart.

Julia took the job seriously and gave every indication that she thought she was the only one who did, though in fact she and Frank shared a similar approach. Historically presenters tended not to attend production meetings. The way that shifts worked out meant it still wasn't always possible and many of the other presenters on the show rarely attended for that reason. But Frank and Julia had both always seen the meetings as part of their jobs. Frank wasn't sure that this was something necessarily welcomed by all the reporters and correspondents and sometimes had the distinct impression that some members of the team preferred the old-style presenters, with backgrounds in light entertainment rather than journalism. He knew some called them 'gobs on sticks' and expected them to mouth the reports they were given unquestioningly despite how thin they might be or how little coherence they possessed. It was hard to mistake the sarcasm with which certain correspondents referred to presenters as 'the talent'.

But neither Julia nor Frank had any desire to present

stories that they themselves couldn't see the point of, or that failed to deliver on the promise of the headline. Frank had become skilful over the years in giving the impression of going along with whatever was the order of the day, whilst actually continuing quite doggedly along the path he thought was the right one. He liked to arrive early in the day with plenty of time to check through the reports and rewrite links. It was a way of curbing the more tabloid or inconsequential impulses of the day's producer. He checked through the stories diligently, watching the packages, subtly pointing out gaps or errors to reporters and rewriting their links as necessary. Much of this work was invisible to Julia who tended to see Frank as spineless. She favoured confrontation and drama and didn't seem to notice that she lost many of the fights that she picked, leaving her fuming as she presented stories she felt lacked credibility.

Frank turned his attention back to the remaining mails:

dear Frank,

I saw you the other day buying wine in oddbins
on colmore row. I expect you need alcol to help
you sleep at nite. you looked very shabby I
thought. I followed you up corporation street
but then you went in house of fraser and I
didn't go in because of the PROSTITUTES.
remember that Jesus is watching you and so am I.

a friend

Frank wondered if he should mention in his reply that he'd never been in that branch of Oddbins. He wondered if that mattered. Did it alter the central premise of the correspondence? Was there a central premise? He thought about the shabby man who had been followed in error. He liked the idea of having a double out there absorbing the sidelong glances and the harmful thought waves. He imagined the man as his tireless protector, his clothes shabby from pounding the city streets 24/7 as Frank, taking the odd drink to fortify himself against the baffling comments people shouted out to him.

As well as respecting her work in its own right, Frank valued Julia because he knew how much worse the alternatives could be. There had been several short-lived co-presenters before Julia started on the programme. The first was Suzy Pickering, who had worked alongside Phil for many years. Smethway and Pickering represented a nostalgic golden era of the show for many viewers and would be the faces forever associated with the programme no matter how many successors came and went. If Phil was a suntan with white teeth then Suzy was a haircut with impeccable knitwear. She had hit on a pageboy bob sometime around the heyday of Purdey and stuck with it throughout the ensuing decades, with the obligatory nod to Diana in the early eighties. Her discreet jewellery was provided exclusively by a boutique named Sally Anne in Knowle in what was a blatant exercise in sponsorship, but went unchallenged. Suzy was old school through and through. A beautiful broadcast voice, a wonderful after-dinner speaker and a marked lack of interest in local news and current affairs. She loved to talk about the old days where everything was marvellous and everyone was a real character. She adored Phil, falling for his faux reverence and delighting in his gentle teasing. The undoubted high-point of her career was an interview with Telly Savalas when he had made an unlikely promotional film entitled *Telly Savalas Looks at Birmingham*. In it Savalas spoke of the wonders of the second city in his trademark honeyed growl: '*I walked on the walkways, sat on the seats and admired the trees and the shrubs in the spacious traffic-free pedestrian precincts.*' In fact the actor was somehow able to resist the allure of the precinct shrubbery and never set foot in Birmingham, recording the script in a studio in London instead. In Suzy's repeated telling of the tale, a twenty-minute Q & A session conducted in a London hotel lobby had expanded to become an entire afternoon of almost unbearable sexual tension and unspoken longing between herself and Savalas. Phil needed only to waggle his eyebrows and mutter, 'Who loves ya, baby?' and Suzy would dissolve into fits of girlish giggles.

Frank got off on the wrong foot with Suzy from the start. In their first week presenting together she had regaled him with story after story from the good old days, most of which he had heard before. After telling the Telly Savalas story she concluded in a studiedly wistful way, 'I often think of how of all the cities in the world something, something perhaps we'll never understand, drew an international superstar of the stature of Savalas to Birmingham, and, well, I suppose in a funny way, to me.'

In retrospect Frank realized that the required response was to say that it had been kismet, or some mysterious transatlantic catnip operating on the bald-headed actor, but instead he said, 'I suppose desperate times, desperate measures. *Kojak* was axed the year before. He did *Telly Savalas Looks at Portsmouth* and *Aberdeen* as well. He would have advertised Don Amott caravans if they'd have had him.'

Despite his best attempts to make amends it was clear that Suzy always considered Frank a very poor substitute for Phil and altogether lacking in old-world charm. After a few years of working together she opted to go part time and remained as one of the seven-strong presenting team, usually doing the early morning bulletins. Julia maintained that Suzy's continued presence was due more to her devotion to Sally Anne's pearl studs than to her career.

After Suzy there was Nicki, who was smiley and petite and in a short space of time became very popular with viewers. She had a natural warmth and vivacity that burned through the screen, and after Suzy's hauteur Frank found her a joy to work with. Because of her popularity Nicki received a particularly large number of invitations and requests for PAs, which she showed no inclination to decline. The weekly society page of the local paper rarely failed to carry a picture of Nicki at a charity dinner, or the opening of a new restaurant, or an awards ceremony for industrialists. As the months passed, she became less petite, her brightness seemed to fade and her slips whilst reading the autocue became more regular. Frank remembered the day he finally reached across and pushed the lift button for her rather than have everyone watch her struggle to control her shaking hands. She resigned due to ill health after just four years.

After Nicki came Lisa, who Frank had found strangely

absent and had a hard job remembering much about. She had worked on the show in pre-sofa days and the producer thought the fact that she was taller than Frank was disconcerting for viewers and so had her sit on a lower seat. Lisa never really forgave the producer or Frank for that. She stayed for two years before moving on to become sole anchor woman of the early evening news on a satellite channel. She was now enjoying, as far as Frank could tell, all the benefits of a full-height chair.

After Lisa was Joy, fondly remembered by all, even Frank's mother, but who moved regions after only a few months. She was followed by the equally short-lived Erica, who collected lizards and was dismissed after an incident involving cocaine, the sports correspondent and the disabled toilets. And then finally Julia arrived.

He looked at his watch and wondered where she was now. He could do with some advice on how best to answer his mail. He gave up on the Oddbins sighting and moved on to the next one:

```
Allcroft, the programme would be a hundred times
better if you were not on it. You are not funny.
I like it best when you are on holiday. Also,
how do you get a job in television?
```

He was uncertain about the last line. From the tenor of the mail he could assume that it was meant rhetorically, with the emphasis on 'you'. But maybe it wasn't. The 'also' suggested to him another tack, an unrelated point. He'd once sent as full and helpful a reply as he could to the request, 'Where do you get your ties?' Only to receive the response: 'I was joking, you wanker. They make me want to be sick.' He remembered Julia had laughed at that, for what he had thought had been an unnecessarily long period of time. As he sat and thought, a new mail appeared in his in-box and he opened it:

Dear Mr Allcroft,

I don't know if this mail will find you or if you will have time in your busy schedule to read it. My name is Sidney Craven and I am currently enrolled upon a 'Silver Surfers' course at my local library which is trying to teach me and some other seniors how to use the world wide web. I think the teacher is finding it a bit of a struggle. It took us a long time to get the hang of the mice.

Last week we learned how to send email. To be honest I can't see what use that will be as I don't have a computer and don't know anyone else who does either, but I think it's good to keep the mind active and learn new things. Anyway I see your email address every evening on the telly and I don't know if that's just a gimmick but I thought I would try anyway.

My wife Margaret died late last year but we used to watch *Heart of England Reports* every evening together. She was a fan of yours and particularly enjoyed your jokes. She also thought you had a lovely smile. You reminded her of someone she

used to know when she was younger and every night
without fail she'd say: 'Oh, he looks just like
Charlie Stoker. I wonder if they're related.'
Well, she had a real bee in her bonnet about it
and would go on and on. Sometimes she'd say, 'I'm
going to write to the programme and ask him,' and
I'd say, 'For goodness' sake, Margaret, they've
got better things to do with their time than
answer silly questions.' If I'm honest I was a
bit short with her because I didn't like her
always mentioning this Stoker chap. It was
jealousy I suppose as I'd never met the man, but
I know that he had been sweet on her before I
came along.

Anyway Margaret's gone now and she never did
write, but when I watch the programme I always
feel as if she's still sat on the settee next to
me. So I thought I'd send an email and maybe you
would read it and I could tell you about Margaret
and ask if I may: are you related to Charlie
Stoker? If you send an answer, I'll get the
teacher to print it out and then I can put it on
the sideboard next to Margaret's photo. I think
she'd like that.

Yours faithfully,
Sidney Craven

Frank sensed that someone was behind him and looked
to see that Julia had arrived at work and was reading

over his shoulder. They looked at each other briefly.

Julia rolled her eyes. 'So this Charlie Stoker looked just like you?'

Frank nodded and said, 'Apparently.'

Julia shrugged. 'That would explain why she ditched him for old Sidney.'

23

Michelle was caught up in a discussion with her producer, so Mo excitedly dragged Frank around the *Tough Love* set while they waited.

'Dad, look, look, this is the Mirror of Truth. That's what Michelle calls it. When the people look in this, they see themselves the way other people see them.'

Frank frowned. 'Isn't that what all mirrors do?'

'Yes, but this one's really big! Michelle gets the people to stand in front of it in a bikini so we can see where they are fat and she tells them what she honestly sees and they cry. That's the tough-love bit – but at the end they come back and stand in front of the mirror again, but now they have new hair and new clothes and intelligent underwear and they cry again, but this time because they're so happy.'

'"Intelligent underwear"? What's that?'

Mo shrugged. 'I don't know exactly. I think it might have a computer in it. It stops the fat escaping.'

Mo stood in front of the mirror and turned slowly with a crazed expression of ecstasy. 'Tough love has turned my life around!' she said, clapping her hands together.

Frank winced. 'Is that what they say?'

'Yes – because their lives were bad before, but after tough love they're really good and all their friends come and clap and tell them how happy they are that they have had a haircut and the fat is hidden.' Mo carried on staring in the mirror. 'I wish Sinead could go on *Tough Love.*'

'Who's Sinead?'

'She's in my class. Sinead Rourke. Some children call her names because she's fat, and she has asthma and she can't run. They shouldn't call her names, should they, Dad?'

'No, definitely not. That's horrible.'

'That's what I said. She just needs *Tough Love* and intelligent underwear. She needs to come on here and find out how to tuck the fat in her pants and turn her life around. She is stuck with a bad life, but she could have a good life.'

'Mo, maybe her life isn't bad. Maybe apart from the name calling she's quite happy. Appearances aren't the most important thing in the world.'

Michelle finally joined them. 'Oh, Mo! What's he saying? That's what all those poor women say, isn't it, at the start of the show? "Appearance doesn't matter to me," and I say, "The point is, love, it matters to everyone else, and yours is a mess." Tough love, isn't it, Mo? You understand.'

Mo looked awkward; she wasn't sure who to agree with.

Frank looked at Michelle. 'Mo was just talking about a classmate who's being bullied for being overweight.'

Michelle was alarmed. 'Oh, oh, I see. Mo, no, love, that's different. It's different for kiddies. The programme's for grown-ups. Kiddies shouldn't worry about their weight – your friend can go on a diet when she's a teenager.'

Frank decided to change the topic. 'Anyway – thanks

for letting Mo come along today. As you can see, she's a big fan of the show.'

Michelle smiled. 'No, thank you, Frank, for agreeing to meet. I'm really sorry we've had to do it here. I'm behind schedule again – as usual – but at least it means Mo gets to have a look around.'

Frank wasn't sure now that he shared that delight but he nodded.

Michelle beamed at Mo. 'Hey, Mo – why don't you go over to the clothes racks and pick out some clothes you think would be good for me. I've got to go to a party tonight – so you go and find something for me to wear.'

Mo was delighted. 'What kind of party?'

'It's an opening.'

Mo frowned. 'Is that like a birthday party?'

'Not exactly.'

'Is it fancy dress?'

'No, not fancy dress.'

'Will you be playing games?'

'What do you mean?'

'After you've had cake – will there be party games? Do you need to be able to run around?'

Michelle laughed. 'No. No games. I just need to be able to stand, sit and drink.'

Frank could see from Mo's face that she didn't think much of the sound of the party, but she set off purposefully to the clothes racks. He felt a sudden pang of love for her as she went and had to fight the urge to run with her.

Michelle led him over to sit on a red sofa in the middle of the set. A couple of crew members moved pieces of furniture in the opposite corner.

'Before I forget. You know you asked me about that photo?'

'Yes.'

'His name was Michael, wasn't it?'

'Yeah. Michael Church.'

'Well, I've no idea if this is connected, but this is why the name Michael was vaguely familiar.'

She fished in her bag and handed Frank a note written on a small sheet of pale blue writing paper. Frank recognized the sloping shaky handwriting from papers at Michael's house.

Phil,

I won't be there next week. Sorry to tell you in a letter but I know if we meet you'll try and talk me round again – like Elsie used to say, you always could charm the honey from the bees.

You're my dearest friend Phil, but you're wrong.

I hope I'll hear from you soon.

Mikey

Frank read it through twice. He assumed it dated back some years.

'Did you find this amongst his papers?'

'No – it came by post a few days after Phil died. Well, actually it didn't come by post – that's how I remembered it amidst all the other letters that were turning up each day. Whoever sent it didn't put enough postage on it so I had to go along to the sorting office to collect it and pay the extra. It would have been waiting there a few days before I got round to going to get it. I had so much going on I didn't pay it a great deal of attention. Is that the Michael you were asking about?'

'Yeah.'

'What's it about?'

'I don't know. A disagreement, I guess.'

Michelle pulled a face. 'It's strange that Phil never mentioned it. Strange that I never even heard him mention this Michael.' She hesitated. 'But that's what I wanted to talk to you about.'

'What?'

'I don't really know where to start – just lots of little things that maybe don't amount to much. I haven't spoken to anyone before, but now I think maybe I should say something.'

'Say what?'

'Okay – put at its bluntest – I just think there was something funny going on at the end.'

'Funny?'

'Suspicious, peculiar. Not ha ha. Definitely not ha ha.' Frank waited for her to continue, but instead she changed tack. 'When did you last speak to him?'

'About a month before he died.'

'And how did he seem?'

Frank remembered the phone conversation. 'Fine, he seemed fine. I mean – the conversation was a little strange, but in himself he was fine.'

'What do you mean strange?'

'Well, he was ringing to apologize for the previous call when he'd had a bit to drink. I didn't mind at all, but he was being really hard on himself, saying he'd behaved ridiculously – you know, obviously very embarrassed about his behaviour – which wasn't really like him. Normally he'd just laugh something like that off, or deny it.'

Michelle nodded. 'When he rang you drunk – had he ever done that before?'

'God no, never. It wasn't his style, was it? Not very debonair and classy. I was looking forward to getting mileage from that little slip for years to come.'

'And when he was drunk, was he telling you he loved you?'

Frank looked at Michelle. 'Yes, he was. I suppose every drunk says that – but that's exactly what he was saying, and that he loved you too – he was full of love that night.'

Michelle sat back on the sofa. 'So you had a glimpse of it.'

'A glimpse of what?'

'Of what life was like in those last two months.' She hesitated. 'This is really hard for me, because it feels like I'm talking about Phil behind his back – well, I am, but I have to talk to someone about it. He became a different person in those weeks leading up to his death. You know how easy going he was, how much fun – well, that changed. He was having these enormous mood swings. At night he'd tell me how much he loved me – I mean we'd always told each other that – but this was different, there was some kind of desperation there. He was drinking more – sometimes he'd actually be crying as he told me he loved me. It was frightening. I knew something was up, but he wouldn't tell me what. Then in the daytime he'd often be tense and short-tempered, preoccupied and tetchy. Other times he'd seem utterly depressed and lifeless. It was crazy.'

Frank was shaking his head. 'But that just wasn't Phil. Do you think maybe he was ill?'

'That's what I thought. I thought it must be something neurological – this complete personality change. He agreed to be checked out, but they found nothing. The doctor said it could be stress, but he didn't know Phil. He thought a seventy-eight-year-old man doing a weekly primetime television show was bound to be overdoing it – but Phil thrived on that.

'I knew something was wrong. Do you know what my first response was when I heard about the accident? My very first split-second thought was *I knew it*. There was just a sense that he was heading towards some catastrophe.' She hesitated before adding: 'I think his death was connected to his behaviour in those last few weeks.'

'It was a hit and run.'

'It's a straight road – no blind corners. The police were completely puzzled by it. The driver never braked.'

Frank didn't think it would help to say that he'd seen the road and thought exactly the same thing. Instead he tried Andrea's theory. 'Maybe the driver fell asleep.'

Michelle shook her head. 'It was suspicious, and the police have never found the driver; their investigation got nowhere. There was something going on, Frank. I feel ridiculous speaking like this – like a character in a film – that's why I didn't say anything before.'

'What's changed now?'

Michelle saw Mo heading back towards them with what appeared to be an orange tracksuit, a black pillbox hat and some red patent-leather stilettos. She was smiling proudly and called as she approached, 'Get ready to have your life turned around!'

Michelle turned to Frank just before Mo reached them and said quietly: 'Now I know about the money.'

24

Rhombus House was designed by Douglas H. Allcroft and Partners. Built in 1974 to house several council departments in the heart of the city centre, its bold, brutalist exterior was striking enough to cause a stir in the local media. Frank recalled sitting with his parents watching the broadcast of his father being interviewed by a reporter for the regional news slot. Years later he discovered that Phil had been the large-collared man conducting the interview. His father's contribution was cut down to a few words and the rest of the report was filled with a vox pop of passers-by.

A middle-aged woman with a clipped voice and pointed glasses spoke as if she had just been waiting to be asked: 'I'm afraid to say I think it is terribly ugly. A blot on the landscape. If that is the fashion, then I'm very glad I'm not "with it".'

A young man with enormous sideburns grinned shyly: 'Iss all right, ennit? I mean it looks modern; it looks now. I dunno where the door is, though.'

The entrance, in fact, was situated thirty feet off the ground and approached via two large concrete ramps forming an apex in front of the building. At some point the rumour started that the architects had forgotten all about the entrance and the ramp approach had been added as a hasty afterthought. It was amazing to Frank that anyone could believe such a clearly improbable tale, but the idea that architects were so out of touch with the needs of ordinary people that they might overlook something as fundamental as a doorway rang true for many.

In the early nineties the council departments had outgrown the building and moved to new premises. Rhombus House, like all of Frank's father's buildings, had been designed in close consultation with the clients, the features and layout tailor-made for their specific needs and the idiosyncrasies of their complex departmental relationships. As a result, no other tenants could be found and its obsolescence combined with an exterior appearance that had passed from being avant-garde and controversial to just controversial meant the council opted for demolition.

Frank remembered the shock of hearing the news. It was the first of his father's buildings to be destroyed. Douglas had always talked about building for the future; Frank was relieved he hadn't lived to discover just how brief that future had been.

Before it was demolished Phil and Frank walked over to the site one evening after work. Phil looked up at the dark grey exterior. 'I don't like this. I don't like it one bit.'

'What?'

'Outliving a building. It makes me feel old.'

'You are old.'

'Mature is what I am. Distinguished maybe. Suave certainly. Not old. Your tie is old.' He looked at the boarded-up entrance. 'I remember doing the report on the ribbon-cutting; I didn't expect to be around at the demolition.'

'I remember watching it and thinking how incredibly suave the reporter was.'

'You're funny. It was a landmark building, though. I remember how ahead of its time it looked then. Your father was very intense. He was talking in terms way over the heads of the viewers. We kept having to retake, get him to just say something simple. In the end we gave up and slapped in some members of the great Joe P. instead.'

'Communication wasn't his strong suit.'

'What do you think of them tearing it down?'

Frank struggled to answer. 'Too many things.' He had a brief image of himself as a boy looking at drawings of the tower on the wall of his father's study. He shrugged. 'It's hard to take in.'

Phil nodded. 'No offence, Frank, but the building has seen better days. It's a bit of an eyesore now. I mean this whole part of town has been redeveloped and here's Rhombus House still stood in the middle in all its concrete glory like an old pair of flares lurking in the wardrobe. I know when it was built your father had the best intentions, and it looked amazing then, but it's better to rip it down now than watch it fall apart.'

Frank had heard this argument before. 'I don't think so. It's the newer buildings that are the problem. The council sold off the area around Rhombus House that was supposed to be a series of tree-lined plazas and gardens. That was an integral part of Dad's plan. You can't just hack the scheme to pieces and then blame the building for looking wrong. The council flogged the land

and let developers build right up against Rhombus House and now they notice that it looks out of place. It was a landmark building – it should have been respected; it should have been planned around.'

'But they gave it that facelift ten years ago and it didn't make any difference.'

'It made it worse. It was a cheap eighties fascia on a seventies building. They should have respected it for what it was, not tried to reinvent it and not tear it down.'

Phil shook his head. 'I don't think it works like that in the real world. Things age, they start to look tired and crap and nobody wants to see them . . . even if they age well. Look at me. I'm an extremely well-maintained, handsome bastard, but I have to change with the times – change my appearance, change my patter, and it's not bloody easy keeping up with it. The fashions change and you have to look like you know what's going on. You have to act like you know why a load of young kids suddenly think you're cool again, or why some twenty-five-year-old git in a trilby wants you in his advert. Facelifts – Jesus, yes, I'm all for 'em. And when that stops working then I'm afraid it's time for demolition.'

Frank shook his head. 'I never understood that advert. Why were you dressed as Mr T? What did that have to do with banking?'

'Irony apparently. It's always irony.'

Frank nodded. 'I bet it is.' He turned his back on Rhombus House and looked at the newer buildings around them. He tried to imagine Rhombus House gone, disappeared from the earth and how that would feel. 'It's not just that.'

Phil frowned. 'Not just what?'

'What I was just saying about the building. It's more than that.'

Phil waited and then finally said: 'Jesus, Frank. Is this pause supposed to be building suspense? What's more than what?'

'I mean this demolition. It's not just because it was my father's building, or about its architectural merits, or the lack of foresight and planning. Even if you disagree with all that, even if you think this building is a hideous mistake, I don't think you should simply erase your mistakes.'

'Of course you don't, Frank. Cling stubbornly to them, keep them as a penance, a constant reminder of how you fucked up. This explains those shoes with the rubber soles you insist on wearing for work. You're punishing yourself.'

'No, I'm punishing *you* with those shoes – that's my only reason for wearing them. Okay, some mistakes can be erased, but I think to wipe out all traces of the past is wrong. Do you remember the mechanized car park they built in the original Bull Ring?'

'Course I remember it. I was one of the few people to use it and get out alive. You drove into a lift thing and then left the car there – the magic of technology did the rest, transporting the car to a space. Total ease and comfort for the motorist, until it broke down on the second day entombing that last Ford Anglia there for the next twenty years.'

'That's what I like about this city.'

'What? That it's crap and everything fails?'

'No. That it has these ridiculous dreams, that it always tries to reinvent itself, to be the city of the future, but then always changes its mind about what the future should be.

I love the little glimpses you catch of the old dreams, the old ideas of what Utopia should be. I think if you get rid of all of them, no matter how embarrassing or naive they are, then you lose something essential about the place.'

'Is that how you feel about your father's buildings? I mean behind all your talk of their architectural significance, is it just that you think they're quaint reminders of what used to seem like good ideas?'

Frank shrugged. 'I don't know. It's different when it comes to my father. I know how hard he worked on this building, on all his buildings. He built them for the future. They were his legacy.' He turned back now and looked at Rhombus House and sighed. 'You know it's an incredibly beautiful building inside? The people who worked there loved it.'

Phil smiled. 'You'll never understand, will you? It's only the outside that's visible. That's all people care about, mate.'

Looking back, Frank thought he did understand now. He'd had a hard schooling. Worcester House, the last but one of his father's public buildings remaining, was due to be demolished the following week. Frank knew that even if all his father's buildings were torn down, his memory would live on in him, but he knew also that such an intangible legacy would have meant nothing to his father.

25

Francis
1975

His mother walks in from the kitchen carrying a tray. Francis studies her closely. He looks at her mouth, her eyes, the line of her shoulders and he knows that today is an orange day. As if to confirm it, she looks at him and flashes a wide smile.

He was very little when he decided that his mother had orange days and purple days. Now he's more grown-up he could use other words to describe the contrast, but the notion of colours has stuck and nothing else seems quite right.

'Well, are we ready for the party?'

He grins and nods.

On purple days his mother pulls plants up in the garden, she looks out of the window at nothing in particular for impossibly long stretches and speaks to her sister in a low voice on the telephone for hours. Sometimes she is cross with Francis whilst at others she doesn't seem to notice he's there at all.

On orange days she tells stories, she invents games, she takes Francis on expeditions and most of all she makes him laugh.

She sets the tray down on the coffee table and Francis surveys the assortment of crisps and sweets, which his mother always inexplicably refers to as 'rocks'. They have been carefully placed as usual in an eccentric selection of crockery. A few Smarties in an egg cup, a heap of cheese snips in a gravy boat, assorted crisps laid out on best plates. She and Francis refer to this arrangement as 'a party', though no other guests are ever invited.

Francis's father is out for the evening attending something called a consultation meeting and when Francis asked his father explained what that was, but the explanation seemed to pass straight through his ears. Francis doesn't know if his father knows about the little parties that sometimes happen in his absence. He suspects that Douglas would not approve of such indulgence and crockery transgression.

Francis sits in his usual place, perched on something his mother calls 'a pouffe'. Sometimes when she rests her feet on the pouffe while reading a book, Francis notices his father's eyes narrowing slightly in the direction of the pouffe, which seems to offend him. The pouffe is black and white and made of leather or maybe plastic. When he was very little, Francis used to pretend it was the driver's seat of a sports car and use a plate as a steering wheel whilst revving away noisily. Now, though, he is older and more sophisticated and is happy enough to sit and just imagine the car around him whilst enjoying the goodies on the table in front of him.

His mother has put fizzy orange pop in the teapot and now holds the teapot high to pour it into their teacups. Francis knows what's coming next.

His mother puts on a funny high voice: 'More tea, vicar?'

'Yes, please,' Francis replies, in what he thinks is a vicar's voice.

His mother then pretends not to notice the teacup that Francis holds out, and with a shocked expression says: 'Oh, vicar, not from the spout! Why, you're no better than a filthy chimp!'

And the idea of a vicar drinking orange pop straight from the teapot never fails to make Francis laugh so much he falls off the pouffe.

Francis wonders if the reason he thinks of his mother's moods as purple and orange might be something to do with her clothes. He remembers a purple dress she used to wear years ago. The fabric was shiny and patterned and the noise it made as it rubbed against her tights used to make Francis's teeth feel horrible. Around the same time she used to wear a bright orange polo-neck jumper made of soft, fluffy wool that he loved to press his face against when she picked him up.

His mother has more purple days now. When he was little, they were very rare – small dark clouds that would drift across an otherwise clear sky. Now, though, the orange days seem rarer. He has noticed too that sometimes what starts as an orange day can suddenly become a purple day for no apparent reason. Last Saturday his father worked in his study all day. At first his mother seemed fine, but by lunchtime Francis noticed that she was banging pans more loudly on the hob than seemed necessary and then she forgot to put chocolate powder in his milk and shouted at him when he asked about it. He has noticed that a purple day never changes into an orange one.

They sit now at the coffee table, he on his pouffe, his

mother kneeling on the floor, munching their way through the smorgasbord and listening to records. Maureen has piles of records from her teenage years and early twenties. She says they are rock-and-roll records and Francis quite likes them too. He hears the sound of the arm moving mechanically and lowering the needle to the record. There are a few moments of hiss and mild crackle before he recognizes the song about the thin girl called Bony Maronie.

His mother laughs: 'Do you remember when I tried to teach you to dance?'

'Which time?'

'Any of them – they always ended the same way – us in a heap on the floor.'

Francis smiles.

'You're made of elastic. I've never known a floppier dancier. It was like dancing with an eel. Nothing like your father.'

Francis looks at her. 'Dad doesn't dance.'

'No, of course he doesn't now, but he used to, when I first met him. He was a marvellous dancer. He took it very seriously.' Her eyes flicker. 'Well – you can imagine.'

In fact, Francis can't imagine at all. He can think of nothing more incredible than the idea of his father dancing to a song about a girl who resembles macaroni. He has to stop himself thinking about it.

'That's why I'm rubbish at rugby.'

'Are you really rubbish, dear?'

'I'm too floppy – everyone pushes me out of the way.'

His mother looks worried. 'Do the other boys tease you?'

Francis shrugs. 'Sometimes they say things, but I don't mind.'

'Really?'

'I think rugby's silly.'

'Well, I couldn't agree more.' She is quiet for a moment and then adds, 'But I dare say you write far better essays than some of those boys, or are better at whistling, or know more about cars. People put emphasis on all the wrong things, Francis – being good at rugby, or being a fast runner or living in a nice big house. They think as long as everything looks good on the surface that's all that matters – but it's not, is it? It's what's underneath that counts.'

Francis doesn't really understand what his mother is talking about, but he nods anyway.

She looks at him and smiles. 'I'm preaching to the converted, aren't I?'

Francis frowns. 'What do you mean?'

'Nothing. Ignore me, Francis.' She reaches over and holds his head tightly with both hands and pretends to try to twist it. She gasps with the effort and gives up: 'No, can't be done!'

'What are you doing?'

'Your head – it's screwed on nice and tight already– can't be budged.'

Francis thinks this may be a new game. 'Shall I test yours is on tight?'

His mother laughs. 'Oh, goodness no. I'm sure it's not – you might twist it right off. I'm sure living with your father for fifteen years has loosened a few of my screws.'

Her laughter dies off and Francis panics that the day is

about to change colour. He scurries off to his room to find Mrs Bumbles, a cuddly cat from his infancy. Mrs Bumbles should have been discarded years ago, but the expression of outright alarm on her face has always amused both Francis and his mother and has led to a colourful history being created for the stuffed toy. Francis runs back into the living room to the pile of records. He finds the one he's looking for and puts it on the turntable. As Guy Mitchell starts to sing, Mrs Bumbles rises wide-eyed from behind the sofa:

(She wears red feathers and a hooly-hooly skirt)
(She wears red feathers and a hooly-hooly skirt)
She lives on just cokey-nuts and fish from the sea
A rose in her hair, a gleam in her eyes
And love in her heart for me

Mrs Bumbles clearly disapproves of the song. She makes repeated attempts to leave the makeshift stage, but is prevented by the other hand holding the album cover showing Mitchell's cheeky face as he prevents her departure and serenades her against her will. Francis crouches behind the sofa performing the puppet show, listening to his mother laugh as she always does at Mrs Bumbles's mounting indignation. When the song is finished, he and Mrs Bumbles take a bow. His mother claps enthusiastically.

'Thank you, Mrs Bumbles. Thank you, Mr Mitchell. And thank you most of all to the puppet master.' She smiles widely at Francis. 'You do make me laugh, darling.' Francis smiles back and tries to believe that it's always like this.

26

They sat at a corner table next to the window looking out on the street. Frank always forgot how bad the coffee was and found himself once more trying to get through a cup of the greasy brown liquid that the café served. It never seemed to cool down.

'Do you think they pipe this directly from the earth's core?' he asked.

Andrea was sniffing her cup of tea. 'This really smells of peas. I mean really strongly.' Frank looked unsurprised.

Andrea took a sip. 'You've got to take your hat off to him. I suspect what he's doing with flavours here is quite cutting edge. He really confounds your expectations.'

Frank nodded. 'He certainly does that.'

They both looked now at Mo, who was diligently transferring a towering Knickerbocker Glory from a tall glass into her mouth a spoonful at a time, legs swinging, her face a mask of contentment. Mo loved JD's Diner. Frank cursed the day they had happened to pass by and she had seen the gaudy photos of desserts in the window. She had begged to try the Knickerbocker Glory and Frank had relented. Now every time they went into the city centre they had to go to JD's. Frank and Andrea perhaps could say no occasionally, but it seemed churlish to deny Mo the immense happiness that every visit unfailingly delivered. JD's was not the kind of place Frank or Andrea would choose to frequent. It was essentially a glorified kebab hut. The plastic tables and chairs were bolted to each other and to the floor, the radio played loudly and everything smelled of bleach. There seemed to be only one member of staff, a lugubrious Iranian man who carried with him an air of deep melancholy. They were unsure if he was in fact JD, but they referred to him as that in the absence of anything else. Sometimes Frank and Andrea speculated as to what the initials might stand for. Frank thought 'Johnny Doom' but Andrea had suggested the more exotic 'Je-suis Desolé'. He reminded Frank of a character in a comic he used to read, who went everywhere underneath his own personal rain cloud.

Mo was always concerned about his sadness. If ever her parents expressed reluctance about going to the café, she'd say: 'But what about JD? Think how sad he would be.' And it was true that they rarely saw other customers in there. When they placed their order, JD would always react in the same way, as if each item requested was a blow he had been expecting. He would nod his head glumly as if to say: 'Of course. What else but a cup of coffee?' Even the Knickerbocker Glory was just another slight. Frank and Andrea had a theory that somewhere on the menu was one item that if ordered would make JD smile. The one thing that he had been waiting all these years to serve. They always intended to try to work through the menu until they hit the jackpot, but each time they visited they lost their nerve in the face of JD's doleful gaze and ordered the same strange non-tea and coffee.

The one thing about the café that Frank liked was its location. It was on a once busy street in town fallen on quiet times as the ever shifting centre of retail energy in the city had moved a few blocks away, like a slow-moving tornado, leaving pound shops and cheap cafés like JD's in its wake. Frank remembered when the street was the heart of the city.

'Hey, Mo. Do you see that Subway over there? That used to be a really good record shop.'

Mo looked and nodded. 'Oh, right.'

'And you see at the end where it opens up into a square? Well, that never used to be there; that used to be a busy road and if you wanted to get across you had to go down some steps and through an underpass, but it wasn't really like an underpass – it was enormous with shops, and phone boxes and thousands of pigeons.'

'Mm-hmm,' said Mo as she attempted to spear a piece of fruit from the bottom of the glass. Frank realized that she wasn't interested, and in the same instant he realized that the reason she wasn't interested was because what he was saying was not interesting. No more interesting to Mo than it was to Andrea when he tried to tell her about shops that had once stood or forgotten news stories he had once covered.

He swore under his breath as he burned his tongue on the coffee for the third time. He wondered why he couldn't just focus on the here and now. It was perhaps Andrea and Mo's misfortune that he felt compelled to share these glimpses of the past with them, assuming that they too would feel his fascination, his responsibility to remember. He decided not to tell Mo about the particular type of cakes you used to be able to eat on the top floor of the department store that had been across the road. Or about the shoe-shop assistant who had won the pools. Perhaps he'd tell her another time.

The door opened and Frank quickly turned his face away. 'Oh bloody hell.'

Andrea looked at the man who had just entered and now stood at the counter.

Frank hissed, 'Will he see me?'

Andrea looked at him as if he was mad. 'Course he'll see you; there's no one else in here. Who is he?'

At that they heard a high-pitched, 'I don't belieeeeeeve it!'

Frank looked up and feigned surprise. 'Oh, Cyril. Hello there. I didn't see you come in.'

Cyril walked over, carrying a cup of brown liquid. Frank hadn't actually seen Cyril in person since their first encounter at the studio years before. Since then all communication had been conducted by phone or email. Frank watched him as he approached and had to conclude that the intervening years hadn't been so kind to Cyril. He looked markedly more haggard than Frank remembered and he had allowed his grey hair to grow long and lank over his collar. He had, though, remained faithful to the Reactolite glasses and leather blouson jacket, but the current one was so stiff and new that it looked as if it was wearing him.

'As I live and breathe! Frank Allcroft in the flesh. This is a rare privilege indeed.'

Frank smiled weakly. 'Good to see you, Cyril.'

'The pleasure's all mine, sir, all mine. I'd come to think of you only as a voice at the end of the phone, or a face upon the flickering screen, but here you are, well and truly alive.'

'Just about, yes.'

Cyril laughed. 'Just about! Just about! I like that. Oh yes. It's the best any of us can say.' He turned now to Andrea. 'Aha – and this would be the old trouble and strife, then, would it? The ball and chain? Eh?'

Andrea gave Cyril an icy stare. 'My name's Andrea. You must be the man who makes Frank pay for bad jokes.'

Cyril hooted at that. 'Oh my goodness, Frank. You've got a live one there! Bad jokes? Is that what he tells you?' Then a look of concern crossed his face. 'Frank, is that what you tell her?'

Frank shook his head vigorously.

Cyril continued to look at him. 'You've told her about Big Johnny Jason? Paddy "Sure I'm only having you on!" O'Malley?'

Frank pretended to try to remember. 'I'm sure I did, Cyril.'

'You have at least told her about *You Gotta Laugh*.'

Frank nodded. 'Yes, I definitely told her about that.'

Cyril grinned and turned back to Andrea. 'That's all right, then. I wouldn't want you to think I had no credentials. Worked with some of the best, I have, and I'd put your husband here amongst them.'

Cyril looked at the fourth empty chair bolted to the table. 'Mind if I join you?'

'Be our guest,' said Frank. 'We have to get off in a minute anyway.'

As Cyril sat down, Frank thought he detected a whiff of whiskey.

'And is this one of your fellow TV presenters, Frank?' asked Cyril, looking at Mo. Mo grinned broadly. 'Yes, I think I've seen her saying very important things about the economic downturn.'

Frank said, 'This is my daughter, Mo.'

Cyril held out his hand and shook Mo's hand very formally.

'It's an honour to meet you.'

Mo smiled. 'Hello.'

He carried on shaking her hand: 'Mo. Mo. That's an interesting name. I used to know a fella called Mo. He had an unusual surname, though. What was it now? Oh, that's right: Thelawn! Mo Thelawn – great chap he was – very green fingered.'

Mo was delighted by this and chuckled into her glass of pop.

Frank watched with disbelief as Cyril gulped down the blisteringly hot coffee without the least sign of discomfort.

'So what are you doing in town today anyway, Cyril?'

'Oh, you know, this and that. A trip to the library to catch up with the papers. I get a lot of material that way. I like to have a few gags on current affairs always on the boil should I need them – sometimes these TV shows call you up last minute needing a few one-liners and it's *boom*! We need 'em now! So you've gotta be prepared. It's a tricky job, though, doing it in the library – sometimes I get a bit too tickled by the gags and start laughing away and the librarians don't like that at all.' He turned to Mo and said. 'Talking of libraries, do you know what my favourite book is, Mo?'

Mo shook her head.

'Ooh, I'd sincerely recommend it. It's called the *The Dangerous Rocky Cliffs* by Eileen Dover.'

Mo nodded and Cyril stared at her intently.

'Cliffs. *Dangerous Rocky Cliffs*. Eileen Dover. Do you get it? Eileen Dover and I leaned too far – aaaaaah, splat!'

Mo was perfectly still for a moment and then burst into uncontrollable laughter.

Cyril turned to Andrea. 'I hope I didn't offend you with my joshing earlier. I'm afraid my mouth gets me into trouble sometimes – the brain's firing off so quick that I don't get time to run it past the censors before it comes out of my big trap. I didn't mean anything by it. Frank always speaks very highly of you.'

As far as Frank was aware, he'd never once mentioned Andrea to Cyril.

Andrea smiled. 'It's all right, Cyril, no offence taken.'

'It's just I'd hate for us to get off on the wrong foot. Frank keeps my stuff alive out there and I'm very appreciative to him for that. Just as I was with Phil. Did you know I worked with Phil Smethway?'

Andrea nodded. 'Yeah, I think Frank mentioned it.'

'Yes, Phil and I went back a way. I was just a spotty kid helping out at the radio station when I first met him. He saw something in me – heard me making a few cracks to the receptionist there one day and told me if I had any more like that I should take them to him. I'd always had lots of jokes – they'd just pop into my head when I was supposed to be doing something else. So I started giving Phil a few gags each week and he'd give me a few bob for them. It all started from there.

'Course Phil moved on, but he never forgot an old mate.

In latter years he couldn't use my material, you see. He had no choice. They had the top writers in the game working on his lines and he couldn't use other sources, even though I know he wanted to. I'd still mail him the odd gag now and again – you know, just for old time's sake, and he'd always take the time to send a thanks, but they were never used. I'd watch his show every week and sometimes I'd be sure one of mine was coming up, but it never did. To be honest, I couldn't see that the gags he was using were any better.'

Frank could definitely smell whiskey now.

'Did I tell you, Frank, that I had the privilege of bumping into Phil in London just before his tragic end? A city like that and we just bumped into each other. You know – of all the gin joints in all the towns in all the world. Unbelievable, isn't it?'

Mo now turned to Frank. 'What's a tragic end?'

Frank didn't want Mo upset. 'We're just talking about Phil. "Tragic end" is just an expression – it just means we're sad that he died.'

Frank wanted to change the conversation but Cyril continued before he had a chance.

'Sad indeed. He was one of the greats and look at the way he ended up. You can never tell what's going on in here.' He tapped his head.

Frank frowned. 'What do you mean? What was going on in there?'

'I don't know – that's my point – you can never tell.' He looked at Mo and grinned. 'I do beg your pardon, Mo – talking about such gloomy things. This is the problem when you get old. Happens to the best of us. Just like my good mate Gerry. Gerry Atric – ooh you should see him trying to cross the road now.' Cyril mimed a palsied old man and Mo once again was reduced to helpless giggles. He stood up suddenly. 'Well, anyway, I shall love you and leave you. It's been a great pleasure to meet you, Andrea and Mo. Mo I shall be looking out for you on the television – and, Frank, I'll speak to you later in the week.' He paused for a moment and his face was serious again. 'Actually, Frank, I was wondering if you might have time to meet up one day – just the two of us. I don't want to bore the ladies here with business.'

'Erm . . . yeah, okay. Give me a ring and we can sort something out. What kind of business?'

Cyril looked blank for a moment. 'Oh, just some new ideas I've had and want to discuss with you. New line in material. New opportunities, that kind of thing.'

Frank managed a smile. 'Great. Look forward to it.'

Cyril gave Mo an exaggerated wink, picked up his briefcase and headed out the door walking like a penguin. After he'd gone, a beaming Mo turned to Frank. 'Oh, Dad. That man's funny!'

Frank watched Cyril disappear down the road. 'Yes, isn't he just.'

27

A sharp wind buffeted the Hilltop estate. Frank had to battle to stop the door whipping back when he tried to get out of the car. The day was bright and the estate looked different from his last rain-soaked visit. The streets had a raw, scoured look about them. Hilltop wasn't by any means a bad estate. The houses and gardens were generally well kept and today with the blue sky and white fluffy clouds moving quickly overhead there was a children's picture-book simplicity to the place.

The block of shops was built in the sixties, like the rest of the estate. A continuous concrete canopy supported by metal posts extended in front of the shops, providing cover for the shoppers. A chequered shopping trolley was bike-chained to one of the posts and a balding ginger dog to another. The local amenities consisted of a bookie's, a baker's, a general purpose convenience store, a boarded-up hairdresser's and a fast-food outlet branding itself Dixieland Chick King.

Frank started with the bookie's. As he passed the dog tethered outside, he reached down to pat its head. The dog sniffed his hand hoping for something to eat and then slumped back down, his head on his paws, an ashtray of drinking water in front of him. Inside was busier than

Frank had expected with ten or more customers standing or seated, clutching plastic cups of tea and newspapers, looking up at the TV screens. He walked up to the woman in the cashier's booth and showed her the photo of Michael Church. He hadn't really rehearsed what he was going to say and only now realized how odd his question might sound. He asked anyway: 'I wondered if you knew anything about this man. He lived around here.'

The woman was unfazed.

'Owe you money, does he?'

'No, nothing like that.'

She smiled. 'They all say that.' She looked closely at the photo. 'No, love. I've seen him around, I think, but not in here.'

A middle-aged man in a baseball cap was standing behind Frank now and was angling his head to look at the photo.

The cashier held the photo up to him: 'What do you reckon, Alan?' Alan gave a firm shake of the head. 'There you go, then. If Alan ain't seen him, he ain't been in here.'

Frank thanked them, took the photo and headed for the door. He saw an old man with sandy hair and a battered sheepskin jacket sitting in the corner, looking gloomy with his head in his hands. Frank identified him as the owner of the dog tied up outside. The resemblance was so striking Frank had to resist the temptation to give him a consolatory pat on the head.

Despite limited floor space the convenience shop next door was trying to offer the same range and level of stock as a major supermarket. It was also attempting to compete on customer promotions. Every display was festooned with fluorescent multicoloured cardboard stars covered in the same spiky black handwriting offering ever more strange and inventive discounts and multi-buy savings:

'Free Bic disposable razor with every 4-pint of milk purchased!'

'Buy 1 litre Teacher's whiskey, get box of Cadbury's Milk Tray half price!'

'33% off any packet of biscuits when three magazines or more are bought!'

Frank was momentarily hypnotized by the dazzling colours and the complex permutations they advertised. He even found himself wondering which three magazines he might buy to get the discount on a packet of Bourbons. He made his way to the counter where an elderly Asian woman sat on a stool. He pulled out the photo. 'I'm sorry to bother you, but I'm trying to learn more about a man who used to live around here. I wonder if you might recognize him?' He pushed the photo towards her, but she carried on looking at Frank's face and smiling. He repeated the question, but trailed off as he saw no flicker of comprehension on her face. He was about to give up when a young man carrying a box of crisps emerged from a doorway behind the counter.

'Can I help you, mate?'

'Oh, sorry. I was just asking if . . .'

The man shot a look at the old woman: 'Have you switched your hearing-aid off again?' He reached over and touched something behind her ear. He shook his head. 'People think she doesn't speak English. Her English is fine. She's just lazy. She turns it off so she doesn't have to serve anyone when I'm out in the stockroom. Isn't that right, Gran?'

The old woman nodded her head in the direction of Frank. 'He's off the telly.'

The young man looked embarrassed. 'I'm sorry. She thinks all English men look the same. She used to think Frank Bough was the one married to the Queen.'

Frank smiled and showed the man the photo.

'Oh yeah, I recognize him. Mr Church. On number three paper round. *Daily Mirror* and *Evening Mail* Monday to Friday, nothing at the weekend.'

'Did he come in the shop much?'

'He'd come in and settle his bill every month – that was about it.' He remembered the box of crisps. 'I need to get these out before the kids are out of school.'

Frank picked up the photo and the old lady spoke. 'My grandson doesn't know what he's talking about. He doesn't even recognize you. He spends so long trying to keep up with the offers at Asda he doesn't know who comes in and out of the shop. That man used to come in a lot. His wife was sick and he looked after her. A very good man. He'd always ask about my husband and I'd ask about his wife. Good manners.' She looked at Frank. 'Is he dead?'

'Yes, I'm sorry.'

She nodded. 'After his wife died I don't think he wanted to live. He stopped coming in, got the papers delivered instead.'

Frank had seen Elsie Church's death certificate at Michael's house. She had died two years ago. He thanked the old lady and took the photo from her.

As he was moving away from the counter, she said: 'My

husband is gone now too, but I'm still here.' Her tone was combative, as if contradicting something Frank had said. He nodded, then left.

Dixieland Chick King was not due to open until 5 p.m. so Frank moved on to Greggs. Two women were behind the counter, one wiping all the surfaces while the other cleared out the few remaining lunchtime sandwiches. Frank bought a gingerbread man for Mo and an éclair for him to eat in the car. He thought the woman serving recognized him, but she said nothing. He showed her the photo.

'Oh, that's Michael. Poor man. Found dead on a bench! Can you believe that? People just walked by him. Terrible.'

'You saw it in the paper? Did you see that the police were appealing for information about him?'

The woman pulled a face. 'Yeah, but what could I tell them? I didn't know him well. His wife used to be a regular, though, didn't she, Maz?'

The other woman came over. She recognized Frank now as well and smiled shyly. 'Are we going to be on telly?'

Frank laughed as if he hadn't heard that before.

The second woman looked at the photo. 'Oh, yeah –it's Elsie's husband. She was a lovely woman. She'd buy a loaf every other day and on Saturdays she'd get cakes for the weekend. Custard slices for him, éclairs for her, or maybe it was the other way round.'

The first woman nodded. 'You should have seen her, though. The weight fell off her, didn't it? In the end he was pushing her up in a wheelchair.'

Though neither woman had asked, Frank thought he should explain his interest. 'I'm just trying to help track any next of kin. I know they didn't have children, but I wondered if you knew of any other relatives.'

The two women blew out their cheeks and chewed their lips as they thought. 'I can't think of any, love. It was always just the two of them – self-contained. I know he looked after her when she got ill. She never mentioned anyone else apart from the nurses who'd visit.'

Maz nodded in agreement. 'She was worried about him, though. Do you remember he'd wheel her in here and she'd send him next door for the paper, cos she wanted a natter without him standing over her? We'd ask her how she was and she'd laugh and say she was only going in one direction. Ever so cheerful, though. Considering some of the people we get in here moaning about all their ailments when there's sod all wrong with them. Anyway I remember she said she worried about him after she was gone. She said she'd always been the sociable one, the one who'd make an effort with friends; he was more of a loner, I think.'

The other woman nodded solemnly. 'Looks like she was right to worry. It's a shame.'

The three of them stood in silence for a moment until Frank spoke. 'Did he come in after she died?'

'Very rarely at first, but then he started back at work and would come and get a jam doughnut to take in with him every day.'

Frank looked at her. 'Work? He was retired, surely.'

'Oh no. You'd think it, at his age, but he kept on. He had his own business. I think it took his mind off Elsie. What was it Maz? What did he do?'

'Oh, you're asking the wrong one here. Something with

machines. Engineering? To be honest, love, I probably wouldn't know even if you told me.'

The other woman closed her eyes to think. 'It was something to do with tools – you know, something like that. It was on the Silver Street industrial estate in town. I remember that because Elsie used to say it had brought them precious little silver for all the time he spent there.'

Frank thanked them. As he was leaving, they asked if they could take some photos of him on their phones. He posed for various shots in front of the cakes, thumbs aloft with a different woman each time.

They said they'd put them up and start a wall of fame. 'Who knows who we'll get in here next. Tell the rest of them about us. Even that stuck-up bit. She looks like she needs to eat a sausage roll or two.'

Frank said he'd be sure to pass that on, grinning at the thought of it, and headed back out into the wind.

28

He could never reconcile the interior with the exterior of Evergreen. The corridors inside seemed to stretch too far and in too many directions to fit inside the visible shell of the building. He sometimes wondered if the disorientation was a deliberate effect intended to match the residents' internal confusion with a wider sense of the dreamlike and unreal. The corridors were thickly carpeted and as he walked along an apparently empty stretch he would often be alarmed to turn and find some diminutive figure had appeared behind him, shuffling silently in his wake. Perspective seemed skewed in the long hallways; bedroom doors stretched ahead of him on both sides, diminishing in size towards a vanishing point that retreated at his approach.

Today he and Andrea made slow progress down the corridor, caught behind two women he didn't know haltingly moving themselves and their Zimmer frames to some assignation.

Andrea looked at the shelves next to every resident's bedroom door: 'Do you think we ever really change?'

'What do you mean?'

'I mean,' she lowered her voice, 'look at these two ahead of us. Do you think in their minds they're still the same teenage girls they once were, walking up the street to call on their mate, hoping she won't be wearing the same cardigan as them?'

'Is that a big worry for teenage girls?'

Andrea ignored him. 'This place reminds me of school. The shelves outside each room where everyone puts their personal trinkets out on display – framed photographs or ornaments or dried flowers or whatever – everyone's trying to show who they really are. Just like at school – all of us having to wear school uniform but doing everything we could to show something else, to say "this is the real me".'

'Did you do that? I find it hard to imagine you at school.'

'Of course I did. I'd wear my tie backwards – with the thin bit at the front and the shameful fat part tucked into the shirt. Then there were the badges on my blazer and most importantly the bag. I'd spend hours copying the typeface from albums – like some medieval monk, painstakingly inking "PiL" onto my canvas bag.'

Frank shook his head. 'You sound like the kind of girl who used to stand at the bus stop and laugh at me when I walked past.'

Andrea was, in fact, already laughing in exactly that way. 'Why? What did you have written on your bag?'

'Nothing. Obviously. You know I was clueless. I really had no idea what was going on. I think I was still wearing flares in 1979. I had a nice sensible haircut – a big wiry helmet, eyebrows that had reached adulthood ahead of the rest of me and taken over most of my forehead, plenty of spots, brutal dental brace, obligatory bumfluff on the upper lip. I'm pretty sure I would have worn my tie the right way round, being unaware of just how sickening that was to everyone else. I wrote Supertramp on the front of my homework diary in pencil – I thought that was pretty wild.'

Andrea was laughing gleefully now whilst singing about kippers and breakfast.

Frank looked at her and shook his head: 'You're such a bully.'

She tried to stop laughing. 'Sorry.' She regained her composure. 'But the reason we used to do all that was to attract boys or girls or whatever.' She dropped her voice to a whisper. 'Do you think maybe that's what the trinkets are for? I mean maybe it's a highly evolved coded language. Maybe a clown with an umbrella means "enjoys bridge" or a rabbit pushing a wheelbarrow means "I'm free".'

'Please stop.'

The two women with Zimmer frames had pulled over and knocked on a door with a toby jug outside. It was opened by an elderly man with a cravat. Andrea widened her eyes at Frank as they passed by and said nothing.

Halfway along the next corridor they finally came to Maureen's room. Frank pointed to the empty shelf.

'Mom's, of course, is bare.'

'Well, she's not the only one – there are some other empty ones.'

'No, they're outside unoccupied rooms. She's the only one with nothing. I suppose the absence says "this is the real me" better than any ornament.'

There was no answer to his knock, so Frank opened the door gently to find his mother dozing in her chair with a newspaper open on her lap. He and Andrea sat on chairs next to her for a while in silence, listening to the gradual escalation of her snores until a particularly violent one woke her up:

'Oh!' She always smiled when woken by her own snores. A mixture of embarrassment and humour. It seemed to Frank like a glimpse of her true self, before the veil of melancholy was drawn up again.

'How long have you been there?'

'We just arrived.'

'Hello, Andrea darling. You must think I'm terrible, sleeping in the day.'

'I do it myself whenever I get the chance.'

Maureen looked around. 'Where's little Mo?'

'She's at a friend's party this afternoon.'

'Oh, that's good. That's where she should be. Having fun, not stuck here in this necropolis. Is it still freezing outside? I looked out of the window this morning and I could just tell that it was a bitter, bitter day. Where on earth are your coats?'

Andrea smiled. 'It's quite warm out, well, warm for October. You should go outside for a walk in the garden. The trees look naked and beautiful.'

Maureen sat forward. 'Ooh, now that reminds me of something. Could you just take a look out of the window for me, dear?'

Andrea got up and walked towards the window. 'What is it? What do you want me to look at?'

'Can you see that small fir tree towards the right? The one that they've squared off at the top?'

'Yes.'

'Aha! Now – what do you think of that?'

Frank joined Andrea at the window. 'What do we think of what?'

'Look at it! Can't you see it?'

'See what?' said Frank, but then Andrea laughed.

'Oh – do you mean the face?'

'Yes. The face.'

'Yeah, I see it. Look, Frank – there are two holes in the foliage like eyes, and just there, level with the birdbath, that's the mouth.'

Frank squinted: 'Oh . . . yeah, I suppose.'

His mother exclaimed in triumph. 'Now you see it! The death's head skull! Grinning at me day after day.'

Frank muttered to Andrea. 'Of course, "the death's head skull". Couldn't just be a smiley face.'

Maureen continued. 'Oh yes, he's there every day baring his teeth. Well, we're old friends now. I get up in the morning and I look out of the window and say, "Not this morning, my friend, but it won't be long." Oh, he's patient; he's waiting for me.'

Frank chose not to engage with this. 'So what have you been up to? Have you been to the lounge at all? Spoken to anyone else?'

'Who is there to talk to? None of the staff speak English. On Wednesday one of them brought me an absolutely frightful cup of tea. Dark brown, the teaspoon virtually standing up in it. So I said, "I like my tea weak." Well, she frowned at me, obviously without a clue as to what I was saying, so I said it louder: "Weak! I like my tea weak." And the light bulb finally goes on and she says, "Ah! Week. Week. No every day. Too many tea!" And she's off laughing away and I haven't had a cup of tea since, the silly woman. I'm living my life trapped in some ghastly farce.'

Andrea said: 'Oh dear. I'll go and talk to someone and explain.'

She left the room and Frank stood with his back to his mother, looking out of the window.

'Why are they knocking it down?'

He turned to see his mother looking directly at him for the first time since he'd arrived.

'Walter showed me the article in the paper. Why are they knocking it down?'

Frank saw now the report about the demolition of Worcester House lying on her lap. He went over and sat by her. 'I don't know, Mom. The owners want to build apartments there – they think they'll get more revenue. They got an immunity from listing and there was nothing more we could do about it.'

She said nothing for a while and then, 'How many are left in Birmingham now?'

'After that one, just one.'

She smiled sadly and looked at Frank. 'If only he'd known. We're going to outlive them all.'

29

Francis
1975

His father's study is littered with architectural drawings. They cover the walls and every surface. Endless, minutely differentiated views of the same buildings showing different aspects or focusing on small details of design. Occasionally, though, perhaps to illustrate scale, the drawings include human forms scattered about lobbies, or descending staircases. These figures are always faceless and Francis finds their blankness horrifying. They have become very real for him. He calls them the Future People. He imagines them moving through tree-lined plazas and along elevated walkways unseeing, unhearing and silent. He thinks that one day they will come to get him and make him like them.

At night he lies in his bed and hopes that he won't dream of them, but still he does. The dream is the same: he's running after his father along a light-filled, glass-lined corridor. He calls out, but his father doesn't hear, and Francis keeps running, trying to close the gap between them. Eventually, after what feels like a whole night of running, his father gradually starts to turn his head and Francis realizes in that final split second that when his father turns he will have no face. He wakes up, heart racing and breathless, before he sees it. He reaches up to his own face and checks that he still has a nose, a mouth.

He turns on his light to check that he can see. He has an old Ladybird book hidden under his pillow. He hides it because Peter and Jane are too babyish for him and he outgrew their books years ago, but when he has the dream he pulls it out to look at their faces and the face of Pat the dog. He likes Jane's smile.

His father goes to work on Saturdays now to work on the new town. Before he would work from his study, but now he announces at breakfast that there is just too much to be done at the office. Francis's mother butters her toast and says nothing. She spends a lot of time in the garden and Francis watches her from his bedroom window. The garden was designed by his father to complement the modern design of the house. He watches his mother dig up the gravel borders and cacti and replace them with soil and flowering plants. He sees her try to soften the geometric edges of the beds and cover the concrete blocks with foliage. He thinks the garden is a type of conversation between his parents. He looks at it and tries to hear what it's saying.

Francis stands at the top of the stairs underneath the picture that isn't really a picture. He isn't sure what it is. A mess of twigs and stones. Dinosaur sick, perhaps. There are pictures like it all over the house. His father chose them especially to complement his design. Francis wishes they had proper pictures instead, of horses or boats by someone who could draw. Downstairs his mother is on the phone, speaking in a low voice to her sister. She is talking about the new town. It is a purple day. Francis can only hear the occasional word. He thinks he hears her swear and he quietly moves down two stairs. He hears her say something about being invisible. He is alarmed and cranes his head round the banister to see if she really is and is half relieved and half disappointed to see that she is still quite visible, her back to him, cigarette smoke coiling around her head. She talks about packing bags, and Francis thinks that they are going away somewhere, but when she hangs up the phone she just returns to the garden.

One evening Francis is carefully carrying a cup of tea to his father in his study when he sees the model for the first time. A neat label reads: PROPOSED CENTRE DARNLEY NEW TOWN – DOUGLAS H. ALLCROFT AND PARTNERS.

Francis stands rooted to the spot, the cup of tea forgotten in his hand. An entire toy town stretches out ahead of him covering twenty feet or more. After a while his father looks up and asks: 'What do you think of that?'

Francis gazes at the streets and houses. 'It's amazing.'

His father assumes he's referring to the elegance of the design. He smiles and nods, getting up from his chair to walk over to the model and point with the stem of his pipe.

'You can see that the town centre is encircled by a gyratory road system with points of access at regular intervals. The passing motorist can navigate around the centre without being impeded by delivery vehicles. The shopping area is in the heart of the town in an enclosed precinct, where the shoppers can buy the things they need whilst protected from the elements. The shoppers' cars go on top of the precinct in a tiered car-parking area. The lorries make their deliveries to the service areas that lie around the perimeter of the precinct. This is how the towns of tomorrow will look. The squalid high streets we now see, Francis, clogged with cars, blackened with soot, their pedestrians assailed by rain and traffic spray, they will be things of the past. The ring road will encircle the centre and pedestrians will be separated safely from cars by a series of subways and elevated walkways.'

Francis doesn't hear a word of his father's presentation. He gazes at the toy town and imagines the lives of the people that live there.

30

He laid the dominos out on the table in preparation. Walter arrived after a few minutes, gripping the local newspaper and looking red in the face.

'Have you seen this?'

Frank looked at the paper where Walter pointed. There was an advert for a local cabaret club. 'What is it?'

Walter shook the paper with fury. 'Third act down! Look at it.'

Frank read aloud. '"An evening of The Whisperers. Come and enjoy the easy melodies and barbershop harmonies of Tamworth's answer to The Drifters in this family-friendly tribute night to the late great Whisperers as performed by Blackjack."' He looked up at Walter. 'Did you not like The Whisperers?'

'Like them? I'm bloody in them! Founder member. Me, Reg Stevens, Vince Capello and Ray Peck. How dare they! How bloody dare they! I've just come off the phone to Ray – he's spitting feathers.'

'The Whisperers? Really? I never knew you were one of them.'

'Not "were", Frank. Not "were", if you don't mind. Am. I am in The Whisperers. We are not "the late Whisperers". Bloody slander that is. Absolute slander. They think they can just come along and steal our gigs? Is that what they think?'

Frank wasn't sure what to say. 'So you're still together as a band?'

'Of course we are.'

'That's amazing, Walter. You still rehearse?'

'We don't need to rehearse. It's all up here.' Walter tapped the side of his head vigorously. 'Last gig we played was the Northgate Theatre, Hanley, as part of a Christmas cabaret night.'

'When was that?'

'December third, 1977.'

Frank looked at Walter. 'That's more than thirty years ago.'

'Well? What difference does that make?'

'Nothing. It's just I suppose that people might have assumed you'd retired.'

'Well, they'd assume wrong. We were just biding our time, laying low for a little while.'

'Why?'

Walter sighed with exasperation. 'Heard of Johnny Rotten, have you, Frank? A thing called punk rock?'

The conversation was growing too strange for Frank. He was only able to nod.

'Oh, we'd weathered storms in the past. Always managed to incorporate the latest sounds in our shows. That was down to Vince – genius arranger he is, pure genius. He'd take the old tunes and make them sound fresh. A touch of Merseybeat in the sixties. Even a spot of disco syncopation in the seventies. But that punk-rock noise. It was too much.'

'But surely that wasn't your audience, Walter. I mean

you must have been in your fifties – your fans wouldn't have wanted you to sound like Johnny Rotten.'

'Well, no one likes to be irrelevant, Frank. We decided the more dignified thing was to sit it out.'

'That was over thirty years ago.'

'Yes. I know.'

'But, Walter, punk didn't last very long.'

Walter stared at Frank, eyes gleaming. 'Well, that's the first I've heard of it.'

They sat in silence for a while. Frank was the first to speak. 'Where are the other Whisperers now?'

'Vince lives on the Isle of Man. Ray's down in Farnborough. Reg isn't too well these days – he's in a place out Lichfield way but I get a Christmas card each year from his wife.' He paused. 'Apparently he doesn't recognize her any more.' He turned away from Frank for a moment. He spoke in the direction of the window. 'I know if we got him on stage it'd all come back to him. It doesn't go away.'

Frank nodded. 'What are you going to do?'

'Oh, Ray's already onto it. He's finding the manager of these Blackjack jokers and getting onto the venue. If they want an evening with The Whisperers, they can bloody well book The Whisperers.'

Frank reached over for his pile of dominos, but Walter stopped him. 'Do you mind if we leave it today, Frank? I'm not in the mood.'

Frank shook his head. 'Course. I'll shove off and see you next week.' He picked up his jacket and stood for a moment. Walter was staring at the advert in the paper again. Frank couldn't think of a single thing to say.

He left the residents' lounge and headed towards the exit.

By the front door was a conservatory extension where a few people dozed in chairs. As he walked past, a frail-looking old woman called out, 'Excuse me.'

She was a tiny shrunken figure, but her voice was surprisingly clear. Frank smiled and approached her.

'It's Frank, isn't it?'

Frank held out his hand to her. Her hand as he shook it was cold and papery. 'Hello, yes, I'm Frank.'

'Hello, Frank. I'm Irene.'

'Nice to meet you, Irene.'

'I've seen you on the telly.'

Frank mock-grimaced. 'Oh dear. Sorry about that.' He sat down on the next chair. He guessed that Irene was older than his mother – possibly in her eighties. 'I've not seen you here before, Irene. Have you been at Evergreen long?' He realized he was raising his voice for no apparent reason; Irene's hearing seemed perfectly good.

'Well, the answer to that, dear, is yes and no. I've been at Evergreen now for many years, but not this branch. That's not the right word, is it? Not this centre – what's it called? Forest of Arden. They have them all over the country, you know. I was out in Northampton – Althorp they called that one. I moved here about nine months ago.'

'What made you move over here?'

Irene tried to smile. 'Oh, silly, I suppose. My good friend, Amy, she passed away and I found it difficult there without her – you know, sad. I thought a change might do me good.' She looked around. 'Though, to be honest, this place is exactly the same. I hardly know that I've moved. I wake up in the morning and I still expect to see her at breakfast.'

Frank nodded. 'I'm sorry about your friend. There are some nice people here. Even some of the staff.'

Irene smiled. 'I'd heard that your mother was here so I was hoping I might bump into you one day.'

'Well, I'm glad we met. It's always nice to meet a viewer.'

She shook her head. 'Oh, I'm not really . . . to be honest. Not wishing to give offence, but I don't really watch your programme. Sometimes it's on in the background, but I find the news depressing.'

Frank realized he'd walked straight into that.

'No, I wanted to talk to you because you used to work with Phil, didn't you?'

Now he understood. People always wanted to ask him about Phil. 'Phil. Yes. He was a great man. Sad loss to the industry. Did you watch his show on Saturday nights?'

Irene shook her head. 'Good gracious, no.'

Frank felt the conversation was getting away from him. 'I stopped watching Phil a long time ago.'

Frank looked at Irene. 'Did you know Phil, then?'

Irene smiled and looked straight back at Frank. 'I should say so. I was married to him for seven years.'

Frank laughed. 'Oh my goodness. Sorry, Irene. We've been talking at cross-purposes. I'm talking about Phil Smethway. The TV celebrity.'

Irene carried on looking at Frank. 'So am I.'

Frank frowned. 'But Phil was . . .' he trailed off.

Irene put her hand on Frank's. 'It's all right, dear. I'm not mad. I was Phil's first wife. We were married when we were young. July first, 1950 – rained cats and dogs all day. I was what they call a cradle snatcher: twenty-five years old to Phil's twenty.'

Frank stared at Irene. He heard what she said, he knew Phil had been married before Michelle, and he knew what Irene said made sense, but he couldn't take it in. He had a vivid image in his mind of Phil's life and the contrast between that and the woman sitting in front of him now was impossible to process.

Irene seemed to read his mind. 'All a bit Dorian Gray, isn't it? Him on telly getting younger-looking every year with his surgery, hair transplants and dolly birds, and here's me, the skeleton in the cupboard, disintegrating quietly in Evergreen.' She laughed. 'Oh, I'm exaggerating, dear. Don't look so shocked. He didn't have me locked up. We were divorced years ago. I remarried very happily, but when my Geoff passed on I didn't want to stay in the house on my own.'

Frank remembered that it was Phil who'd first recommended Evergreen for Maureen. He'd said he knew someone there; Frank had had no idea he'd meant his ex-wife. For no clear reason he felt ashamed of Phil. 'Did he ever visit you here?'

'Phil? You are joking, aren't you? We stayed in touch. Christmas cards, the occasional phone call, that kind of thing – we were always on good terms – but Phil wouldn't step foot in somewhere like this. He'd be terrified.'

'What do you mean?'

'You must have known what he was like. The vainest man I ever met – even when he was a lad he was always very particular about his clothes and hair. He hated the idea of these places. He told me as much when I first moved into one. He said: "How can you stand to be surrounded by old people?" I said to him: "I am old, Phil. So are you." He thought he could run away from it. Poor Phil. I was terribly upset when I heard what happened to him, but I was ill at the time, you see, and couldn't make it to the funeral.'

Frank imagined if Irene had been there how alien she would have seemed amongst all the celebrities and fans. He had a picture in his head of her standing at the grave-side in her lilac cardigan and neatly set and curled hair next to Michelle in her Italian sunglasses and crocodile-skin boots.

'My children . . . well, they're not children now – I'm a great-grandmother – but anyway they find it hard to believe that I was married to him. They say: "Why did you let him go?" Which I think isn't very nice to their father, really. I tell them, "Well, if I hadn't, you wouldn't be here, would you?" That was the reason, you see. I left him, not the other way round. I did it because he didn't want children. He couldn't stand the thought of moving aside for someone else – even his own child. Too much of a child himself, I suppose. Poor Phil.'

A member of staff approached from the side. 'Irene?'

'Yes, dear.'

'The life-drawing class is starting now. You put your name down for it.'

'Oh yes. Sorry, I was blathering on to this man. I'll come now.'

The member of staff helped her up and Irene said goodbye to Frank. He stood to watch her being led slowly by the arm down the long corridor.

31

Phil
January 2009

His jaw aches like hell. He has pins and needles up his right forearm and the handle is slippery with sweat in his palm. He looks at the clock on his office wall. Michelle will be back in another hour. He tries to focus. He's wasted the last God knows how long thinking what he might have for dinner before remembering there won't be any dinner. He shifts the barrel in his mouth. He needs to get in the right frame of mind. He tightens his grip on the gun. He assumes it works – he's had it hidden away since National Service. He wonders if guns have best-before dates.

The final blow came suddenly: shooting a trail for the show, a quick fifteen-second to camera piece – 'Join me tonight when our special guests include . . .' He keeps mispronouncing the name of the singer. Some slappable-looking kid from a talent show. The truth is Phil isn't even sure who the kid is. He's got him mixed up with the one who won the year before, or maybe the year before that. They've all got the same faces, the same voices – how's he supposed to keep up? He fluffs the link maybe seven or eight times, then he sees it. A couple of crew members exchange a look – one of them rolls their eyes and smirks. He is an object of derision. In an instant he knows. There won't be another reinvention. He's come to the end of the road. He can't keep up any more, doesn't have the will or the energy. He knows he's finished.

'Past it,' he says aloud now to the empty room. He squeezes his eyes shut and wills himself to pull the trigger, but still nothing happens.

People think success is down to luck, but he knows luck has nothing to do with it. It's sheer graft. Critically assessing himself all the time and making changes – making the right changes. Always making the right decisions. A constant process of reinvention, making sure he's giving people what they want.

He started noticing the effects of age around forty. After that they kept coming, like space invaders – never-ending lines of them descending the mirror in front of him. They start off superficial – the changing hair colour, the skin sagging and bagging. Nothing a little work can't fix: hair dye, hair transplants, nips, tucks, Botox, whatever's going. He thinks where a lot of women go wrong is that they overdo it. The aim is to look very, very good for your age, not to try to look forty years younger – that way you only end up looking embalmed.

In the last year or two, though, it's all moved beyond the surface: a massive falling away of his physical abilities, a general feeling of frailty, little lapses of memory – forgetting people's names or where he went on holiday four years previously. He's seen the doctors, he's had all the tests; they tell him it's normal.

'Nothing sinister, Mr Smethway, just old age.'

What, he wonders, could be more bloody sinister.

Ahead of him he sees only decline. Maybe he could bear to watch it, but it's the other eyes he can't take, that gaze that never ends. Even when he retires, people will always know the way he once was and the way he has deteriorated. Worst of all for him is the thought of Michelle witnessing this transformation. If he thought she might leave him for another man, it would make it less hard, but he knows she won't. She will stay by his side. She will look after him. She will forget him as her best friend and lover, and know only the dependent patient, wiping his face whilst wiping away more of the man he once was.

He looks again at the clock. He's been here for two hours.

'Do it,' he says. Nothing happens. He lets out a howl of despair and slams the gun down on the table.

Whether it's the thought of the pain he will cause Michelle, or simply his own cowardice, he doesn't know, but he realizes he can't do it. He moves his jaw up and down, trying to work some life back into it and turns his desk lamp on. He looks at his distorted reflection in the base of the lamp – his mouth twisted into a grin. He shuts his eyes. He needs help and in that moment he knows exactly the person who will help him: the most capable person he knows, the person who always helped him out of a jam. He thinks of Mikey.

32

It wasn't the kind of modern, purpose-built industrial estate that Frank had expected, but rather a ramshackle affair, clustered around a courtyard in the shadow of a large paper factory. Frank looked at the board listing the companies based there. Amongst them were a tattoo artist, a manufacturer of ball bearings, a car valeting service, a sandwich bar, a precision tool maker, a supplier of party inflatables, a company called SK enterprises and in unit eighteen something describing itself as the Ministry of the Risen Christ. He wondered if the tenants found much to say to each other when they met in the sandwich shop.

If the woman in the bakery had been right, then Burkett Precision Tool Makers in unit six seemed the obvious choice for Michael's place of work. Frank walked across the courtyard, past the car valeting boys with their radio blaring and up an exterior staircase to the door of unit six on the upper level. Burkett's appeared to be closed for business, the lights off and the door locked. Frank knocked at the door anyway and then squinted through the wire-grilled windows. Inside he saw a neat workshop lined with machines and a brown warehouse coat hanging on the back of a chair. He could just see a pile of post inside the door but failed to make out the name on the top envelope.

He went back down the steps to Azad's Kleen 'n' Kustom Kars. A young man with an intricately razored haircut was heat shrinking some black-plastic tint onto the rear window of a Seat Ibiza and talking loudly to a man who was reading the paper and giving no indication of listening.

'She wanted the full valet, right, but you shoulda seen it inside. She had like four hundred Snickers wrappers all over the floors and the seats. Nothing else – no Kit Kat, no Monster Munch, no road atlas – just Snickers everywhere. And she's like skinny, man. Like a size zero. So I thought to myself, *Fine. Whatever. Bulimia.* But the thing is I thought they were supposed to hide it. Where was the shame and all that self-hate stuff? She seemed pretty happy with herself to me. She looked at me as if I was something she'd trod on, you know, like: "Yeah? I eat twenty-six Snickers bars a day and I still look hot." So I just took the keys and said nothing, you know, cos we're professionals.'

The other man raised his eyebrows and then saw Frank hovering nearby.

Frank approached. 'Are you Azad?'

The man regarded Frank with some suspicion. 'Yeah, that's me. Who wants to know?'

'My name's Frank.'

Azad nodded. 'All right, Frank, can I help you?'

'I was just wondering if you knew if a man called Michael Church worked in the unit above.'

Azad walked over towards him. 'Mike? Yeah, there's a Mike works up there. He ain't in today, but you can leave a message if you like. I'll make sure he gets it next time he shows up.'

Frank wasn't sure if they were talking about the same man. He pulled the photo out of his pocket. 'Is that the Mike you mean?'

'Yeah, that's him. I ain't seen him for a few weeks, but . . .' Something in Frank's expression prompted him to ask, 'Is something wrong?'

'Well . . . Michael died three weeks ago. I'm just trying to trace any next of kin or close friends.'

Azad closed his eyes for a second and then let a long stream of air out between his teeth. 'I fucking knew it, man. I knew there was something wrong. I said to the owner of the estate when he come round last week – I said, "Not seen Mike about. Maybe you should try and call him." I was worried, you know.'

'You knew him, then?'

'Yeah, I knew Mike. That's sad news.'

'Could I talk to you about him?'

Azad looked over at the kid tinting the window. 'You be all right if I go get a coffee, Sy?'

'I'm a professional, Az, this is what I'm telling you.'

Azad shook his head and led Frank over to a couple of plastic chairs outside the sandwich shop.

'You're not chasing up debts or anything like that, are you?'

'No, nothing like that. It's just that Michael died alone. He was a friend of a friend and I'm just trying to help find out a little about his life.' He decided to spare Azad the details of Michael's death.

Azad lit a cigarette and took some time before he spoke. 'I never used to talk to him at first. He was just another face you'd see around here, you know, like the Jesus people. We'd nod or whatever, but that was it. I know he was working here long before we came and set up below him. I'd see him going in each morning at eight thirty on the dot with his little lunchbox and then again at five going home, and that was all I knew about him.

'Then one day I was here on my own, Sy was off sick and it meant I could turn off the radio for once. I mean don't get me wrong, I love music, but Sy doesn't listen to music – he just likes distorted bass rumbling around the boot of a car. To be honest, it gives me a bit of a migraine by the end of the day – getting old I guess. So I was sorting through invoices or some shit like that in the workshop and I heard this other music coming from upstairs. I didn't notice too much at first, then I started listening and – I can't explain it, but it was so beautiful. It was old music, I could tell that, but there was something about it, you know, kind of sad and happy at the same time. I don't know . . . it got under my skin.

'Anyway, in the end I had to know what it was so I walked up the stairs and knocked on the door. Mike opens it, wiping his hands on a rag. He looks at me and you know the first thing he says? He goes: "Is the music too loud?" I thought, *Bloody hell, man, how loud is our music normally and he's asking me if he's disturbing us!* That was the first time I spoke to him.'

Frank nodded. 'And you got to know him after that?'

'Yeah – we just got on and I started to go up there most days to eat my lunch. Mike'd have corned-beef sandwiches and I'd have Pot Noodle and he'd play his records and tell me a bit about them. It was weird, really. Sy thought it was well weird – I mean you'd think we wouldn't have anything in common, but we just got along.'

'Did he ever mention any family or people outside of work?'

'A bit. Mike and Burkett worked together for years, but Burkett died some years back. I think really the business was winding down anyway and after he died Mike could have retired, but he felt some duty to Burkett to carry on the business – he didn't want to let it all fade to nothing. He was very loyal, you know. He thought his mate had worked all his life to build up the business and it was up to him to carry it on. To be honest, I don't think he had many customers, but he'd still come in every day.

'He told me something amazing once – apparently back in the day, every Thursday night, he and Burkett would clear the workshop upstairs, push all the machines to the sides and throw covers over them. They'd light some candles, get it all looking nice and then at seven o'clock their wives would come down and they'd do an hour or two of ballroom dancing. Can you believe that? I love that story, man. I like to imagine the men in dickie bows and the women in those big, pink ball gowns they wear on telly with numbers on their backs sweeping up and down the unit. I'd have loved to have seen that.

'Anyway those days were long gone by the time I set up here. Mike'd just come in every day, work on his own and go home. It went on like that for a few years, then Mike's wife got ill and he started taking time off to go with her to the hospital and stuff. Then eventually he just left to nurse her full time.'

'But he came back afterwards? He was still working here till recently?'

'Yeah – he came back. I never expected him to. I thought if his wife died – well, *when*, really, it was obvious from what he said that she wasn't getting any better – I thought he'd call it a day then. But he came back. He was really low, you know. He didn't say anything, he was all business on the surface, but you could tell. He didn't have any customers by then. They'd all gone elsewhere when he was off nursing his wife. He just used to come here because it was what he did when she was alive. I think he could pretend she was still at home waiting for him when he was in his workshop. He still made stuff. There's boxes of little intricate things he made up there, but it was just a hobby, really.'

Azad chewed on a broken nail. 'I've been worried about him these last few weeks. You can ask my wife – she knew all about Mike. I told her how I didn't think he spoke to anyone else but me, up there in that empty unit all day long and then back to an empty house in the evening. It was hard. My wife was always saying I should invite him over for dinner one evening, cook him something proper but . . . I dunno, I thought it'd make him awkward, you know – it'd be crossing a line. I knew nothing about him, really. Not where he lived. Not even his surname.'

Frank thought for a moment. 'What about Burkett's wife – is she still around?'

'She emigrated to Australia after the husband's death. Mike had a postcard she'd sent stuck to his wall. I don't know where in Australia.'

Frank nodded. 'Did he ever mention anyone else?'

Azad paused to think. 'Yeah, there was someone else I

remember. He'd bumped into some old mate of his from the old days – this wasn't that long ago, a year maybe, since his wife died anyway. Anyway this bloke – Phil – he knew him from when they were kids. They'd done National Service together. Mike thought a lot of him. He mentioned him quite often for a while – they were back in touch with each other. I suppose it was someone to focus on other than his wife.'

Frank had forgotten that Phil had done National Service. He very rarely spoke of it – probably because it allowed people to age him. He thought of the note that Michelle had shown him. 'Did he ever mention a falling out with Phil? A quarrel over anything?'

'No, man. I can't imagine Mike arguing with anyone – he was a peaceful bloke – you know, very chilled. You can't ask the Phil guy either, I'm afraid, cos I know he died some months back. Mike mentioned it. Can you believe that? I don't ever want to get old, man, and just see everyone I know die around me. I don't think Mike had any room left to feel grief.'

Frank started saying his thanks and goodbyes to Azad, but then asked him, 'What was the music, by the way? The music you heard that first day.'

Azad grinned. 'Nat King Cole, "Mona Lisa". Mike had loads of his records. He'd play them on his little portable record player up there. I loved them all, man. His voice and those strings, they do something to my heart.'

Frank smiled. 'Do you still listen to that stuff?'

'Oh yeah. Mike gave me all the records. He couldn't listen to them after his wife died, made him too sad – he made me take them all. I've got them at home. Sometimes when we've got the kids in bed, I put one on and my wife and me dance in the living room, just like Mike used to with his wife.' Azad smiled. 'I'll miss him.'

Michael Church would be missed. Frank shook Azad's hand, and wondered if that's all he'd wanted to hear.

33

It bothered Mo that her grandmother rarely left her room and often seemed so sad. Mo was sure that the problem could be resolved with enough thought and application. She was always on the lookout for ways to improve the quality of Maureen's life. She kept an eye out for new products and innovations, she scoured the adverts in the TV listings magazines they had at home and picked up leaflets on hints for the elderly whenever she saw them in the chemist.

Through a process of trial and error she had come to the conclusion that perhaps there wasn't one single solution to the problem, but she remained optimistic that a combination of small measures would gradually alleviate her grandmother's sadness. Her ultimate aim was for Maureen to be like the old people in the posters and brochures for Evergreen: admiring a rose bush in the garden with a man in a cravat, clapping her hands in delight at something on the Scrabble board, standing with open arms and an expression of joy as a young child approached. Smiling always.

Today Mo had been a long time in Maureen's en suite bathroom. Frank had gone to get them some tea and cake and Maureen began to worry that there was a problem.

'Mo, dear. Are you all right?'

'Yes, thank you.'

'You've been rather a long time, is everything okay?'

'Yes. Everything is okay. Finished now.'

At that the door swung open, making Maureen jump. Mo stood looking pleased with herself.

'I've just been doing some work in your bathroom.'

'You're not ill?'

'Ill? No. I'm not ill.'

'Oh . . . good.'

Maureen started to return to her seat. Mo went after her.

'Granny, don't you want to see it?'

'See what, dear?'

'The improvement. I have made an improvement in your bathroom.'

'Ah – an improvement, I see.' Maureen looked at Mo. 'I don't know where you get all these ideas for improvements.'

Mo answered with great satisfaction. 'Research.'

Maureen nodded. 'Research. Yes. I rather thought so. I hope you don't spend too much time researching on my behalf.'

'I like doing it.'

'Well, it's jolly nice of you, dear, but really there are no improvements to be made. This,' she said, gesturing vaguely at the room around her, 'is all perfectly . . . adequate. I barely notice the place anyway.'

Mo was undeterred and led Maureen back into the bathroom.

'Can you spot it?'

Maureen looked around vaguely. 'I'm afraid not.'

Mo laughed. 'Actually, it's a bit difficult to see. Look.' She pointed at the toilet roll hanging on its holder.

Maureen peered at it. 'Oh, it's a different colour, is it? Ooh pink. Lovely! My favourite colour. Much better than whatever was there before. Well done, Mo – that's a great improvement. I shall be much happier each time I visit the bathroom now.'

Mo frowned. 'No. I didn't change the toilet roll. Look more closely.'

Maureen obliged by lowering her head and examining all aspects of the toilet roll and its holder. After a few moments she let out an uncertain: 'Ah . . . I think I see.' Mo was nodding and smiling. 'You've . . . erm . . . stuffed toilet paper inside the toilet roll. That's the improvement, is it?'

'Exactly. Do you want to know why?'

'Yes – that might be an idea.'

'I read it in this leaflet.' Mo pulled a folded pamphlet out of her back pocket. On the front were the words 'Tips and hints for the elderly'.

'It's full of very good ideas.' Mo opened up the leaflet and pointed out different parts. 'They are all very practical! Look – a whole section for people in wheelchairs: "Win appreciation from welcoming hostesses by drying your wheels with a tissue before entering their house. This will avoid unsightly tyre marks and ensure a subsequent in-vitation."'

Maureen's eyebrows were raised. 'Goodness. I'd imagine it would be quite difficult for someone to clean their own wheels.'

Mo wasn't listening. 'And look – this is the one I've done

today: "A fast-spinning toilet roll can be disconcerting for the elderly or the one-handed. By padding out the inner tube of the toilet roll with toilet paper, the speed of rotation will be reduced.'"

Maureen stared at Mo and then at the toilet roll. 'Well, Mo. I'm quite lost for words.'

Mo beamed. 'That's okay. Here's Dad.'

Frank was standing in the doorway to the bathroom. Maureen looked at him.

'Mo has been making improvements.'

'Yes. She did mention something about that in the car on the way here.' He was relieved to detect a trace of amusement in his mother's face. 'Did you find yourself often disconcerted by the fast-spinning roll?'

Maureen looked very serious. 'Goodness, yes. Mo really has put my mind quite at rest. Visits to the bathroom shall hold no fear now.'

Mo skipped out of the room in the direction of the residents' lounge, eager to spread the word about this simple but effective measure. Maureen's face changed as Mo left the room.

'I wish you wouldn't make the poor child feel she has to cheer me up.'

Frank laughed. 'It has nothing to do with me. Mo does what she wants.'

Maureen ignored him. 'I sense you behind all her efforts – trying to jolly me along. All bright and breezy, like on television.'

Frank found himself getting annoyed. 'Why would I encourage her to try and cheer you up? Why promote such a futile waste of time and effort?'

'Yes, a waste of time and effort, that's what I am. I tell you that all the time, but still you come, every bloody week.'

'Why are you being like this? Why can't you just enjoy her company? Enjoy anyone's company? Why is everything a source of suffering?'

'Well, I'm sorry I'm not like the other grinning fools. Clapping their hands in gratitude at the dawning of each new glorious day. I'm sorry I see things differently. I must be a terrible disappointment to you.'

Frank stood looking at his mother, furious at her and himself, completely baffled as to how the situation had soured so rapidly.

'You really are,' he said, before picking up Mo's coat and leaving.

34

He had watched the clouds of the economic downturn roll in. The press and national news bulletins had reported on the global crisis with escalating frequency and alarm. Soon the gentle patter of stories started to fall in the local news and gradually built to a downpour. There were apparently signs of recovery in the wider economy, but not, it seemed, in Frank's region. The recession did at least lend a certain cohesion to the programme. Instead of the usual succession of non sequiturs and oddments, the ripples of cause and effect were discernible across the evening bulletins.

On Monday he reported another downturn in the local housing market. House prices had fallen from the previous quarter. On Tuesday he told viewers that four hundred staff were being laid off by a manufacturer of building and digging machinery. Tonight the story was about one of the region's leading property firms who was halting all building projects. The company had a large portfolio of sites around the region, most notably an old football ground and the former home of a car-manufacturing plant.

Frank remembered reporting on the plans for the empty car plant just a few months previously. He recalled the artist's impressions: glass-fronted apartments, a central plaza with a water feature and young trees, the inevitable faceless human form walking a faceless dog. He was reminded of the childhood fear he had of those faceless figures. The local councillor had expressed her satisfaction at the new jobs the project would bring and the start of the regeneration process for the area.

As he read through the report, Frank found something about the halt in development that snagged his attention. The constant flickering of change and renewal in the city was usually incremental, invisible. Here, though, the old and the new and the usually invisible transition between them was revealed, as if a projector had stopped abruptly, leaving the two frames frozen on the screen. He thought of the massive hulk of the car plant coexisting now for some undefined period of time with the artist's impression of the new apartments and shops. The past had gone, the future had yet to come and what remained was a stalled present. The local residents were still weighed down with facial features and memories and broken cars and debts. Frank thought again of the embryonic faceless form on the artist's impression. No others would come now; it was alone, a ghost of the future stranded in the present.

His thoughts were interrupted by the arrival in the newsroom of Donald Bucknall, greeted by ironic applause from Mustansar.

'A cameo appearance from Bucknall! Are elections upon us already?'

Bucknall continued to his desk acknowledging Mustansar only with an arm-stretched V-sign. Over the course of his thirty years in the job, the *Heart of England Reports* political correspondent had succeeded in whittling down the time he spent in the news room to the bare bones. He worked chiefly from the corner table in the Old Albion, venturing out occasionally for a round of golf at the Belfry with a councillor, which he considered to be news-gathering.

After a few minutes at his computer he put his jacket back on and wandered over to Frank's desk. 'Come on, then, Allcroft. I'm buying. Let's mark the occasion.'

'What occasion?'

'What do you mean what occasion? I hope you're joking.'

'It's not your fiftieth birthday again, is it?'

'Ah yes – a spontaneous Allcroft one-liner. Very good – soon you can stop paying for them. Come on, you insufferable tit, let's go.'

Frank looked in amazement at Donald. 'You don't see them at all, do you?'

'See what?'

'Desks, computers, filing cabinets, phones – all the accoutrements of the modern office. They're invisible to you, aren't they? When you walk through those doors, what you see is a gentlemen's club – with a few absent-minded old duffers sat about just waiting for the first sherry of the day. Donald, I have work to do.'

'Oh please, don't make me laugh. The only work you have to do is make sure your wig's on straight. Do you really not know what the occasion is?'

Frank shook his head. Bucknall sighed and then in a loud voice directed at Mustansar. 'Unlike some of these leaking glowsticks I respect the achievements of my colleagues, and today, sir, is your turn to be saluted.'

Frank continued to look at him.

'Because today, God help us, is the twentieth anniversary of your first stumbling lurch into the world of television – a once great institution that you have single-handedly turned into a cheap joke.'

Frank grinned. 'Is it really?'

'It is indeed. I remember it well. You did a report on the morning bulletin and were so nervous managed to mispronounce your own name. I realized then I was witnessing the birth of a legend.'

Frank laughed. 'Well, what can I say, Donald? I'm touched that you've followed my career so closely.'

'Yes, it's been one long slow-motion car crash I've been unable to tear my eyes from these past twenty years, fifteen of those as the almost perfectly named anchor. Come on, let's get a pint.'

Frank looked at his watch. It was almost lunchtime. Donald looked around at the rest of the team.

'Anyone else fancy a quick drink? Celebrate twenty years of Allcroft magic? Come on, Julia. Twenty golden years. Think of all the laughs you've shared.'

Julia looked at him. 'I'm wracking my brain.'

'Come on, Julia – just a little bitter lemon to keep your acid levels stocked up.'

Julia ignored him and looked at Frank. 'I actually can't. I need to get to the bottom of this hospital story – it's a mess.' She paused and then with an effort added: 'Happy anniversary, though.'

The pub was located in a former bank, built in the days when banks were made to look like churches rather than cheap hotel lobbies. The epic grandeur was now, though, tinged with shabbiness around the edges. It was easy to marvel at the domed ceiling and not notice the occasional mouse making a dash across the tiled floor, the shrapnel of a stale Pringle gripped in its teeth. Donald ordered a pint of mild and Frank, conscious of needing to return to work, had half a shandy. They sat at a table at the back.

Donald raised his glass. 'Happy anniversary, then, Frank. Thank God there's still a few of the old guard about.'

Frank took a drink and then held his glass up again. 'And to those who went before us.'

They drank to that and Donald shook his head sadly. 'I fear another comrade is about to bite the dust, though.'

Frank frowned. 'Don't say you're retiring – we'd hardly notice.'

'Not me, you fool. Why would I retire? I'm still a spring chicken.'

'Are you actually drawing a pension already?'

Bucknall ignored him. 'I'm talking about Bosker.'

'Black Glove Bosker?'

'Being put out to pasture.'

'No!'

Donald nodded and sipped his pint. 'I ran into him yesterday afternoon. He'd just come from a meeting with Martin and the big bosses. They said they were restructuring and there was no place for a special correspondent any more.'

'But Bosker's a legend. The correspondent without portfolio. They just sacked him?'

'They offered him general reporter, but he told them

to shove it. They know he's not going to learn how to use a video camera at his age.'

Frank shook his head. 'I suppose it's been coming. He doesn't really fit in with the programme now, but bloody hell, Steve Bosker. End of an era.'

'He doesn't fit in because he has a personality. He's not just some pretty-boy replicant off the production line.'

'Those leather gloves were his trademark, those and the tinted glasses – he was the assassin. There was something very theatrical about him.'

'They're not interested in that local-colour stuff any more. He said they didn't want stories about inanimate objects.'

'What?'

'Haunted houses. Historic stretches of canals. Industrial heritage. Inanimate. The viewers are like panting dogs – they like to follow moving objects. Living, breathing things – kids in hospital waiting for operations, pensioners who've had their medals stolen, gang members shooting each other.'

Frank sighed. 'I suppose that's understandable.'

Bucknall took a long drink of his mild. 'Do you remember that phase he went through of always being filmed between branches or partially obscured by leaves?'

'Yeah – "Citizen Kane" Phil used to call him.'

'He was wasted on us really. The auteur of local news.'

'The best Bosker story, though, was the Tamworth child snatcher.'

Bucknall frowned. 'I don't remember that.'

'It was ages ago – maybe early nineties, I'm not sure. Anyway some bloke in a van was hanging around primary schools in Tamworth and making inept attempts to snatch kids – you know, offering them lifts to the sweet shop, that kind of thing. He actually got one, but she managed to jump out at some traffic lights. There were loads of complaints to the police and so we ran the story over a few nights. There was a lot of panic; every parent in Staffordshire thought their kid would be next. I mean, to be honest, I never thought this bloke was much of a threat – he seemed a bit of a joke to me – but you can imagine the hysteria. Anyway, on the second night the police had given us an artist's impression based on the kids' descriptions. Do you really not remember this?'

Bucknall shook his head.

'Well, we showed the artist's impression and as the report was running Phil turned to me and said, "Did you notice anything about that image?" I hadn't really looked at it. So I took a look and that was it. Both Phil and I were in bits. It was a real struggle to get our act together back in time for the next item.'

'What was the joke?'

'The face of the child snatcher – it was Bosker. The tinted glasses, the wiry hair – I mean it was a striking resemblance. In fact, if it wasn't for the fact we knew exactly where he'd been at the times of the incidents, we'd probably have shopped him. Anyway, as bad luck would have it, the next item straight after that was a Bosker special – a report on some new water-park open-ing in Coleshill. I swear the moment his face appeared on screen the phones started ringing. I think we had over a hundred calls alerting us to the fact that the Tamworth child snatcher was working for us.'

Bucknall laughed.

'Luckily they got the bloke in a few days, but Bosker never worked in Staffordshire after that for fear of reprisals.'

'Those were the days, eh?'

'Yeah.'

'I mean you wouldn't get any of those gimps we have reporting now being mistaken for predatory paedophiles.'

'Sad times indeed.'

'Talking of sad times, I've got to get off to have a chat with Rentaquote Reeves to see what words of wisdom he has to say about the suspension of the regeneration project.'

'I suspect he'll be outraged.'

'I suspect you're right. If his party was running the council, the local car industry wouldn't have hit the wall, the global recession wouldn't have happened and Britain would win Eurovision every year.'

'Why, you sound jaded, Donald. As if you've heard it all before.'

Bucknall finished his pint. 'Well, we have, haven't we, Frank. All of the stories, all of the faces. Heard them, seen them a million times.'

35

He was watching what he assumed was Evergreen's Sing Something Simple group. He'd seen notices for them pinned about the place and when he'd heard the music in the corridor he'd followed it to the glass door where he now stood.

They sat on a circle of plastic chairs – their walking sticks, newspapers and cardigans scattered about them. Someone he didn't know played the guitar and the group sang along. Frank recognized 'Over the Rainbow'. He had heard it a hundred times and it had always been a song that floated past and never stuck to him. Hearing it now, though, Frank felt a soaring sensation in his chest. It was the same reaction he experienced sometimes on catching a glimpse of Mo, or Andrea's silhouette separating from a crowd, or on seeing a sudden hurtling of vivid yellow leaves along a black road. For a moment he was overwhelmed, the very rhythm of his heart affected by the impact of what he saw and heard. He found the sight now of these few people each holding on to their stapled sheets of song words, combined with the melody and the lyrics, pierced him deeply. Each time the chorus came round the members of the group raised their heads, freed from the need to follow the words, and looked across at each other as they sang the well-known lines. Frank believed that what he was experiencing was not the power of one song, but the power of music itself, the transcendental, transformational magic, and he'd never felt it so purely before.

After the song finished there was a brief moment of stillness, a savouring of the suspension of the world, before time and place asserted themselves once more. Song sheets were passed back to the man with the guitar, assorted belongings reached for, cups of tea considered, the difficult business of standing up negotiated. As the circle broke apart, and chairs moved backwards, Frank was able to see figures previously obscured by others. He noticed for the first time that Walter had been sitting on the left-hand side of the group and as he leaned backwards to reclaim his newspaper Frank saw someone else he recognized by his side. It took a split second for him to realize it was his mother. He quickly pulled his head back, and turned and walked away from the room.

He returned to his car without really knowing why and sat with the heater on, looking at the exterior of Evergreen. Damp bark chippings covered the ground and wire cages encircled the skinny trunks of bare sapling trees. A garden intent on suppressing life.

A few nights previously he had spent hours looking through old family photographs that Mo had pulled out when looking for photos of her grandfather. The piles of battered Kodak photo wallets tumbled over the table, a chaos of negative strips spilling out and mingling promiscuously across the packs. Andrea was impressed by the photos of his parents before they were married. The images seemed poised and graceful – of a far higher quality technically and formally than any photos Frank and Andrea took now with a more sophisticated camera. The wallets were in no order and so they zigzagged through time from tiny, white-bordered, black and white rectangles, to gaudier, full-gloss jumbo shots and back again. Frank changing from scowling baby to smiling father to squinting young boy shielding his eyes from the sun.

Andrea had seen them all before but enjoyed seeing them again. Her enjoyment turned to outright hilarity around the time of Frank's thirteenth birthday as she howled at the photos of teenage Frank with his sensible haircut and jumpers. As the evening wore on, Frank found himself focusing most on the face of his mother. He compared the very old photos of her with later ones and tried to work out what it was that had changed beyond the simple process of ageing. It was something to do with her smile. At some point it had lost its softness, and took on a brittle, artificial quality. Her face showed effort, her eyes squinted. It was as if one day she had forgotten how to smile naturally and was forced to follow instructions from a manual.

He hadn't expected to see his mother at the singing group, had never expected to see her joining in, but most of all he had not expected to see a brief flash on her face of an open smile. He felt as if he had glimpsed something he shouldn't. He thought enough time had passed now for her to be back in her room. He gathered his things together once more and headed back towards the front door. He knew already that neither of them would mention it.

36

Sometimes Frank would see a film, usually American, set in and around a news room. He struggled to find any parallels with his own work environment. The journalists were always either hard-bitten cynics, or wide-eyed idealists – never the kind of shuffling unspectacular plodders that he felt himself and many of his colleagues to be. Their patter was fast and littered with one-liners, not the direction-less drivel that passed between him and the others on slow afternoons as they asked each other about their sandwich fillings. Their Hollywood counterparts drank black coffee, never milky tea, ate Danish pastries, never Penguin biscuits, and they never seemed to cover stories about controversial new traffic-calming measures.

As Frank looked around at his colleagues in the morning production meeting, he thought wistfully of the kind of glass-sided meeting rooms with large oval tables where these meetings took place on-screen. Never once in a movie had he seen a hard-nosed news team crowded around a stained sofa next to a fridge that smelled of sour milk in a staff kitchenette. He noticed that the science correspondent had taken his usual policy of wearing casual, if not to say palpably dirty, clothes below the waist a step further and appeared to be wearing carpet slippers.

Martin, the producer, was talking about an item on a line of new eco-friendly fire engines being introduced in Coventry. 'Apparently they're made of a special kind of plastic, hence much lighter, hence use far less fuel.'

Mustansar chipped in. 'Plastic? Won't they melt when they attend fires?'

This was greeted with a few groans and half-hearted laughs, but Martin jabbed the air with his pen. 'Good one, Mustansar. Frank, could be a nice little joke in there – could you work something up for us for the link? You know – a bit of Allcroft magic to make the item a little less dull.'

Julia replied before Frank could. 'Less dull? How about dropping it altogether? That would be less dull.'

Martin ignored her and carried on to the next story. 'Obviously Bonfire Night tonight. Now we had a nice feature last year about a lady in Walsall who makes replicas of world landmarks out of clothes pegs and then burns them on the night. Does everyone remember?'

Julia muttered to Frank. 'Who could forget that scoop?'

'So I thought we'd do something with her again. Sadly they're not lighting the bonfire till seven, so we're not going to be able to get any footage of the actual burning, but can we think of something else to do on her?'

Julia interrupted. 'Why are we covering her again? We did her last year. Isn't it enough that we run a weak item once?'

Martin shook his head. 'The viewers will love a return visit, Joolz. She's a local character. It's a nice story. Come on – any ideas?'

A reporter spoke up. 'How about at the top of the

programme we run a little clip of the lady hanging out some washing, focusing on the pegs, and ask the viewers, "What's going to be keeping her busy tonight?" You know, a little teaser.'

Martin nodded. 'Yeah. I like it – bit of a mystery to catch their attention. What do we reckon?'

Frank thought it sounded pretty weak. He could feel the indignation seeping out of Julia like heat.

The same reporter spoke again. 'Or . . . or – another possibility. At the top of the programme Frank says, "Tonight on the programme the White House" – or wherever it is she's done this year – "in flames! More later."'

'Great idea,' said Julia, 'because (a) obviously it's funny to pretend the White House is burning down and (b) our viewers would totally expect that kind of story to be covered on *Heart of England Reports*. Sounds brilliant.'

Martin ignored her again. 'Nice suggestion, Hugh – I think the viewers would take it in the light-hearted spirit it was intended. By the way, what is it she's made this year? What's the landmark? Where's Sally? She's the one who suggested this. Sally? Are you here?'

Sally had been lurking towards the back of the group saying nothing. 'Um – yeah, I'm here, Martin.'

'Sal, what's the landmark this year?'

Sally looked awkward. 'Yeah – I didn't actually know what it was when I suggested it. I've only just got off the phone with her and found out.'

Martin was impatient. 'Yeah? And?'

Sally grimaced. 'Well . . . apparently, this year she's made a replica of Al-Masjid al-Ḥarām.' There were a few gasps.

Martin looked blank. 'What's that, then?'

Mustansar looked at him with disbelief. 'That would be the Sacred Mosque of Mecca.'

Martin slumped in his seat and said, 'Bollocks.'

But Julia looked up. 'And she's going to burn an effigy of it? In Walsall?' She was beaming now. 'Oh yes, the viewers will certainly take that in the light-hearted spirit it was intended. I take it all back, Martin – you're a genius!'

Back at their desks, Frank said to Julia: 'You enjoyed that, didn't you?'

'It was a small recompense for sitting through the rest of that crap. That man is such an idiot. He has such a low opinion of the viewers. He thinks they're imbeciles.' She paused, but Frank could tell she was only just getting started. 'He's not the only one, of course. I wonder sometimes who we are making this programme for. People who are desperate to hear us repackage press releases from the fire service? People who demand no greater interactivity than an email address on the screen? People who can't focus on anything for longer than a minute and a half? All we do is bombard people with these random, decontextualized jumbles of facts and faces. Don't you ever wonder who actually watches this programme?'

'Well, people do watch us – there are viewing figures.'

'Watch us? Really watch us? Do you reckon? Okay, maybe older people who've always watched us. But the bulk of those figures – we're just on in the background. A familiar noise while they're eating their tea.'

Frank shook his head. 'But regional news is important. The small-scale, the local – that matters to people, it matters to me. Why shouldn't we be able to see stories that happen here? Why shouldn't we have a sense of our own identity?'

Julia laughed. 'Are you joking? What identity are we talking about? What is this region? Our patch covers about a third of England. Who in Birmingham gives a toss about some ASBO gang bothering an estate in Stoke or a farming issue in Hereford? If they want to know about the rest of the country, they'll watch the main stories on the national news. If they want local news, they want news about their locality. The only identity this programme reflects is whichever fool has been put in charge of the controls for the day.'

'Sometimes we get it right.'

'Rarely – more by chance than design. Most of the time we're dicking about in no-man's land with stories that are neither specific nor broad enough to interest anyone. Sometimes I feel as if we have a deliberate policy of avoiding the news, of reporting anything that actually matters.'

Frank reflected on this. 'It's just a time of transition – we've been through them in the past. The internet has changed everything and we're still trying to work it out, but I think we will. In the meantime I don't think we're doing anything evil or wrong.'

Julia smiled. 'No. Just utterly pointless. I like working with you, Frank – you know that, and don't take any offence – but this is just the place you come every day for a few hours. It's just a job for you. You've got family and stuff outside of work and you never let this be that important to you. But my work means everything to me. I want it to define me. If I think I'm doing a shit job, I feel worthless – it eats away at me.'

Frank smiled a little.

'What's funny?'

'It's nothing.'

'What?'

'I was just thinking how you actually sound like the kind of journalists you see in films – you know, fire in the belly – you sound like the real thing.'

Julia nodded sadly. 'I've got to get out of here, Frank.'

'I'm not sure you'll find things very different wherever you go.'

'Landmarks made out of pegs? Come on.'

'The odd bit of local colour – there's no harm in that.'

'Year after year, the same bloody rubbish.'

Frank suddenly felt tired, worn out by Julia's anger. He sat heavily in his chair. 'Well, that's just life, isn't it?'

37

As he approached his mother's room, he heard an unfamiliar sound. For a moment he wondered if she could possibly be listening to the radio that had sat gathering dust on the sideboard since he'd bought it for her four years ago. As he stood outside to knock, though, he realized that the source of the sound was something unlikelier even than that. He could hear his mother laughing softly. His first thought was that her long anticipated dementia had finally kicked in. He knocked on the door urgently and the laughing stopped. He heard his mother clear her throat and call out 'hello'. He opened the door, braced for the worst, but was thrown completely by the sight of Walter sitting in the chair where his mother usually sat, and Maureen standing by the window. Frank was struck by the symmetry of the composition, a geriatric version of Hockney's *Mr and Mrs Clark* – without Percy.

Walter stood up. 'Hello, Frank, how are things?'

Frank was slow to respond. He found himself strangely shocked by the scene. 'Erm . . . fine, Walter. Don't get up. Don't leave on my account.'

Walter hesitated but Maureen said: 'No, Walter was just leaving anyway. He's got better things to do than sit around here all day.'

'Well, that's certainly not true,' said Walter as he made his way to the door. 'Watch out, Frank, she's on top form today.' Just before he left he turned back to Maureen and laughing once more said: 'Oh dear . . . "emitting pellets"!' And he left, chuckling to himself.

Maureen started to smile, but bit her lip. 'Bye now.'

Walter closed the door and Maureen shuffled back to her chair, sat down in it and assumed her usual expression of mild pain.

Frank stared at her until it became clear that she intended to offer no explanation. 'What was all that about?'

'What was all what about?'

'The laughing – the pellets. You seemed to be having a nice time.'

'Really, Frank, don't exaggerate. Walter just came by to borrow the newspaper.'

Frank thought of the previous week when he'd seen Maureen and Walter singing together in the group.

'You never mention Walter when I ask you what you've been up to.'

'Well, why on earth would I?'

Frank was about to counter that she seemed to be seeing an awful lot of Walter, but stopped himself when he realized that he was sounding like a jealous husband. He knew his mother couldn't stand to let him see her happy.

'So how have you been anyway?'

'Oh, the same as usual – staggering onwards in the dark.'

'Really,' said Frank.

'My knees have been sheer hell this last week. I lie in bed at night and it's as if someone is hammering nails into them.'

'Have you spoken to the physiotherapist?'

'Oh, what's the point? It's just the usual decay. The gradual falling apart at the seams.'

Frank felt his frustration rising and tried to change the subject: 'I meant to tell you, I think we've had some good news.'

'Well, that would make a change.'

'You know the Renwick Building?'

'I know it was one of your father's – don't ask me which one.'

'It's the block of offices in Edgbaston.'

Maureen put her head back for a moment: 'Did it have a pond or something?'

'Yeah – a large rectangular ornamental pond set in front, supposed to reflect the building, but it was usually too dull to reflect anything. I remember being very excited by the pond as a kid. It looked like a swimming pool on the plans. I imagined the businessmen changing into their swimming trunks at lunchtime.'

Maureen half-smiled. 'I don't suppose that ever happened.'

'No, I think its only successful application was as a kind of floating rubbish installation. Crisp packets and juice cartons float about on it like lily pads.'

'It's not been demolished, then?'

'No, that's what I was going to say. It's his only public building left standing in Birmingham and I think we've got a good chance of getting it listed. It's an important building; it has an architectural significance and uniqueness that's hard to argue against. The owners haven't applied for an exemption, so I think it should be okay.'

Maureen said nothing and Frank felt the need to press for a response. 'So that would be good, wouldn't it? After all the destruction, to save one building, to leave some trace?'

Maureen looked directly at him. 'Oh, Frank. Let them demolish it if they want to. Things move on. Your father was the first to say that.'

Frank was taken aback. 'But . . . I don't think he was in favour of the complete obliteration of the past, of rewriting history.'

Maureen said nothing. They sat in silence for a while. The light outside was fading and Frank thought he should turn the light on, but momentarily couldn't summon the will to do so. His mother's breathing was heavy; he thought she might have fallen asleep and was surprised when she spoke again.

'Just before your father and I were married he made your Aunt Sylvia a beautiful doll's house. He designed it and made it all by hand. You really couldn't imagine the detail – right down to the tiny cutlery – it was breathtaking really. She would have been about Mo's age and he presented her with it on Christmas morning. I think she would have married him there and then if she could. He could be so thoughtful.' Maureen turned towards Frank: 'Your father had an amazing ability to focus, did you know that?'

Frank shrugged. 'I suppose I did, yes.'

'Incredible really. He could block everything out and just direct all his thought and energy to one thing. It was quite a remarkable thing to find yourself the object of that beam. It was like the sun shining just on you.'

Frank had a flash of memory of the dream he used to

have. He was running after his father, calling for him to turn round.

'But your father wasn't a sentimental man. The object of his beam was always shifting – never a backwards glance. Do you know what was the most important thing in the world to your father?'

Frank shook his head.

'The next thing.' There were a few moments' silence before she continued. 'Of course it's not so good to be the previous thing. The thing moved on from. But we know that, don't we?'

Frank looked away, unable to meet his mother's eye, uncomfortable with her directness.

'Well, now it's the turn of his buildings. Their turn to be erased and forgotten. So let the bulldozers come. I can't really bring myself to shed a tear.'

38

Francis
1975

He tiptoes down the stairs carrying a box filled with Matchbox cars and an eclectic selection of plastic figures: cowboys, Indians, German and British infantry, assorted farmyard animals. He is sneaking into his father's study for the sixth Saturday in a row. His father is at work; his mother is in the garden ferociously tearing up some bamboo stalks. He's not sure that he really needs to creep about.

In his bedroom he often tries to construct roadways for his cars to race along, or battlegrounds for his soldiers to fight upon. He uses opened books for tunnels and pillows for hills but the results are always unconvincing. The model town, however, is perfect. What it lacks in colour it makes up for in detail.

He knocks before entering, just in case, and he quickly closes the door behind him. He heads straight for the model, trying not to catch a glimpse of any of the Future People on the drawings around the room. He places his cars and figures about the town, trying as best as he can to put them exactly where they ended up last time so that the story can continue.

The roads aren't quite wide enough to allow for two-way traffic, but one Matchbox car can just about fit on the carriageway. The big circular road that surrounds the town is soon clogged with an exotic mix of sports cars and emergency-service vehicles all needing to get to different destinations. Some of the drivers become short-tempered and occasionally one car pushes another right off the road and Francis has to try and arbitrate and alleviate the problem. He isn't able to place his men inside the buildings, but he can position them on the pavements, in the empty squares, on the elevated pedestrian walkways and even on the roof-tops. Each character has a name and a story. Colin waits for a taxi that's caught in the gridlock. Fingers and Johnny plan a robbery outside a bank. Martin lies shot dead in a side street. One lone Apache scout called Little Cloud stands on top of the tallest building and looks out at the baffling universe beyond the protective perimeter of the ring road.

Francis calls the town San Francisco. This is partly because the name serves as shorthand for every exciting American city he has ever seen on television – with skyscrapers and guns and children who can drive – and partly because it has his name in it. His role in the town is a combination of mayor, sheriff and God. On interminable dark winter afternoons at school, while the teacher works out simultaneous equations on the board, Francis thinks about San Francisco and all that is happening there.

He always clears out of the study before his father's return. He hears his mother moving around in the kitchen preparing lunch and he reluctantly begins to disassemble the town. He imagines the panic in the streets as his hand descends and plucks the citizens out one by one.

He returns the people and the cars to the box, placing them tenderly on top of one another. When they are all put away, he checks the model over one last time. San Francisco is depopulated, the pavements deserted, but he is sure that he still hears the voices echoing in the empty streets.

Today, though, he is caught up in a difficult situation. An outsize Friesian cow is causing chaos in the shopping precinct. Francis had thought that this was surely the very kind of job the cowboys would be able to deal with, but they have shown themselves to be incompetent and cowardly, terrified by the sheer scale of the animal. They huddle at the entrance to a pedestrian subway. A British infantryman has taken the extraordinary decision to release a lion into the crowded precinct to capture the cow. His colleagues call for assistance, but everyone knows there is no direct vehicular access to the precinct. It looks as if Little Cloud will have to save the day with a well-aimed arrow from his rooftop perch. The British, the Germans, the cowboys and the Indians are all looking up at Little Cloud waiting for him to draw back his bow when a breeze sweeps across San Francisco, followed by:

'What on earth . . .?' And Francis turns to see his father standing in the doorway. For some reason his first reaction is to reach out and remove the cow from the shopping precinct, as if that one detail is simply too much for his father to take.

His father speaks quietly.

'What exactly do you think you're doing?' Francis finds he can't speak. His father stares at him. 'I asked you a question.'

Francis looks down at his feet. 'Playing a game.' He hates that his voice wobbles when he answers.

'Does it say "playroom" on the door?'

'No.'

'Does it say anywhere upon that handmade, extremely delicate and intricate model "toy"?'

'No.'

'Are you ever permitted to come in here alone?'

Francis just shakes his head.

'No. Well, I'm glad we agree. I thought perhaps I was mistaken. I thought, when I walked in and saw you clumsily throwing your toys around the architectural model and showing no regard either for property or for the rules of this house, that something must have changed.'

Francis stands with his head down waiting for his father to shout. He has never seen his father lose his temper. He has a strange desire to hear him shout, just once. Instead his father sighs.

'What disappoints me, Francis, is that a boy of your age looks at a model like this and sees only the potential for childish games. You see only a toy and I think that's really most disappointing. If I were you, I should be very excited indeed at the idea of building a new town, about looking to the future and providing better lives for people.'

Francis thinks his father is right and that there is something wrong with him. He doesn't find the simple subject of buildings and roads and roundabouts, unadorned with Friesian cows and cowardly cowboys, as interesting as he should. He vows to try harder.

His father is still talking. 'Our cities are overcrowded and insanitary. There are parts of Birmingham where people are living in appalling slum conditions. Yes, we can redevelop our cities and I've played a part in that, but new babies are being born every minute and new cities need to be born too to house those citizens of tomorrow.' He has the sense that his father has forgotten he's still in the room. He is speaking in the same strange tone of voice he often uses when speaking of his work, as if to a room full of people.

'We have to focus on the future. We have to move on. You should remember that, Francis. When you finish something, don't slap yourself on the back; don't waste time telling yourself what a good job you've done. That's what the other fellow does. Your job is to move on to the next thing and the next thing and the next thing. We push forward and we find new and bigger challenges. I started off designing tiny details of buildings, I worked my way up to designing whole buildings and now that I've done all I feel I can do with those I am moving on to designing a new town. A new challenge: that's what gets us out of bed in the morning.'

Francis has stopped listening. He is fixed instead on his father's mention of the 'citizens of tomorrow'. He waits for his father to stop speaking before he asks, 'Dad, are you working for the Future People?'

His father looks at him. 'Well, yes, that's what I'm saying. Of course I am. That's what we all must do.'

Francis realizes that he had suspected it all along. His father is a slave to the faceless figures. He is building them office blocks and new towns even though he has no idea what they look like, or what they will say. Francis suddenly feels sorry for him.

39

'Mo, don't sit so close to the television.' Mo shuffled back without taking her eyes from the screen. Over the next few minutes she gradually edged closer again, sucked in by the glow. Andrea was trying to ignore the television and read her book, but it didn't seem to be working. Every few minutes Frank would hear her sigh or tut at something she heard.

The husband on the screen smiled nervously. He was in his own living room, but it was difficult to relax because there was a TV crew there and a glamorous presenter interviewing him.

'So, Neil, how long have you and Carol been married?'

'Twenty-two years now.'

'Wow. Twenty-two years. That's great. Congratulations. That's a real achievement.'

Neil nodded and smiled.

'And is that a photo of your wedding day there? Can we have a look?' Neil picked up the frame and handed it to Michelle, who held it for the camera to see. It showed a considerably slimmer Neil with a full head of hair, next to a laughing blonde woman.

'What a beautiful couple. Is that really Carol? It's hard to believe.'

Neil laughed. 'Well, we've both changed quite a bit. I don't think I'd fit into those trousers again!'

Michelle laughed too. 'Oh, I know what you mean. But Carol is unrecognizable.' Michelle looked earnestly at Neil now as if about to deliver some important news. 'Carol is a beautiful woman.'

Neil was abashed. 'I know –'

Michelle cut him off. 'You just wouldn't know that to look at her now, would you, Neil? I mean she just hides that beauty, doesn't she? Shuffling around in those great big jumpers of hers.'

'Well, I guess a wedding dress isn't that practical for day-to-day life.'

Michelle didn't laugh. 'Course not, Neil, but I mean we can still take care of ourselves, can't we? Have some pride in our appearance. You work in business, don't you, Neil?'

Neil was wrong-footed. 'Erm . . . that's right, I'm a sales manager for a leading manufacturer of doors.'

'Right, well, I know about working in sales, and I know there's a lot of schmoozing with clients, wining and dining. You and Carol must be out a lot. Are you proud of the way she looks when you go out on these nights? In front of these clients? Do you think she's presenting a good image?'

'I think she always looks very nice.'

'Very nice, Neil? In that sequinned kaftan I found in her wardrobe? Come on. You must be embarrassed.'

'To be honest, I don't really notice what she wears. I'm not that into fashion.'

'Well, that's one thing you have in common, my love. But I mean come on, Neil. What about on a more intimate level? Don't you ever look at Carol and wonder where the woman you married went? When she's standing there in the bedroom in those big grey pants, can you honestly say you feel in the least bit romantic?'

Neil was visibly uncomfortable now. 'The way she looks just isn't that important to me. I love her.'

'I don't think you see her at all, Neil. I think you look straight through her. She's become invisible to you. No longer a woman. I think you take her for granted. Well, she is a woman, Neil! And you need to value her more!' Neil was at a loss for words. 'Don't you wish she loved herself more? Don't you wish she had a higher opinion of herself?'

'I know she has very low self-esteem. She's put on weight since we married and it doesn't bother me at all, but I know she gets quite depressed about it. She can't fit into the kinds of clothes she used to wear and that makes her feel bad. When I first met her, I thought she was a stunner, I still do, but she thinks that when people look at her all they see is an overweight, unattractive woman. I tell her she should be more confident. I tell her that I love her and that's she's beautiful. Of course I wish that she had more pride in herself. I want her to have a high opinion of herself.'

'And do you see, Neil, that that high opinion, that good self-image starts with the outside? How can she feel good about herself when she's wearing a sack? We need to throw the sacks in the bin – yeah? Throw them in the bin! Do you see that?'

He nodded uncertainly.

'So what do we say about the big baggy jumpers?'

It took a moment for Neil to work it out. 'Throw them in the bin?'

'And what else?'

Neil tried to remember. 'Erm . . . the sequinned kaftan and the grey pants – throw them in the bin!'

The scene now changed to a white studio. Michelle sat next to Carol on the couch.

'Now, Carol, Neil had something he wanted to tell you, but finds it difficult to say to your face.'

Carol frowned as Michelle pressed a remote control and they watched Neil saying: 'When I first met her I thought she was a stunner.' Carol rolled her eyes. Neil's face filled the screen. 'She's put on weight over the years.' Carol tried to smile, but couldn't quite manage it. 'She can't fit into the kinds of clothes she used to wear.' Now on screen was some footage of Carol in the supermarket wheeling a trolley along an aisle with Neil's voice-over: 'People look at her and all they see is an overweight, unattractive woman.' The camera cut back to Carol, tears rolling down her face as she watched her husband say: 'Of course I wish that she had more pride in herself.'

Michelle put her arm round Carol. 'It's okay, love. It's hard for men to say what they mean sometimes. They don't like to hurt our feelings. When sometimes what we really need is *Tough Love*.'

The screen filled with the *Tough Love* logo and cut to adverts.

Frank turned to Andrea. 'Bloody hell.'

Andrea looked up from her book. 'I told you.'

'It's quite harsh, isn't it?'

'Yes, I think they've imported tactics from Mao's cultural

revolution. She's still in the midst of her re-education. She'll be a model citizen by the end of it.'

'Michelle's quite scary on it, isn't she?'

'Yeah, now maybe you'll appreciate why I didn't fancy meeting her last week. She's turned into the devil.' Andrea looked anxiously to check Mo wasn't listening, but saw that she was still glued to the television. 'We should never have let Mo watch this. All she's learning is how to hate herself. It's horrible.'

Frank looked at Mo. 'Maybe I could get Michelle to talk to her. Tell her it's just a role. Tell her it's all nonsense.'

Andrea looked unconvinced. 'Well, good luck with that. I'm not sure Michelle sees it that way.' They were silent for a few moments, both watching Mo, until Frank spoke again.

'I keep thinking about what she said about Phil.'

'Who?'

'Michelle.'

'What? The moodiness?'

'It was more than moodiness. It just all sounded really strange. There was the money missing from the bank account, Michelle told me there was a cash withdrawal of £20,000. And the mysterious hit and run . . .'

'It wasn't particularly mysterious, was it? It was a hit and run – the driver doesn't stick around and offer an explanation or apology.'

Frank ignored the interruption. '. . . and the note from Michael Church.'

'What's the note got to do with anything?'

'Well, it was strange, wasn't it. What was he saying Phil was wrong about?'

'I don't know. Maybe a disagreement about an episode of *Terry and June*. It might seem strange, but we don't know the context – it was probably something completely banal.'

'Maybe, but it's a bit odd, and turning up when it did . . . It says, "I won't be there next week." They must have arranged to meet around the time of Phil's death.'

Andrea tried to keep a straight face. 'Hmm. Very mysterious.'

Frank looked at her. 'Are you laughing at me?'

Andrea was by now laughing. 'Wow, Frank, are we *Hart to Hart*? Let's get our safari suits and go and track down some clues!'

Frank laughed, but was silenced by Mo clearing her throat loudly and saying: 'It's quite hard to hear the television.'

'Sorry, Mo.'

Frank was silent for a while before turning to Andrea and speaking quietly. 'Maybe you're right.'

'About what?'

'You told me when I started looking into Michael Church's life not to go weird. Do I sound like a nutter?'

'It just all sounds a bit conspiracy theory. I'm worried you're going to start getting interested in UFOs.'

'Or writing in to local television.'

'Watching local television even.'

Frank threw a cushion at Andrea. They sat and watched the end of *Tough Love* with Mo. Michelle delivered a piece to camera.

'Sometimes we have to be honest. It's hard but it's worth it. We look at the person beside us and we can see that they've lost their way, they've let themselves go. We say nothing. Like Neil we use love as an excuse. But love alone isn't enough. Is it, sweetheart?' The camera pulled out to reveal Carol standing next to Michelle shaking her head.

Michelle smiled. 'What is it we really need, Carol?'

'Tough love.'

They both laughed and the end title sequence began.

40

Henry had him in the corner again. '"Points make prizes!"'

Frank shook his head.

'"Cheap as chips!"'

'What? Henry! No, that's not me.'

Henry shrugged with indifference before the finger shot up again. '"Play the game or take the train!"'

'Is that a catchphrase?'

'Oh yes. Oh yes, quite definitely. Somebody said it. Was it you?'

'No, it wasn't me.'

'Ooh I know I've seen you on something. I'm wracking my brains. Wracking them. Wrrrrrrrrrrrrrracking them.'

Henry was getting so much pleasure in repeating the word that Frank thought he might make a getaway, but Henry focused on him again. 'Oh, all right, then! Give me a clue. Come on. Just what is it you say?'

'Hmm. I sometimes say, "Good night." Or maybe, "Have a good night." Or other times, "Take care."'

Henry stared at Frank, the humour draining from his face. '"Good night"?'

'Yes.' Frank shrugged. 'I don't really have a catchphrase.'

Henry's eyes searched Frank's face as if seeing him for the first time. 'Well, what's the bloody use of you?' he said in disgust as he walked back to his armchair in the window.

Frank considered the question and really couldn't think of a satisfactory answer.

He left the residents' lounge and walked in the direction of his mother's room. As he passed the dining room, he saw Irene drinking a cup of tea. She smiled and waved when she saw him.

'Hello, Frank, visiting your mother, are you?'

'Yes, well, partly. I haven't actually made it to her room yet. I got trapped in the residents' lounge by Henry.'

Irene looked blank. 'I don't think I've met a Henry. Is he a fan of yours?'

'I don't think so.'

'Oh, I see.'

Frank hesitated. He knew he should let it go, but found himself reaching into his pocket for the photo.

'Actually, I wanted to see you too. There's something I should have asked you last time, but I just didn't think. Can I show you something?'

He waited while some complicated business with glasses was completed. Irene eventually found the right combination and, wearing one pair whilst holding the other a few inches from the photo, she peered at the image.

'My God, look at Phil – he's just a boy. He wasn't much older than that when we met. Look at that smile! That was the first thing I noticed about him. When Phil smiled at you, everything was all right. That's how he got away with murder.' Her smile faded. 'Photos are cruel things. It's terrible to see what's happened to us. I can't look at mine any more. They're too sad.'

'I'm sorry,' said Frank. 'What about the other boy? Do you recognize him?'

Irene angled the glasses again and extended her neck backwards as if avoiding an unpleasant smell. 'Oh . . . it's Mikey, isn't it?'

Frank nodded. 'Michael Church.'

'That's right, we always called him Mikey. I've often wondered what happened to him. I asked Phil about him a few times but they'd lost contact.'

'Do you remember much about him?'

'A fair bit. He was Phil's oldest friend. They were friends from when they were lads. Well, you can see that from the photo. He was best man at our wedding. I think it was a bit of an ordeal for him, having to make a speech. He was a shy lad.'

'Did you see him much?'

'A fair bit in the early years. He'd often come round to call for Phil. They'd go for a drink or a game of cards. They did their National Service together and I wasn't really interested in listening to their stories. Phil was always going on about Mikey being a good shot – what is it? A marks-man? I don't know – but apparently Mikey was really something with a gun and Phil thought that was marvel-lous. Poor Mikey always looked embarrassed when he'd start going on about it.' She looked at the photo again. 'Is he still alive?'

Frank shook his head. 'I'm afraid not. He was found dead recently. I heard about it and half remembered meet-ing him one time with Phil. I thought I'd see if I could trace any family. He died alone.'

'Oh, poor Mikey. He was a lovely boy.' She stopped for

a moment to think. 'I know his mother lived up near town, but she'd be long gone by now, of course. He didn't have any brothers or sisters. I think Phil and he were like brothers when they were young.' She put the photo down and looked towards the window.

'I liked Mikey. He was nothing like Phil. He was a quiet lad, a bit of a dreamer. Married his childhood sweetheart. He'd stand by quietly while Phil rattled off his usual nonsense. I don't know how they ever drifted apart, really – I mean Phil thought the world of him. But then Phil could be careless; he moved around and he didn't make the effort to keep in touch and I could imagine Mikey as the type who wouldn't want to bother Phil when he got more famous.' She paused. 'Phil was all chat and smiles, but there wasn't much else underneath – I found that out for myself. This lad was quiet, but I think underneath he had something Phil never had.'

'What was that?'

'I don't know. There was just something there, some substance. He seemed solid somehow.'

Irene looked up at the ceiling, trying to think. 'There were far worse men to be married to than Phil, I know that, and I know he was your friend, but he was a weak man and he knew it, as he was drawn to people who weren't. I think that's what he saw in me, some strength he didn't have, and I think it's what he saw in Mikey. He never told me much about their past, but he did say that Mikey was bullied at school because his dad had been German – he'd done a runner years before, but of course everyone knew. Phil said Mikey would get a beating from the other lads most days, but he'd always fight back. I asked Phil what he used to do while his mate was getting beaten and to give him his due he was at least honest: he said he used to hide. I suppose it's to his credit that he was the only one who was friendly with Mikey. He said he'd try and make Mikey laugh on the way home. He'd pretend to be a commentator and give his analysis of the fight, or he'd do impressions of the bullies and Mikey would laugh. Phil said he loved the sound of Mikey laughing. I suppose that was what Mikey admired about Phil, his gift of the gab, his ability to make him laugh, his charm. Everyone admired that about Phil and it made him think that that was all you needed in life, a nice surface.' She peered at Frank through her glasses. 'You're not like that, are you?'

Frank smiled and shook his head. 'I don't think too much of my surface. I wouldn't wear jumpers like this if I did.'

Irene laughed. 'It does look like it's seen better days – just like me.' She looked again at the photo and her face changed. 'Poor Phil. He was nice enough in his own way, but I'm glad I found a real person to marry in the end.'

41

Phil
February 2009

As the video clip ends, the doors at the back of the set open to reveal the two guests waiting in a cloud of dry ice waving at the audience. Phil greets them warmly and guides them down to the front of the stage. He has his arm clamped tightly round the waist of the member of the public, keeping her steady and walking in the right direction. With the celebrity his touch is lighter, just a guiding palm. The audience claps and whoops. He looks out into the roaring blackness and is able to make out a few banners being waved; some audience members are standing to applaud. This pair are the favourites to win. As he smiles into camera one, he has a flash of pure blind panic: he can't remember the guests' names, he can't remember his own name, he can't remember what show this is. It's gone in less than a second. He's back in control. The guests are Jane and Toby. He is Phil Smethway. It's Saturday night and the show is *Two Can Play That Game*. Eleven million people are watching.

Through Jane's chiffon blouse he feels tiny subcutaneous vibrations and spasms of terror and excitement. He's often thought how handling civilians is like handling horses. Easily spooked, quivering and blinking, they need to be spoken to reassuringly. She's generating enough heat to power the studio. He gets the two of them to their marker.

'Now then, you two. That was quite an interesting little film we just watched!' The audience whoop. 'What on earth were you doing, Toby? Tuna and bacon? What kind of a sandwich is that? Were you trying to put poor Jane here out of business?'

Toby looks rueful and shakes his head. The audience laughs wildly. 'I was trying to innovate.'

Phil pulls a sickly-looking face for the crowd. 'Innovate? You'll make 'em regurgitate, more like.' The audience groans and laughs. Phil shrugs with mock innocence. 'No, but seriously. Toby. Jane. Thank you for being such wonderful sports. Haven't they been wonderful, ladies and gentlemen?' Rapturous applause. 'How would you sum up your week doing Jane's job, Toby?'

Toby's face is serious now. 'All joking aside, Phil, I have a hell of a lot of respect for this woman here.' The applause starts again. 'This woman here,' he struggles to be heard over the sound of the crowd, 'is quite simply a marvel!' The audience goes wild and he waits for them to quieten down. 'I had no idea how challenging running your own sandwich shop could be. You know, Phil, you and I both work in TV, and I'm sure we both sometimes like to think we know stress, but, take it from me, you haven't seen stress till you've got a queue of twenty workmen with big appetites all making demands.'

Phil doesn't have to say anything; he just cocks an eyebrow at the audience and generates a chorus of high-pitched squeals of delight.

Toby carries on talking about sandwiches and Phil examines the side of Toby's face. He admires the quality of the skin and wonders what products he uses. The colour is perfect. Phil thinks it's Californian Fall. It makes his own Caribbean Caramel look cheap and overdone. Toby's had some good work done on his brows too. Phil remembers seeing him for the first time a few years ago on some kids' programme. He was a good-looking lad, but he's worked hard since then, or someone's worked hard on him. Now he's fully formed. His hair is spectacular. Phil counts at least four different low-light tones in there – a really beautiful job.

He turns now to Jane. 'Well then, missus. What about you, eh? One minute you're at the wholesalers stocking up on coleslaw, next you're the quiz mistress of *Clue Sniffers*! Now, what did I tell you before you went off and did the job swap? What did I expressly tell you?'

Jane grins. 'You told me not to be too good.'

'Exactly. Don't be too blinking good, I said, and make the rest of us look like amateurs, and you went and let me down, Jane. How could you?'

Jane laughs and starts to tell the audience about the exciting week she's had. Phil thinks that she's not in bad shape for a civilian, but she could be a different species to Toby. The lack of dental work alone gives her away. Her skin is dull, despite the make-up and Phil spots a chicken pox scar above her eye. In her ear lobe he sees the traces of three or four closed-up holes. Teenage piercings – another small sign of lack of care. She has great warmth, though; the viewers have taken her to their hearts.

At the end of the series the winning team will choose a charity to donate the prize money to. Phil will stand behind the piles of bank notes and ask them to nominate the good cause. He will listen gravely as they outline the important work the money will support. He thinks now of the cash he gave to Michael. He wonders if the audience would applaud that donation so enthusiastically. Would they judge that cause to be a good one?

The two guests are thanking each other now and urging the viewers to vote for them. Phil watches Toby in action and feels a thousand years old. He's conscious of eleven million pairs of eyes mercilessly fixing on his every wrinkle, every age spot, every grey hair. He sees himself laid out naked on an autopsy slab on high-definition plasma-screen TVs across the nation. A brutal overhead light shines down on his withered body and he wants to scream out for someone to turn the bloody lights off. Instead he turns to the cameras and says: 'Thank you, everyone here in the studio, and there at home, for watching. You've been a marvellous audience and we hope to see you again next week. Think you could do better than our guests? Well, just remember: two can play that game!'

He waves, smiling at the camera, and thanks God that this will all soon be over.

42

Frank looked at the day's menu, presented on parchment in an elaborate curling font:

Baked winter squash and goat's cheese cannelloni

*Slow-cooked lamb shank with thyme
and roasted winter root vegetables*

*Pan-fried salmon with crab and herb crumb, and
asparagus and shellfish dressing*

Walter appeared at his side. 'Would a shepherd's pie be too much to ask for? The occasional egg and chips? I don't know where they get these chefs from.'

'It always sounds lovely, Walter – like eating in a top restaurant every day.'

'I don't want to eat in a top restaurant every day. Who would? I'm not Michael bloody Winner. I like to eat everyday food every day. I can't stand this fiddly stuff – it's no good if you've got arthritis in your hands. The other week I spent fifteen minutes chasing two tarragon-buttered prawns around my plate before giving up. I'd be skin and bone if it wasn't for the cheese and crackers in my room. Course the Gestapo have got wind of those so I get regular little talks from the nutritionist. I've told her about the menu, told her it's not appropriate, but it's balanced apparently – that's all she cares about. I told her: "Well, it's not the food I was raised on. I'm not bloody French." That was an error, though. Turns out her husband's French and she thought I was making a point. Me and my big mouth.'

Frank laughed.

They sat at a table and Walter shook the dominos out. Frank looked over at the television while the tiles were arranged. A middle-aged couple in blue T-shirts were jubilant that the plate they'd bought for £15 at a car boot sale, had sold for £18 at auction. The man punched the air and whooped. Someone changed channels.

Walter placed his first tile. 'You remember Leonard, don't you, Frank?'

'Of course.'

'I went up to see him today.'

'How's he doing?'

Walter shook his head: 'That bloody place.'

Leonard was now looked after in the Golden Days facility at Evergreen. Back when Maureen had first moved to Evergreen, Leonard had been a fellow resident of Helping Hands. He had seen himself as a kind of self-appointed social secretary, liaising with Evergreen's activities co-ordinator, planning various excursions and evenings, and went out of his way to make Maureen feel welcome. Frank had watched with a mixture of amusement and pity as Leonard's efforts were met with Maureen's steely determination to be miserable.

His optimism, though, had remained undimmed. 'I think I may have found the key, Frank.'

'Oh yes?'

'Yes, indeed. Now, we've established, have we not, that she's not interested in trips to local markets, country and western evenings or the majesty of the Peaks.'

'Yes, I think we've established that.'

'They are all, Frank, rest assured, crossed off my suggestions list for Maureen.'

Frank didn't doubt that such a document existed.

'But I think I've come up with something to get her up and about and involved.'

'Really?'

'Yes, Frank. Next Saturday, a brass-rubbing excursion to Lichfield Cathedral – all materials provided.'

'That sounds great, Leonard.'

'Right up her street, I reckon.'

'The thing is my mother's never really been a team player – she likes her own company . . . well, I'm not sure she even likes that, but she's stuck with it. I mean – don't feel bad if she doesn't go along. She just isn't a joiner.'

Leonard nodded. 'I know that, Frank. I know some people like to keep themselves to themselves and that's the end of the story, but I don't think that's true with your mother. I think there's something else there. I think she wants to join in; she just doesn't know how.' Frank thought Leonard was as wrong as he could be, but said nothing. Leonard smiled. 'You'll see. I'll get her enjoying herself yet.'

As it turned out, though, Maureen's will had outlasted Leonard's. The first time Frank noticed anything wrong was when Leonard suggested a day trip to Salisbury Cathedral. When Frank said that a three-hundred-mile round trip seemed a bit too much for one day, Leonard had frowned at him and told him he'd often made the journey in fifteen minutes. As the months went on, Leonard became more confused about where he was, often thinking he was back in the Wiltshire village he had grown up in and waiting for his mother to bring his sandwiches. Six months ago on a trip to Warwick he disappeared from the group and was lost for hours. He was found by police walking along the hard shoulder of the M40 believing it to be the road to Swindon.

He moved into Golden Days shortly afterwards.

'What's it like up there?' Frank asked.

'It looks the same as down here. Same decor, same bloody menu even, but . . . bloody hell, Frank, is that what we've got to look forward to? People joke and say it's better than the alternative, but I don't think it is.'

'How's Leonard?'

'Oh, he's okay, I suppose. Happy if you take him some sweets; beams at you, he does. Hasn't a clue who I am or where he is. But what chance has he got? You could go in completely compos mentis and you'd lose your marbles within a week. There was one old fella up there with no legs in a wheelchair. Almost knocked me over, whizzing across the floor, face like thunder. He goes haring across the room and I think he's going to smash into the wall, but he brakes right at the last minute in front of some mirrored doors. Starts shouting: "Out my bloody way, you bugger!" and all this – turning the air blue. He doesn't recognize his own reflection, Frank, thinks there's some old codger in a wheelchair blocking his way. The nurses wheeled him away eventually, but he was still shouting.

'Then some old dear next to us started crying. So I went over and said, "Come on now, love. It's not that bad." But she looked at me, and her face – you've never seen such pain, like she'd just lost everything and everyone. She was in a terrible state, really wailing. Then this nurse came over, a Philippine woman. I don't know her name. She says: "What's all this, Eva? Today's not a crying day, it's a smiling day!" She takes the old dear's hand and shakes it gently like it's a baby's rattle. "Yes, a smiling day today. We're all smiling all day. Not a crying day." And do you know what?'

Frank shook his head.

'She stopped crying.' Walter's eyes were wet now and he had to fight to control his voice. 'Completely stopped crying. She started to smile – a big bright smile. Jesus Christ, Frank.'

Frank could think of nothing to say and they played in silence. After a while he noticed that Walter was smiling.

'Your mother was saying the other day how much she loved the sea.'

'Was she?'

'Yes. It's something we have in common. Funny really, both lived here, as far as you could get from the sea all our lives, and yet always had this hankering.'

Frank felt a little defensive. 'I could take her to the sea if she wanted. She's never said. I mean – I'm always asking her where she'd like to go.' He wondered if he should add that Walter could come too, if he should acknowledge the friendship that seemed to be developing between the two of them. He decided against it. His mother wouldn't acknowledge it – why should he?

It was a while before Walter spoke again. 'You know, I feel just the same.'

Frank looked up. 'Sorry?'

'Inside. I'm seventy-seven now and I feel just the same today as I did when I was forty-seven or twenty-seven even. Nothing's changed in here.' He tapped his chest. 'This fella' – he indicated his heart – 'is still the same stupid bugger he always was.'

Frank considered Walter for a few moments before answering. 'I guess that's a good thing, isn't it?'

Walter smiled. 'I think it is, Frank. I think it is.'

43

They stood on the landing with the ladder between them.

'Are you sure you want to come up here with me?'

'Yes. I'm going to help. Mom says you're not very good at throwing things away.'

'Well, Mom shouldn't say that. I'm very good at throwing things away that are broken or unwanted. Your mother specializes in throwing away perfectly good things, things we still want and use. That's not a virtue, Mo, that's a mental illness. She throws away my clothes all the time – perfectly good clothes.'

Mo, who had helped her mother do the last sweep of Frank's wardrobe, said nothing to this. She remembered how they had both laughed at a sweatshirt of Frank's they'd found with a picture of a dog on it.

Frank looked up at the loft hatch. 'Because you never used to like it up there.'

Mo rolled her eyes. 'That's when I was a baby, Dad.'

Frank nodded. 'And you don't get scared of things now, right?'

Mo shook her head emphatically.

'It's just, how can you know you won't be scared when you haven't been up there for years? You know, Mo, I remember the last time. You insisted that you wanted to come up and then when we got up there you didn't like it. Do you remember? I don't want to go through that again. We couldn't calm you down. People in Birmingham could hear you scream.'

Mo tutted. 'You're an exaggerator, Dad.'

'I'm not. I promise you I'm not. Do you remember what set you off?'

Mo shrugged.

'Remember the coat on the hanger. You thought it was someone hanging.'

Mo smiled weakly, but Frank could see that she'd forgotten about the coat until now. He saw her bite her lip.

'So, for the last time, are you sure you want to come up? You don't have to. I can clear it out on my own.'

Mo nodded.

'Sure?'

She nodded again, but her face still showed uncertainty.

Frank started up the ladder and turned back. 'Would you like me to go up first and take the coat down?'

She shrugged, but when Frank raised his eyebrows she cracked and nodded rapidly.

Frank climbed the ladder and wondered if the clear-out was really necessary. The sale seemed to be going through, but after so long waiting he still couldn't quite believe they might finally be leaving the house. The buyer was a solicitor and his family relocated to the area. News of their interest and subsequent offer had caught Frank and Andrea unawares and after so long thinking only theoretically about where they would ideally like to live they were now having to find somewhere quickly.

He removed the coat from the hanger and called Mo up.

They stood at the top of the ladder near the hatch and looked at the scene around them. There was an overhead light, but Mo had insisted on bringing a torch and shone it now from one perfectly visible pile to another.

'What is it all, Dad?'

'Stuff.'

'It looks like as much stuff as we have in the whole rest of the house.'

Frank nodded slowly. 'Yeah. I think you're right.'

'Where did it all come from?'

'My parents' house mainly. When Gran moved out of her house she could only take a few things to Evergreen. So we put it all here. A lot of it should have been thrown away back then, but we didn't. It's easier to put things off, isn't it, rather than do them straight away. It's a terrible habit, Mo. I hope you haven't inherited it.'

Mo shrugged and Frank stood looking around at the piles of paper and mounds of boxes – he pushed at the edge of a suitcase with his toe.

Mo waited and after a while said, 'Are we going to do something, Dad?'

'Yes. Right, exactly. Chop-chop. Now – Mom's suggested a job for you. You see the rail of clothes at the end? They're all old dresses of Gran's. Special dresses for occasions and dinners and things. Mom thinks we should be able to sell them on the internet – they're vintage, apparently, like wine. Do you want to go and put them in bags?'

Mo clambered in the direction of the rail and Frank turned to the nearest pile covered by a dust sheet. He pulled the sheet back to reveal a stack of papers and ledgers. He took the top few and saw that it was paperwork taken from his father's office at home. Sitting down on the floor he started to leaf through them. The first thing he came across were drawings of Rhombus House. Some of the early prototypes were markedly different from the final structure. Frank looked at the different approaches pursued. Many of the drawings had scribbled notes in his father's handwriting around their edges. There were so many different images tracing the project from initial conception through to final design that it seemed strange to Frank that they should stop there. He imagined the sketches carrying on through time beyond the completion of the building. The faceless figures would develop faces and coats and carrier bags containing their lunches, their silhouettes changing with the passing fashions. One sketch would show the skateboarders who would come and make new use of the access ramp outside office hours. Later drawings would show the neglect of the exterior followed by the inappropriate facelift. A later one still would show the office workers moving out, Manila folders and houseplants in boxes. Then a series of images of the empty building, buses passing in front, the leaves on the trees coming and going. Then the JCB, like a dinosaur, taking the first of many bites out of the building, reducing it to rubble and dust and finally to its present state, a vacant plot of land.

He looked at the piles and piles of drawings and notebooks documenting all his father's projects. He thought that there in the dusty attic all the stories stopped at just the right place, finishing at the optimistic start.

Mo called from the other end of the roof space. 'Dad, did Gran really wear these dresses?'

Frank squinted down towards the rack. 'Yes, she really did. We've got photos of her in some of them.'

'But, Dad, they're like the kind of clothes people wear in space.'

'Well, it was the sixties – it was all a bit futuristic.'

'But Gran isn't futuristic.' She paused. 'She's totally pastistic.'

'Well, that's just getting old, Mo. When you're young, life's all in the future; when you're old, it's all in the past.'

'My life is present, Dad.'

'Yeah, I know. That's the best way.'

'Dad? Can I keep this dress?' Mo held up a short, silver A-line dress.

'I thought we were supposed to be getting rid of stuff. Anyway, isn't it a bit too big for you?'

'When I wear it, I will be a bad robot.'

Frank shrugged. 'In that case, you'd better keep it.'

He turned back to the piles around him and wondered if the library might be interested in his father's archive. Maybe the library was full of plans for buildings that no longer stood, just waiting for the day when someone came and reassembled the city as it had once been. Dead buildings risen from their graves.

Mo had finished sorting the clothes and now wandered into the far corner of the attic. Frank heard her exclaim and turned to see her standing in a cloud made by the pulling of a dust sheet. She managed to say. 'Dad! Look at this!' before sneezing.

Frank started to walk over to where she stood.

'It's one of your old toys.'

Frank frowned. 'I don't think so – they're all long gone.'

He reached her and saw what she was looking at. 'Oh . . . that.'

'Did you used to have little toy figures to put on the streets and in the buildings?'

He smiled. 'I did, actually, but I wasn't supposed to.'

'Why not?'

'It wasn't mine, Mo. It's not a toy.'

Mo looked at it again. 'But it's a town.'

'I know, but it's not a play town. It's an architectural model. It was my dad's.'

'Didn't he let you play with it?'

Frank laughed. 'No. You didn't play with his stuff, Mo. You didn't touch it. Well, I did, but only when he was out and Mom was off somewhere else.'

Mo walked around the model slowly. 'So this was a model for a real town?'

'Yes.'

'Is the town still there?'

Frank was staring at the model now, lost in thought. He remembered Little Cloud standing on top of the tallest building.

'Dad?'

He'd done a good job putting it all back together after his father's death. The fine lines where he had glued the shards back in place were barely visible.

'Dad?'

'Yes?'

'The town? What's it called?'

Frank looked at Mo and realized he hadn't been listening to her.

'The town? It's called San Francisco.'

44

Michael
October 2009

Elsie and Michael often saw Phil on television. They'd watch him sometimes on Saturday nights, surrounded by his glamorous assistants, his skin glowing, his teeth and eyes catching the light like glass, and he was the same old Phil to them. He was still the boy with too much oil in his hair who wanted to be Stewart Granger. Elsie would say, 'You should drop him a line,' and Michael would nod and agree that he should.

He remembers Phil's wedding. Michael didn't think he was right for best man. He thought Phil should pick someone better with people, better with words and speeches. Phil told him he didn't care about any of that. What he wanted was a best man who would look after him on the scariest day of his life. He said that Michael had always looked after him, that he relied on him. Michael found that funny. He'd always thought it was the other way round.

He supposes now that the usual things happened to them: wives, jobs, house moves. They saw less of each other over time. They'd send a few scribbled lines in Christmas cards, but then a new address got missed and they drifted out of touch completely. It would have been easy for Michael to contact Phil through the television, but because Phil was in their living room so much he never really felt as if they'd lost touch.

Elsie sometimes worried that Michael was too self-contained, but Michael didn't think that was true. She contained him; he had no need of anyone else.

He and Elsie walked a lot when they were courting. He had never been a great talker and she had never made him feel that he should be, but when they walked they talked. Nothing, they'd be the first to admit, of any great consequence, just the easy flow of observations, memories and thoughts possible only with each other. They always ended up in the park, under the tree they thought of as theirs, lying in the long grass, glimpsing the sky through the leaves and feeling the earth spin beneath them.

When she had the fourth miscarriage, he held her tightly all night, not letting her slip away. They cried and knew it was the last time. He promised her they'd be okay, just the two of them, told her they didn't need anyone else. He knew it was harder for her, but for him it was true – he already had everything he wanted.

Even now, he's never lonely. He stands at bus stops on busy streets and no one sees him. He sits in the lounge at night listening to the stairs creak. He spends his days in the unit crafting fine-precision tools that no one, as far as he can tell, wants. But he's never lonely. He has no desire to attend the coffee mornings at the local community centre. He doesn't want to talk to the limping young vicar who knocks at his door once a month. He doesn't reply to the invitations that come from the school to their annual old-folks' party.

He feels no connection to his hands and feet. He stares

at them and wonders who they belong to. He watches with fascination as they put teabags in cups and shuffle to the post office. He isn't lonely. He doesn't want company. His Elsie has gone. His Elsie has gone.

45

Julia was off for the week. She'd said she was going away on holiday, but she told Frank in confidence that she just needed a week to sort her head out and work out what she wanted to do with her career and her life. Her disillusionment with the programme had reached breaking point recently. Sitting next to her on the little couch as the cameras rolled, Frank would feel something bubbling under the surface. Some days he thought it might dramatically break through and Julia might resign live on air with a blistering speech. He had an image of her as a bedraggled Peter Finch shouting at the camera: 'I'm as mad as hell and I'm not going to take it any more.' But he had to concede that was fanciful, perhaps even wishful, thinking on his part. It wasn't really Julia's style.

In Julia's absence Frank was presenting with Suzy for the week. She breezed in each day in her immaculate knitwear, hair like a helmet with tales of marvellous engagements at the golf club or the local chamber of commerce. She had no interest at all in getting to the bottom of the stories or in discussing with reporters exactly what it was they were trying to say. She was a presenter and her job as she saw it was to be a reassuring presence to viewers. She might pick up on a grammatical error on the autocue, but she would never question the internal logic of a report or the worthiness of it. Frank had to admit that for that week, after Julia's recent thunderous moods, she was a delight. Whilst he and Julia held more or less similar points of view about the programme, about the standards they should aspire to and about what made a decent story, he found keeping up with her constant level of outrage to be exhausting.

On their last day working together Frank asked Suzy if she fancied getting a drink after the programme.

'No thanks, Frank. I need to get off.'

'Oh, well, that's a shame. I just wanted to say that it's been nice working together this week.'

Suzy smiled to herself and shook her head.

Frank picked up on something. 'What?'

'It's nothing.'

'No, what is it?'

She looked at him. 'You think I'm a bit of a joke, don't you?'

Frank was taken aback. 'No. Certainly not.'

She rolled her eyes. 'You could at least be honest about it.' Frank didn't know what to say. 'I'm seen as "old school", aren't I?'

Frank shrugged. 'Well, that's not an insult.'

Suzy laughed. 'I think it is, Frank. I think we both know that.' She carried on bustling with her handbag and coat and then stopped to look again at Frank. 'Can I ask you, Frank, how old you are?'

'I'm forty-three.'

'Well, I'm fifty. Not a huge difference, is there? And yet there you are on the main evening show and I'm tidily tucked away in the broom cupboard of the morning bulletins, where hopefully not too many people will notice me.'

'Nobody tucked you away. You chose to move to the morning slots.'

'Oh yes. I chose, but I was given a lot of helpful advice and guidance in making the decision when I was coming up to forty.'

'By who?'

'The powers that be. The same people who are giving me helpful advice now about perhaps retiring. You know, I've put in the years apparently, so why not take it easy and retire? Put my feet up? Take a well-earned break?'

'Why do they want you to retire?'

'Oh, come on, Frank. I'm fifty. I'm a woman. It's fine for a man of that age to be presenting. It's fine for a man of that age even to move to national television, to embark on a new phase of his career in front of a wider audience, to marry a woman half his age. But women? No, we're supposed to fade away decorously sometime in our early forties. We may reappear in adverts for Saga holidays, or financial services aimed at the elderly, we may do the occasional voice-over on radio, but to be the face of the news? Who wants to see that?'

Frank realized that he was shocked not by what she was saying, but that she was saying it at all. He realized with some shame that he'd always assumed Suzy was somehow unaware of her own sidelining.

'I'm sure Julia thinks that they replaced me with her because of her journalistic integrity, her rigour. Well, you might want to tell her one day that such things make no difference at all. There have been many female presenters before her on our programme and others – and they've run the gamut from brilliant journalists, to straightforward, professional presenters, but none of them makes it past fifty.' She looked quite closely at Frank. 'You see, Frank, your wrinkles lend you gravitas, mine make me unemployable.' With that she left the newsroom.

A reporter named Clive had been standing nearby and had evidently been eavesdropping. He looked over at Frank now and pointing at his temple made the universal 'nutter' gesture. 'Menopause – sends 'em mental.'

Frank looked away and felt complicit in the whole shitty nature of things.

He was still thinking about Suzy when the phone in his pocket started to ring and made him jump. He answered without looking who was calling.

'Aye, aye.'

'Hello, Cyril.'

'Nice show this evening, sir, nicely done.'

'Oh, thanks.' Frank couldn't remember a thing about it.

'Just thought I'd see what's coming up tomorrow. I can get my thinking cap on tonight and come back to you fresh in the morning with some crackers.'

'Okay . . . give me a second, Cyril. I'll just have a look . . . Hmmm, I don't know, it's all quite serious stuff to be honest – job losses, arson court case, a cowboy builder who's swindled thousands from pensioners, a parish refusing to accept a female vicar . . .'

'Hold up, Frank. There could be something with the lady vicars. Always good for a giggle that. Did you hear about the female vicar who wanted to say "awomen" not "amen" at the end of the prayers, eh? She insisted the parishioners sang "hers" not "hymns".'

'Cyril, those were old jokes when I was a boy . . .'

'Yes, I know, I know – I'm just saying there are plenty of possibilities – what you might call juice to be squeezed. And if there's a drop of juice there Cyril's the man to wring it out. Don't fret, Frank, I'm onto it. I'll have a think tonight and give you a choice of three tomorrow.'

Frank didn't worry too much; he was fairly sure the story would be dropped before the following evening's show.

'All right, Cyril, I'll talk to you tomorrow.'

'Yes. Tomorrow.' Cyril hesitated. 'I was wondering . . . did you have a chance to think any more about what I said?'

Frank's mind was blank. 'Which bit of what you said?'

'Remember, the other day when I met your lovely daughter and fiery wife. You're a lucky man, Frank – she's just the kind of woman I like. She reminded me of a tiger, a blazing tiger.'

Frank had to try and shake the image of a big cat on fire from his mind. 'Oh yes?'

'I said about us meeting up again, just the two of us. Just wanted to have a chat with you about a couple of things.'

Now Frank remembered. The new business opportunity. He wondered if it was possible to say he was busy before Cyril had even suggested a date. 'Right. Yes.'

'How about next Monday after the show? I'll come down and meet you at the studio.'

Frank tried to think of an excuse. He had a suspicion that there was no new business opportunity, and whilst that was cause for relief it would mean the only reason Cyril wanted to meet up was to get maudlin about the old days and Big Johnny Jason.

The silence prompted Cyril to add: 'Or any day, really. I'm free any time.'

Frank had a brief glimpse of Cyril's solitary life. He thought of Michael Church. He realized that giving up one evening to spend with someone who clearly wanted a bit of company was hardly the greatest sacrifice.

'Monday's fine, Cyril. I'll see you then.'

'Aye, aye, Cap'n.'

46

They stood leaning against the car looking at the exterior of the Renwick Building.

'So what number is it, Dad?'

'What do you mean – what number? On the street?'

'No, on the list. What number is it on the list?'

Andrea touched Mo's arm. 'Being listed doesn't mean it's on a list. Well, it does, but I mean not that kind of numbered list. It just means that it's protected – for now anyway.'

'But if there was a list.'

'What kind of list?'

'Like . . . the hundred best buildings in Birmingham. What number do you think it would be, Dad?'

'I don't know, Mo. Ninety-nine maybe.'

Mo shook her head fervently. 'No way, man.' She'd started saying that a lot recently. 'It'd be in the top twenty – definitely. I think it would be number seventeen at least.'

Frank nodded. 'Hmm, the seventeenth-best building in Birmingham – that has a ring to it.'

'Will there be a sign to say that it's listed with your dad's name on?'

'I don't think so. Lots of buildings are listed; they don't have plaques.'

'I can't believe there won't be a sign. What's the point in being listed?'

'It just protects the building.'

'So no one can ever demolish it? Ever?'

Frank hesitated. 'Well, you can't say forever and ever. But it means it's very difficult to get rid of it.'

Mo looked at the top of the building. 'I think in four hundred years people will be coming here for day trips. They'll have question sheets to fill in about the name of the man who built it and the shapes of the windows like we had to do at Aston Hall. Maybe they'll have to colour in a picture of your dad! I bet loads of them will look at the building and say, "Wow! What a great building. I wonder if he had any grandchildren." And they'll try and imagine me, but they won't be able to because I'll be so long ago and mysterious.'

Andrea nodded. 'Mo the Mysterious, that's what they'll call you.'

Mo liked that. She walked up and down the street in front of the building, inspecting the block as if it was her ancestral home. Frank was glad it was a Sunday and none of the office workers were around. He worried that Mo might have tried to charge them admission.

Andrea turned to Frank. 'Do you think your father would have been happy?'

'I don't think he'd have been too thrilled about the seven that were razed to the ground.'

'But at least this one will remain.'

'I'm not sure even that would mean that much to him.

I think he lost interest in individual buildings towards the end of his life. He didn't seem to think they counted for much.'

'I suppose everyone becomes disenchanted.'

'No, he wasn't disenchanted. The opposite, really – he was more fervent than ever, but his ambitions had moved on. He was obsessed with the new town he was planning. He felt he'd always been limited by his environment, by history, by other people's ideas and mistakes. With the new town, he was going to start from scratch. It's all he thought about.'

'We should take Mo. She'd love that. She'd think she was the Lady Mayoress.'

'Take her where?'

'To the new town. You've never shown me, either. Darnley's only in Worcestershire, isn't it?'

Frank said nothing.

'I mean I've seen the model; it'd be good to see the disappointing reality.'

Frank was silent for a few moments. 'The reality is more disappointing than you imagine. We can go and visit Darnley New Town any time you want, but it has nothing to do with my father.'

'What do you mean?'

'He never got the contract. It went to the Langdon partnership.'

Andrea stared at Frank. 'But . . . you've spoken about it so much, his obsession, his endless work on it.'

'It feels like he did build it. It dominated our lives for so long, dragging on and on. Endless public meetings and consultations and planning applications. He seemed to be perpetually presenting his plans. It was a long drawn-out beauty contest and they eventually narrowed it down to my father's company and the Langdon partnership. They had to go away and develop the plans further before the decision was finally made. It had been a huge investment of time and energy for him. I mean he'd never been around much, but he seemed to leave us completely. Even when he was physically there at the dinner table his eyes never seemed to fix on us. It's hard to believe that it all came to nothing.'

Andrea was quiet for a while and then said, 'But I suppose he was used to that kind of thing, I mean for a practice like his that must have happened all the time – losing out to competitors.'

Frank shook his head. 'Not to my father it didn't – not often, anyway. In Birmingham he was the golden boy; he seemed to get everything he tendered for. I think he'd started to take it for granted that he always would.'

'He took it badly, then?'

Frank could see quite vividly his toy town lying in pieces on the floor of his father's study. 'Yes, I think he did.'

'Did he say much about it?'

'He didn't have much opportunity. He died a month later.'

Andrea looked at Frank: 'God, Frank – I never realized.'

He shrugged: 'Maybe they weren't connected.'

'But you obviously think they were.'

Frank looked over at Mo who was now poking the pond in front of the building with a twig.

'I'm not sure that in the wake of losing his next big thing

it might have occurred to my father that he had anything left to live for.'

Andrea reached out and squeezed Frank's hand.

'I've been wondering recently why I wanted to try and save this building. What would it matter if all his buildings disappeared? I mean lots of people die and seem to leave no trace – like Michael Church. But when you go back and scratch at the surface you find the people who knew him and who he'd meant something to or who he impacted in some way. He left traces. Then at the other extreme there are people like my father who leave behind this very tangible, physical legacy. Concrete proof that he existed, but if all his buildings went, what traces of him would remain?'

Andrea frowned. 'Well, you remain.'

'Yes I do, but he looked straight past me . . . and Mom. He'd grown bored of us long before. He was focused on the future; he was never really there with us in the house, in our lives. When you take away his works and all his talk about his works, he just slips through the fingers.'

Mo was walking back towards them, her face still glowing with some misplaced sense of ownership of the building.

Frank smiled at her but directed his words at Andrea. 'I've no idea who he was, and this,' he said, indicating the building, 'never brought me any closer to knowing.'

47

Phil
March 2009

He does his second lap of the park. Sweat drips down his back. Adrenalin pumps through him. His eyes flick from side to side; he twitches at every movement in the bushes. His mind is a ticker-tape machine: Now. Or now. Or now . . . It runs on and on.

He tries not to think of Michelle. He tries not to think of the warmth of her body in bed last night, of her smile this morning as he left the house, but he thinks about them anyway. He'd got it wrong recently – revealed his desperation, gripping her too tightly, scaring her with his intensity. Last night he had the excuse of their anniversary. He kept it simple and honest. He told her she was everything to him and she smiled and relaxed for the first time in weeks. Later at home, she looked at him in a way that made him believe that he was still the man he had been – for a while at least.

He looks at his watch for the hundredth time. Now. Or now . . . Or when exactly? Where is Mikey? A dog emerges from the bushes and Phil yelps in surprise. He tries to breathe. He's in control. Everything is under control.

He didn't linger this morning when he kissed her goodbye, allowing only a brief glance at her eyes. He just smiled, stroked her hair and shouted a breezy, 'Take care.'

Mikey's solid, Phil knows that, even after all these years. Something about him has never changed – some quality of self-containment that Phil has always envied. Mikey knew Phil. He knew his weaknesses and still he'd do anything for him. Any minute now. Mikey wouldn't let him down.

48

Frank had a biscuit with his cup of tea. It was just a plain digestive: there was nothing more interesting on offer.

His mother watched him closely from her high-backed chair. 'Is that nice?' She was looking at the biscuit.

'Yes. It's quite nice.'

'Oh, I wish I could eat biscuits.'

'What's stopping you?'

'They're far too sweet for me.'

'So you don't like them.'

'No,' she said sadly, 'never have.'

Frank sipped his tea and decided that the triggers for his mother's melancholia were infinite. The mere act of watching someone else eat a biscuit was capable of sinking her further into the gloom.

He noticed for the first time that the room had been re-ordered. A pile of books that had sat on the shelf for as long as he could remember had moved. The collection of coats that hung on the back of the door had shrunk down.

She noticed him looking around. 'Oh, I've been having a bit of a sort through. Weeding out the rubbish, you know.'

Frank frowned. 'You've hardly got anything in here anyway – I can't imagine you had much rubbish.'

'The clutter mounts up and then sits there collecting dust, adding to the general sense of disrepair and decay.'

Frank looked around at the sunny, pastel-shaded room. His mother could never just say she wanted to tidy up. It was always the 'd' words with her: doom and death and decay, like an adolescent locked forever in a gothic phase.

'Andrea can't stand clutter. The house move has given her the perfect excuse to purge. I'm scared when I get home each night to see what else will have gone. I think I'll be next.'

His mother peered at him. 'You were always a hoarder, Frank. Never threw anything away.'

'I threw rubbish away, just not things I wanted to keep. Not mementos.'

'Yes, and everything was a memento for you. Everything reminded you of something. Nothing was allowed to be forgotten. I can't imagine anything worse.'

Frank shrugged. No matter what her motivation, he was actually pleasantly surprised by his mother's activity. It was the first time she had shown any interest at all in her surroundings for years. He noticed some fresh flowers in a vase on the window sill.

'Those are nice,' he said.

'Oh those. Yes.' She showed no sign of volunteering where they'd come from. 'So, how are the preparations for moving going?'

'Oh – okay, you know. Mo's very excited. She's developed some complicated colour-coded method of packing, but she won't let us interfere – says she has it all under control.'

Maureen smiled. 'She'll be happier in the city I think. She's too lively to be stuck out in the middle of nowhere.'

'I think we'll all be happier. We weren't really cut out for country life. Well, I wasn't anyway.'

'No, not enough clutter in the countryside for you. Not enough mementos of your past.' She hesitated and then added. 'I've been thinking about your move.'

Frank was surprised to hear this. He had the idea that he and his family didn't figure much in his mother's thoughts. She always seemed very vague on the details of their lives. She never knew how old Mo was and still thought Andrea had the job she'd briefly held fifteen years ago. He waited for her to continue, but she said nothing.

'What were you thinking?'

'Well, it's just that it makes this place even more inconvenient for you, doesn't it?'

It had never occurred to Frank that his mother might worry about such a thing. She spent so much of her time telling him to forget all about her that it was odd to think she might ever fear he actually would.

'Oh no, honestly, it's nothing – an extra thirty miles or so. We'll still come and see you just as much as we do now.'

She looked at her hands. 'No, I mean I wasn't worried about that, you know I'd never worry about that. Quite the opposite really. I just think it's too far, especially for Mo. I really don't think you should come so often. I mean you're here once or twice every week, and it just worries me that you're here that often. You must have better things to do with your time.'

Frank couldn't quite work out his mother's tone. She seemed to be taking the usual martyr tack, but there was something different there.

She spoke more quietly now. 'I mean with you moving away it doesn't really matter where I am, does it? I've no reason to be in this particular location. If I didn't have to worry about you visiting so often, I could live anywhere I wanted.'

Frank was confused, and didn't know what his mother wanted him to say. 'Worry about us visiting? I didn't realize we caused you worry. That was never the intention.'

'I didn't mean it like that exactly. I just mean that I worry that you take too much responsibility for me. I don't want to be a burden.'

'And I always tell you that you're not.'

'Well, maybe I could be less. This could be an opportunity.'

Frank looked at her. 'Mom, I've no idea what you're talking about.'

Maureen took a deep breath. 'Well, the fact is I've been thinking that I might like to move too.'

'Move? What? Back into a flat of your own? Is that a good idea?'

'No,' she said impatiently, 'not a flat of my own. I've got no interest in having to cook and clean and worry about all the bills. I mean another residential home.'

Frank was concerned. 'Is there something happening here? Is there a problem with a member of staff?'

'No, of course not. I just thought a change of scenery.'

Frank puffed out his cheeks. 'Well, I think they're all much of a muchness. I mean we can go back and look at some of the ones we looked at before here, maybe some new ones have opened up since.'

'I wasn't thinking of round here. That's my point. A change of scenery.'

'Well, where were you thinking?'

'The south coast . . .' She paused. 'Or the east coast, maybe even the west. Not the north, I couldn't stand the cold. I think the south might be easiest for you to get to.'

Frank looked at her. 'The coast?'

'Yes, Frank, the coast. It's not so very strange. I've always wanted to live by the sea.'

Frank shook his head. 'Why do people keep saying that? You never told me before.'

'Oh, I'm sure I did. You probably just weren't listening.'

'But it would be an incredible upheaval.'

'What upheaval? I have two bags, at most. I could do it in a jiffy.'

'But you'd be totally on your own; you wouldn't know anyone there.'

Maureen was quiet for a moment before saying, 'Well, what if I did know someone there? Would you worry less then?'

'Who would you know, Mom? You've lost touch with all your friends.'

'Well . . . maybe someone from here is considering a move as well.'

'Someone from . . .' Frank began, but then realized that he knew the answer. 'Walter?'

His mother looked away. 'Well, yes, as it happens. It seems Walter is thinking of relocating to the coast as well.'

Frank looked at her for several moments. 'You and Walter have decided to move to the coast together. Why can't you just say that?'

'Oh, Frank, I can't see that it matters how I say it.'

He couldn't for the minute even focus on how unlikely the situation was. The idea that his mother had made some positive plans for the future, had embarked upon some kind of a relationship, had shown any interest at all in life, was too big to take in. His immediate response was taken up by his frustration with her.

'Because . . . I don't know, it just doesn't seem honest. If you and Walter are . . . friends, well, that's fine, I'm happy, but why can't you just say it? Do you think I'm going to disapprove?'

Maureen didn't answer. She walked over to the window and looked out at the garden. It was a long time before she spoke.

'I was very proud of your father, you know, when we were first married. I'd talk about him to anyone who'd listen. Talk about him as if he were a possession. "My husband" – well, it suggests ownership, doesn't it? I didn't realize then that we don't own anything, least of all our own good fortune. You're left feeling very foolish when it slips away.

'I didn't make that mistake with you. I never boasted about your achievements. I didn't want someone up there hearing me and thinking they'd take me down a peg or two. I came to think that it was better to protect yourself by expecting the worst – that way you can build up quite a shell.

'Like everything else I've ever done, I've no idea if that was the right or wrong thing to do, but I'm afraid it's not a very easy habit to break.' She turned to look at Frank. 'But I know I'm tired of this place. I don't want to stay in this room any longer. I need some air. I need to breathe.'

49

They joined the canal in the city centre, but within a few minutes they had left the cafés and bars behind them and were walking in the shadows of factories and warehouses along the black tow path.

'I hope you don't mind meeting outdoors.'

'No, it's fine.'

'This is my life now, Frank. Traipsing the highways and byways of the city like a vagrant, the only way I can have a smoke. They treat us like lepers, doesn't matter that we keep the economy afloat. People bang on and on about civil liberties in China, but I'd swop places any day. They love their fags there – can't get enough of them. I tell you what, I could live with never standing in front of an approaching tank if it meant I could smoke when I wanted – seems like a win-win situation to me if ever there was one.'

Frank wondered if this was how it was going to be: an evening with Cyril Wilks – the man and his thoughts.

Cyril seemed to pick up on this. 'Thanks for coming, though, Frank. I do appreciate it. I know you're a busy man.' He started walking in the direction of a bench on the tow path. 'Do you mind if we sit down for a bit?' He lit another cigarette and Frank noticed his hand shaking.

'We look like a right pair of fairies, but never mind.' He inhaled deeply. 'You know this place is crawling with them, don't you? I've learned a lot about the homosexuals since the smoking ban. You wander along the canals and there's some chap asking you the time, or watching you from under the bridge. *Hombres furtivos* I call them. It's a shame I'm not that way inclined as it would make the trudging around outdoors a little more rewarding. You know – kill two birds with one stone. "Got a light?" "I've got more than that, mate." "Ooh . . ."'

Frank interrupted him. 'Cyril, what was it you wanted to talk about?'

Cyril exhaled a long plume of smoke. 'I'll come clean straight away, Frank. I owe you an apology – there is no new business venture. I'm sorry for getting your hopes up. It was a cruel trick.'

Frank tried to look disappointed. 'Oh, I see.'

Cyril didn't seem inclined to say any more so Frank prompted him. 'Was there anything in particular you wanted to discuss?'

Cyril looked out at the water. 'It's a funny game – writing.'

As Frank had suspected, this was going to be a slow trip down memory lane. He wondered how long before Bryce Spackford hove into view. For some reason he found himself not minding, though. Sitting on the bench, watching debris float by on the surface of the canal, listening to Cyril reminisce was strangely calming.

'Specifically writing for other people. It's like being invisible. The only clues that you exist are in the lines that occasionally come out of other people's mouths.'

Frank frowned. 'What makes you do it?'

Cyril gave a short laugh. 'Not for the money, that's for sure. I suppose it's just nice to watch a television programme and hear something you've written. Proves that you're there. You need that sometimes. Sometimes the rest of life doesn't feel quite real. You'll laugh, but it's as if until I've heard you say it, it doesn't count. Sometimes I almost have to fight the urge to ring you up and tell you stuff to make it count. Imagine that on the news: "Bong: Cyril Wilks went to the library today."'

Frank smiled. 'Is that what this is about? Breaking Cyril News? Washed the car today, did you?'

Cyril changed the subject. 'You were a good mate of Phil's, weren't you?'

Frank was caught off guard. 'Phil? Yes . . . I suppose so. I mean we didn't live in each other's pockets, but we always kept in touch.'

Cyril nodded. 'Phil and I weren't so close. We went back a long way, but it was always more of what you might call a working relationship. He was the face on the screen and I was the invisible man behind the curtain. No one knew about my role and that's how I liked it most of the time, but sometimes it's nice to have some recognition, to let people know about your part . . . or at least tell someone . . .'

'You don't need to tell me, though, Cyril. I know about the work you did for Phil and for the others, for Big Jackie –'

'Johnnie. Big Johnnie Jason.'

'Yes, him, and the others . . . and me.'

Cyril chewed his lip for a moment and then said. 'What

would you say if I told you Phil's death wasn't an accident?'

Frank frowned. 'I'd ask if this was a joke.'

Cyril shook his head. His cigarette had gone out. Frank mustered all the patience he could as he watched Cyril pat every pocket several times over looking for his lighter before finding it on the bench next to him where he'd left it. After taking another drag he finally spoke. 'I told you before, didn't I, that I bumped into Phil before he died? Well, it was actually the night before it happened. I was down in London chasing a bit of work and went into a hotel bar near Oxford Circus for a snifter and there he was. He was a fair bit worse for wear – you know – greeted me like some long lost loved one, insisted I join him, bought me a double. We started off talking about the old days, but he kept veering off into frankly very depressing territory: ageing, decay, humiliation, doom and general gloom. It was bloody miserable, to be honest. I thought, *Note to self – avoid social drinks with Phil in future.*' Cyril gave a forced laugh.

Frank thought of what Michelle had told him; he thought of his own last conversation with Phil, but said nothing.

Cyril continued. 'Then, just when I thought it couldn't get any worse, he told me he'd decided death was the only option.'

'Why was he telling you all this?'

'Bad timing, Frank. Story of my life. Always in the wrong place at the wrong time. Of all the times I could have bumped into Phil it had to be that night, when he was half cut and desperate to confide in someone. When I first saw him, all I'd wanted to do was sell him my gag about Prince Philip and the Polish maid but I could see that wasn't going to be appropriate in the circumstances.'

'So what are you saying? He was suicidal? He was just drunk, Cyril.'

'Yes and no. Yes he was drunk and no he wasn't suicidal . . .' Cyril hesitated. 'Or at least that's not quite the right word.'

'What do you mean?'

'He was past suicide. He'd tried it already and couldn't do it. That was why he'd come up with his plan.'

'What plan?'

'He'd pay someone else to kill him.'

Frank stared at Cyril. He started to have a very bad feeling. He wanted to believe Cyril was mad, to nod benignly, humour him and then escape home to something solid and sane like an Ocean Pie, but he couldn't. He hesitated before asking. 'Pay who?'

'Some old boy from his National Service days.'

Frank closed his eyes. Somehow he had sensed it. 'Michael Church.'

Cyril turned to look at him. 'Bloody hell, Frank. Stop me if you've heard this one before.'

'Just carry on.'

'Yeah – Michael, that was his name. They'd met up again after years out of touch. Apparently Michael had lost his wife to cancer not long before. He told Phil about how she'd suffered at the end, how awful it had been to watch. Phil listened to it all sympathetically and then asked Michael to kill him.'

Frank put his head in his hands. 'Jesus, Phil.'

'This Michael – well apparently he was good with guns

– had been some crackshot in their army days. Phil had some lunatic idea of Michael walking up to him in the street, shooting him with an old National Service revolver and walking away. You know – Jill Dando style. It'd be just another unsolved mystery, Michael would never be connected with it, Phil would get what he wanted and Michelle would never know the truth. That was his main concern – that Michelle should never know.'

'And he paid Michael twenty grand to do this?'

Cyril looked at Frank again. 'You have heard this.'

'No. I'm just putting it together. Carry on.'

'Michael said he didn't want the money. Phil said he could donate it to charity – to the hospice where his wife had died. He posted it to him so Michael couldn't refuse. Phil told him to think about how his wife had suffered at the end of her life. He asked him could he stand back and watch Phil suffer in the same way? Never mind that there was sod-all wrong with Phil – but . . . he was a persuasive man and Michael was his old mucker. In the end he agreed.'

Frank stared out at the oily surface of the water. He tried to suppress both the terrible shocked laughter that he felt lurking in his chest and the tears that burned at the back of his eyes. He thought he should feel anger towards Phil for his stupidity, his selfishness, but he didn't feel it yet. For now he just felt sorrow. Despite his shock he could somehow believe it all of Phil. He could quite easily imagine his terror of the slow decline. He could imagine too his persuasion of Michael, his tenacity with an argument, the history they shared. He thought about what Irene had said about Michael. About his strength and Phil's weakness. He thought how little Michael had to live for after Elsie died. He kept seeing Michael's eyes. He was the loyal, steady friend who would do anything for Phil.

Cyril was staring ahead at the canal. 'It wasn't so easy, though. Michael let Phil down three times. Dates and times would be arranged. Michael would show up, but he couldn't pull the trigger. Phil was going out of his mind, making Michelle's life hell, but still he couldn't give up on it; he thought the alternative was worse.

'That day I saw him was the eve of the fourth attempt. Phil was going to go for a run along the country lanes near his home and Michael had said he would do it.'

Frank had a sudden image of Michael's sloping hand-writing. 'I won't be there next week.' Michael coming to his senses in the note that Phil never received.

'Phil seemed jubilant and terrified at the prospect. He kept saying, "Ten thirty on the dot – all over, Cyril. All over." It was too much for me, Frank. I hadn't wanted to know any of this stuff and there I was being told by Phil that he was going to be killed the next day. I lost my patience. I told him to pull himself together, think of all the luck he had. I told him to stop drinking, go home to his wife and I left him in the bar.

'I tried to forget about it on the way home, think of something else, work on some gags, but Phil's nonsense kept popping into my head. I had to have a few when I got home just to get to sleep. The next morning I was up at the crack of dawn with a hell of a hangover and still all I could bloody think about was Phil. The bugger had somehow made me responsible. I couldn't just stand back and let him go ahead with it. I knew I'd have to do something.

'I tried to call him, but all I got was his voicemail. I thought, *Well, there you go, I tried*. But that kept the brain happy for all of two minutes and then it started up again: *You should go down there, talk to him face to face*. In the end I gave in and got in the car.

'Traffic of course all the way down there. By the time I found his house it was ten fifteen and there was no answer. I had fifteen minutes. I headed off, driving around the country lanes, not having a clue where I was going. Those lanes are like a maze, endless hedgerows on either side – bloody claustrophobic. The headache was pounding. I was glad I had the bottle of Johnnie Walker on the seat beside me – hell of a lot more effective than paracetamol.

'As I drove round in circles, I rehearsed what I was going to say to him. Maybe he was getting old, losing his edge, getting a bit soft in the head – but that happens to all of us, doesn't it? I mean everyone else puts up with it. Apart from that, what did he have to complain about? A success-ful career? A devoted audience? A beautiful wife? I wanted to tell him that there were worse ways to live. Far worse. Imagine if he didn't have any of that. Imagine if no one ever begged him to do another series. No one doubled his fee to keep him with the network. What if no one returned his calls and no one remembered his name? I'd ask him to imagine a life in which no one was won over by his charm. Women didn't catch his eye and men didn't offer to buy him a pint. Ever. A life spent working on his own in the same room that he slept in. A life of invisibility.' He paused for a moment. 'Perhaps then he'd have a point.'

He lit another cigarette and had smoked most of it before he spoke again. 'So, anyway, I'm haring round another bend and I see him up ahead of me in the distance. Bright red tracksuit – can't miss him. I put my foot down, racing to get to him, but it's after eleven. This Michael character has let him down again.

'It's only then that I really feel for him, that I understand his pain. *Poor Phil*, I think. *Poor, poor bastard. Another bloody morning to face.* God, I know how that feels. Pale light bleeding under the curtains. Weeping into your pillow. Sometimes a few Johnnie Walkers sort you out, but sometimes they don't. Sometimes the day starts bad and ends bad. Do you know what I mean? Sometimes it's impossible to see when the bad days are going to end. I'm getting closer to him. I see him more clearly now. I can see the whole story in his silhouette. He's shattered, broken. Let down again. Do you know that feeling, Frank? Trapped in fucking pain? Have you ever felt like a fly smashing into a window over and over again? Desperate to get out, hurling yourself at the glass. All you want is a way out. I take a last swig from the bottle and put my foot down on the accelerator. The engine roars, my head spins and the car flies forward. I close my eyes and I'm soaring through the air. I sense a lifting inside me; I can taste freedom; I'm hurtling towards the light. But then comes the thud that brings me back down. That same bloody thud as I smash into the same bloody window again.'

Cyril and Frank sat silently side by side for some time. Cyril was crying.

'When I open my eyes, I'm back on that country lane. Blue sky above, tarmac below and no sign of Phil.'

50

One month later

His mother's room had a new occupant now. He walked past and noticed the display shelf outside her old door was covered in ornaments and photographs. The ornaments included some curious ceramic representations of half-rotten pieces of fruit with cheeky mice poking out of them. He imagined how amused his mother would have been to see these grisly tableaux of decay constantly reminding residents that not everything was evergreen.

He eventually found Irene's room. The door was open and she sat on a floral-print chair just inside with her hat and coat already on.

'Am I late?'

'No, dear. I just like to be ready.'

He wondered how long she'd been sitting there clutching her handbag waiting for him to arrive.

They took a detour on the way to the church. It ended up being more of a detour than originally intended as Irene's directions were based on the road layout she remembered from the mid-fifties. Every now and again they'd come to a dual carriageway or a flyover and Irene would emit a small 'oh' and Frank would realize that another U-turn was necessary. She wanted to show him the area where she had lived when first married to Phil, the same area that Elsie and Michael and Phil had grown up together. She looked out from the car window at the vast Golden Cross estate.

'I don't recognize anything. It's all gone.'

'It can't all have gone. There's always something.'

Eventually after much reversing out of one-way streets and double circuits of roundabouts they came across the back of an old Victorian school.

'I think that might have been where Phil and Mikey went to school.'

They drove up the side of it and emerged onto a major dual carriageway that Frank recognized. He saw a bench on the far side of the road. He realized that this was where Michael's body had been found. He said nothing to Irene and they carried on to the church.

There were more people at the service than he'd expected. He recognized Azad and the women from Greggs, but there were another fifteen or so faces he didn't know. He found out later that the women from Greggs had gone to some effort to track down Elsie's old friends and spread the word amongst the few neighbours who had known Michael. He led Irene to a seat near the front and sat beside her.

The police had never found any next of kin for Michael. Eventually they advised the coroner's office to release the body for a local-authority funeral. When Jo rang Frank to let him know, he asked if he could pay for the funeral instead.

The service was simple. Frank's only request was that something other than the twenty-third psalm form the main reading. There were no hymns, but Azad chose a

Nat King Cole track to play at the end of the service. The melody tugged at Frank. He didn't know the song, something about a boy 'a little shy, and sad of eye'. It seemed corny and haunting at the same time.

Michael was finally buried alongside Elsie five months after he died. The cemetery sprawled over an incline overlooking the M6 motorway and a fine mist of rain fell. It was hard to imagine a bleaker setting. The vicar said a few more words and some of the mourners threw handfuls of soil on top of the wooden casket.

A woman from the hospice where Elsie died came and spoke to Frank afterwards. She told him of the day some months earlier when Michael had turned up with a large brown envelope. She seemed to assume that Frank knew all about it. She said the new family room had been built now and she had wanted to invite Michael to a small event marking its opening. She said they would always be grateful for his great generosity. His name was on a plaque at the entrance. As she walked away, Azad approached Frank. 'It was good of you to do this for Mike.'

Frank shook his head. 'I didn't do anything.'

'Yeah, you did: you asked around, you found the people who knew him, you let people know that he'd gone.'

Frank looked at the graves stretching away from them in all directions. 'That's my speciality – things that have gone.'

'It's good to remember. People forget without meaning to.'

'But they're not really my memories. I only met Michael once for a few seconds.'

'Yeah, but you gave people a chance to remember. It's

like my wife. She remembers everything – dates, places, faces. I forget our anniversary every year. I see the card waiting for me on the table and can't believe it's happened again. I don't want to forget it; it means a lot to me. She says it's okay, says she'll remember for both of us.'

Frank smiled. 'She's a nicer person than me. My wife never remembers our anniversary. I enjoy making her feel bad about it all year.' The other mourners had moved away from the graveside now. A council worker hovered nearby beside a small mechanical earth mover. 'I meant to say I liked the song you chose.'

Azad smiled. '"The greatest thing you'll ever learn is just to love and be loved in return" – I thought Mike would have liked that.'

51

The new producer was younger than Martin had been. His name was Benedict and he told Frank to call him Ben. He wore narrow black-framed rectangular glasses to which his eyes seemed attached. Throughout their meeting Frank had to try to fight the impression that when the glasses came off so did the eyes. He found the image of a blank expanse of skin above the nose stuck in his mind and proved quite unsettling. Ben apologized for not formally sitting down with Frank earlier but explained that he wanted to watch the team in action for a few weeks before speaking to individual members.

'So, Frank, I notice that the jokes appear to have dried up.'

'Erm . . . yes. There haven't been any for a few weeks.'

'The viewers aren't very happy about this. Quite a few have got in contact and we've actually already noticed a drop in viewing figures. Apparently your bon mots used to brighten up the day for many viewers.'

Frank had known this was coming. 'I'm sorry. It's just that the man who used to write the jokes . . .'

Ben looked at Frank; his eyes seemed to fill their tight black frames. 'A man? Someone used to write those jokes for you?'

'Yes.'

'I'd always assumed . . . well, I mean they seemed so . . . ad-libbed.'

'Oh no, they were scripted by a professional.'

'Right.'

'Anyway, he's retired, I'm afraid.'

Frank had received a short note from Cyril. He wrote that he'd decided he needed looking after for a while, something his sister had apparently been saying for the past few years, and so he had gone to live with her and her family in Bootle. He said he would be writing exclusively for his two young nephews from now on. He asked Frank if he had been to the police and gave his new address in case they needed it. He ended the note with a one-word apology, and Frank wasn't sure what it was for: his part in Phil's death, burdening Frank with the information or withdrawing his puns and one-liners.

Ben was nodding. 'I see. Are you planning on providing your own jokes?'

Frank shook his head. 'I don't think I'd be able to do that. It takes – well, a special kind of mindset to find the humour in every situation.'

'So are you thinking of finding someone else to write them for you?'

Frank felt his heart sink. 'Do you think I should?'

Ben looked at Frank for a few moments. 'Frank, do you actually like including jokes in your pieces to camera? Is it very important to your image of yourself as a presenter?'

Frank didn't have the energy to explain to Ben about Cyril and Phil. About how this had all been foisted upon him. How it was nothing he had ever wanted, and didn't figure at all in his image of himself as a presenter. He simply settled for: 'No.'

Ben smiled. 'Good.'

Frank looked up. 'I'm sorry?'

'Let's leave the jokes, then.'

'What about the viewers? The drop in figures?'

'To be honest, Frank, I'm thinking of making a few changes around here. There's going to be a period of transition, we'll lose some viewers, but hopefully we'll gain new ones. I've just been discussing some of my ideas with Julia and I know we share a great deal of common ground, which is very exciting. From what she's said I think you're on the same wavelength too. I greatly respect your work, Frank. I know you're a professional with high standards. I was just dreading having to persuade you that puns and one-liners didn't form part of my vision for the future.'

Frank left the meeting feeling uncertain. He thought that during his time at *Heart of England Reports* he'd perhaps seen enough new visions for the future, enough rebrandings, repositionings and refocusings. At that precise moment in time he found the whole idea of yet another change of direction filled him only with weariness. He tried to focus on the positive: no more jokes – he should have been walking on air, but he found himself slightly sad at the prospect. At least Julia would be happy.

He looked at his watch and realized he was running late to meet Michelle, a meeting he had been putting off since learning the truth about Phil's death. He knew he had to tell Michelle what he'd discovered, but that didn't make it any less difficult. He'd discussed it over and over with

Andrea and she thought the same. It was up to Michelle what she did with the information.

She was waiting in the bar as he rushed in.

'I'm sorry I'm late.'

'It's okay – makes a change.'

He pecked her on the cheek. 'You look really well.'

'Oh, thanks. I take it that means I looked like a bag of dog food last time we met.'

Frank had no idea how this always happened when he tried to offer a simple compliment.

Michelle laughed. 'It's all right, Frank. No offence. I hope I do look better. I'm feeling a lot more myself. That's why I wanted to see you.'

Frank was sure that it had been him that suggested the meeting. He was keen to do what he'd come to do, to just get it over with and yet now found the conversation being hijacked by Michelle.

'Look, Frank, I just wanted to apologize about the last time we met.'

'Apologize for what?'

'For worrying you. For being a mental case. For talking all that rubbish about Phil.'

Frank looked at her. This was his opportunity. He hesitated a beat too long and she was speaking again.

'I've been thinking about it a lot over the last few weeks. I realize that I'd just let things get out of all proportion. I'd be mad to let just a few months cloud the happy years Phil and I spent together.'

Frank nodded uncertainly. He didn't know what to say. 'What about his mood swings? The erratic behaviour you were talking about?'

'He was coming up to retirement, Frank. He was due to quit the show the following year. I wasn't seeing things from his perspective. It was going to be a massive adjustment. Of course he'd get moody: he had to get used to the idea of putting his feet up, relaxing, letting me look after him – all the things he hated most! The transition was probably like a second adolescence for him – I mean it could have been a lot worse really.'

'Right. Yes, I suppose that makes sense. What about that money you mentioned, though?'

'Oh, that was ridiculous. I never had any idea what Phil did with his money. He was always protecting me from that side of things. I just seized on that £20,000 cash withdrawal when I saw it on his statement as evidence of something strange – something I was almost hoping to find. In reality it could have been anything – a charity donation, a poker game, whatever.

'And yes, I know, the hit and run. To be honest, I still think it's a bit odd, but the point is that odd things happen sometimes. I'm not going to waste the rest of my life cooking up crackpot conspiracy theories. I was thinking about it all and I suddenly had this crystal-clear vision of myself in ten years' time on one of those daytime shows – you know, "Thinks her celebrity husband was killed by Mafia" scrolling under my name. You can convince yourself of these things. Once you get an idea in your head everything can be made to match that theory. Well, why can't the theory be nice? Why can't I now build on the idea of all the happy years Phil and I spent together instead of trying to concoct something out of a few bad days and a load of supposition?'

Frank envied Michelle. He wished very much that Cyril had never told him. He thought about Phil, of how much he had loved Michelle and wanted in his strange way to protect her. He thought perhaps some knowledge was overrated. He looked at her and answered, 'No reason at all.'

52

Three months after his mother's move and Frank still found each visit to Evergreen Sea Breezes a uniquely disorientating experience. Everything, from the artwork on the walls to the faces of the staff, was almost but not exactly the same as Evergreen Forest of Arden. Identically carpeted corridors led to different rooms, the television in the residents' lounge was located in the opposite corner, silver-haired heads would turn to reveal unexpected faces. He invariably turned the wrong way out of every doorway, and had mistaken Mrs Burton's room for his mother's so many times that she no longer smiled when she passed him in the corridor.

Aside from the spatial confusion, his visits to the home followed much the same routine as ever. His mother's room for a cup of tea and then a game of dominos with Walter in the residents' lounge. His mother still chose to rarely mention Walter, though occasional references might be made to 'a friend' having said something or been somewhere. It was only during the games of dominos that Frank would hear of walks they had taken, or tea shops they had visited and gain any sense of the friendship between them. Where Maureen was circumspect, Walter was open and forthcoming. He frequently told Frank how wonderful he thought his mother was. Frank never knew quite how to react, and sometimes found himself defaulting to a polite, 'Thank you,' in the absence of anything better.

'I've never been happier, Frank. Can you believe that? I'm seventy-seven and really I've never felt more content and settled. I know your mother feels the same, though of course she doesn't make a song and dance about it like I do.'

Song and dance were certainly lacking in his mother, but so, Frank had detected, was the sense that she was simply waiting to die.

He sat in her room now with Mo who was looking at the sea view through the window using a magnifying glass she had bought in one of the fossil and souvenir shops in the town.

'Interesting,' she said. 'Very, very interesting.'

'Mo,' said Frank, 'I don't think it works for things in the distance, only up close.'

'It works for both. Up close it magnifies, in the distance it blurs.'

'Oh right – it blurs – that's good, is it?'

'Take no notice, Mo,' said Maureen. 'I think most things look far better when they're blurred.'

Mo nodded. 'I can pretend that I'm looking back in time and there are no people, only dinosaurs.'

'Well, that might be an improvement. I'd imagine dinosaurs talk a lot less rubbish than plenty of people I know. So what's the plan for this afternoon?'

'I'm going fossil hunting with Mom and Dad.'

'Hunting for fossils?'

'Yes – this is the Jurassic Coast – there are loads of them.'

Maureen smiled. 'Well, I know that, dear. I take breakfast with them every day.'

Later they walked across the beach looking for a good picnic spot. Andrea reached the middle of the beach and dropped the bags. 'Here's as good a place as any. What do you reckon?'

Mo nodded. Frank shook the rug out and laid it on the pebbles. Andrea started getting foil packages out of the carrier bags. Mo opened her backpack and pulled out her new fossil-hunting kit. It contained a hammer, a chisel, clear plastic bags, protective glasses and a small book on hunting for fossils. She put the big plastic glasses on to read the book.

As they drank tea from the flask, Mo looked up from her book and asked: 'Do you think that one day in a trillion years someone will find our fossil? They'll be sitting on a big rock eating a picnic and they'll look down and there we'll be – looking out at them?'

Frank pulled a face. 'That'd put you off your sandwiches.'

'But could it happen?'

'I don't think so. I think one day, a long time in the future, after we die, we'll probably be buried or cremated and we'll eventually become dust or soil.'

Mo was unimpressed. 'Dust? I don't want to be dust. Being a rock would be much better.'

Frank shook his head. 'Do you really think? Being trapped in a rock forever sounds horrible to me, like being

305

imprisoned, but if you were dust you could be blown by the wind and go wherever you wanted.'

'But, Dad, nobody notices dust.'

Frank jabbed the air with his sandwich. 'Well, maybe they should.'

They finished their sandwiches and then Mo set off with her hammer and chisel to look for fossils. Frank and Andrea watched her as she walked back towards the cliff. She tried to keep her balance on the mass of rounded stones beneath her feet. As she walked away, the contrast in size between her and the wall of rock grew, until she reached the bottom and stood dwarfed at the very foot of the cliff. They saw her remove her parka and lay it on the ground. She sat down on it at the base of the cliff, with her back to them and the sea, and with her magnifying glass clutched in front of her eye examined the surface closely for any signs of past life.

53

Michael
October 2009

It's dark now – or as dark as it gets in the city. He sees no stars in the sky above him, just an orange glow from the street lights. The last bus left hours ago. At some point he realizes that he's never leaving the bench. There are worse ways to go. He thinks of Elsie. He thinks of Phil.

Phil told him that he'd saved his life once. He said, 'All I'm asking is for you to undo that.' Michael hadn't realized that's how it was supposed to work.

He'd agreed to do it because Phil asked him and because he thought he could. He thought his hands could do anything. After Elsie died they had carried on tying his shoelaces in the morning, polishing the furniture in the lounge, cold-bloodedly functioning through it all. Why not hold a gun and pull a trigger? There didn't seem much difference.

But his hands surprised him. They faltered and refused. The cold metal lay inert in his palm. His busy hands stilled. His fingers limp. They wouldn't let him do it.

Phil thought that age would rob him of everything. Michael told him it couldn't. He told him to look in the mirror and he'd see something in his eyes that had never changed and never would. Michael had seen it in Elsie's eyes, even at the end, still there burning through everything else. Still Elsie.

A smile flickers on Michael's face. Poor Phil. Always scared. Always running before he needed to. Michael always tried to tell him that running never solved anything.

Elsie was standing under the tree at the side of the park. A breeze moved the shadow of the leaves across her face, revealing and hiding glimpses of her as he walked towards her. For months all he'd had were photos and letters and memories and now he wanted to see all of her. She was looking towards him, her face impossible to see. Eventually he broke into a run, laughing at the corniness of the gesture, the returning soldier, running to embrace his sweetheart. She came out to meet him, walking out of the shadows, into the daylight and he saw she was laughing too, the happiest most beautiful thing he had ever seen.

The park has gone now, buried under the ring road, the bandstand has been replaced by a traffic island and there is no trace left of the trees. Except for their tree. It too has gone, but a bench marks the place where it once stood. It's a strange place for a bench. He's walked past it hundreds of times and never seen anyone else on it. He wonders if it's been waiting for him.

Some people say they feel the presence of the dead. They sense some disturbance in the air and they know their dead husband is standing beside them, their dead cat curled on their lap, their dead wife still battling with the pile of ironing.

He's never once felt Elsie's presence since she died. He

watched the last breath leave her body and then the world changed. She was gone.

He feels her absence, though, all the time.

It's there in specific things:

the dip in the bed where she used to lie,

the shape of the crack in the vase that she dropped,

and it's everywhere:

the air around him,

the colour of night in their bedroom,

the shapes he sees on the insides of his eyelids.

He understands now. Our absence is what remains of us.

Acknowledgements

The BBC regional news programme *Midlands Today* is not the model for *Heart of England Reports*, and neither are the characters in this novel based on anyone working there past or present. I am, however, greatly indebted to the team for their assistance with my general research into regional news and their great patience in answering my dim-witted and at times bizarre questions. Special thanks to Naomi Bishop for acting as guide and to Sue Beardsmore for all her time and expertise.

Thanks also to MACE and Ian Francis of Seven Inch Cinema for introducing me to the 1984 Central TV documentary *Reclaiming the City*. Although Douglas Allcroft is not based upon John Madin or any other Birmingham architect, the 1965 BBC documentary *Six Men* about Madin was particularly instructive. Similarly the chapter entitled 'What Went Wrong with Tomorrow?' in Chris Upton's *A History of Birmingham* (published by Phillimore & Co. Ltd) was essential and fascinating reading.

I am indebted to the website www.britisharmedforces. org and its webmaster Keith Petvin-Scudamore for sharing the wonderful National Service memoirs of William Hawksford. I am further indebted to Mr Hawksford's family for their kind permission in allowing me to borrow from Mr Hawksford's account of life in Port Said for background detail in Michael and Phil's posting overseas. Neither Michael nor Phil are based upon the late Mr Hawksford in any way.

Mo's attempts to improve the quality of Maureen's life would not have been possible without the excellent *Tips and Wrinkles* by Mary Sansbury and Anne Fowler (published by Pan Macmillan).

The fictional Silver Street industrial estate was certainly influenced by my memory of the documentary *Five Units on Fazeley Street*, part of BBC Radio 4's *Lives in a Landscape* series.

I'm grateful to Sandy and Don Fletcher for the insights they gave into care homes for the elderly. Their expertise was built up during daily visits to Sandy's father Bill Hughes who sadly died during the writing of the book.

Thanks to Jim Hannah for early read-throughs, discussions and an amazing ability to follow the thread of incoherent, rambling spoken synopses. Thanks also to Francisco Dominguez Montero for introducing me to the wonders of the real Byron's Common. I'm grateful to Luke Brown for much more than just taking care of discarded canapés. Thanks to Lucy Luck for her endless encouragement and support, to Kate Barker and to Helen Atsma for their belief, their comments and their understanding when the schedule was unexpectedly hijacked.

Thanks above all to Peter and Edie Fletcher for everything.

Not
The End

Go to channel4.com/tvbookclub for more great reads,
brought to you by Specsavers.

Enjoy a good read with